Vines and Daggers

Powerful Pawns: Book 1

Rauri Rose

Contents

Helomasi
???
Ptheryeth

TIKILIUM
ARALETOS

Content Warning

Vines and Daggers is an adult reverse harem romance fantasy book that contains **strong language** throughout and content some readers may find distressing including **sexual themes**, **bondage**, and an instance of **attempted sexual assault**. Please keep your own triggers in mind before proceeding. Your mental health matters.

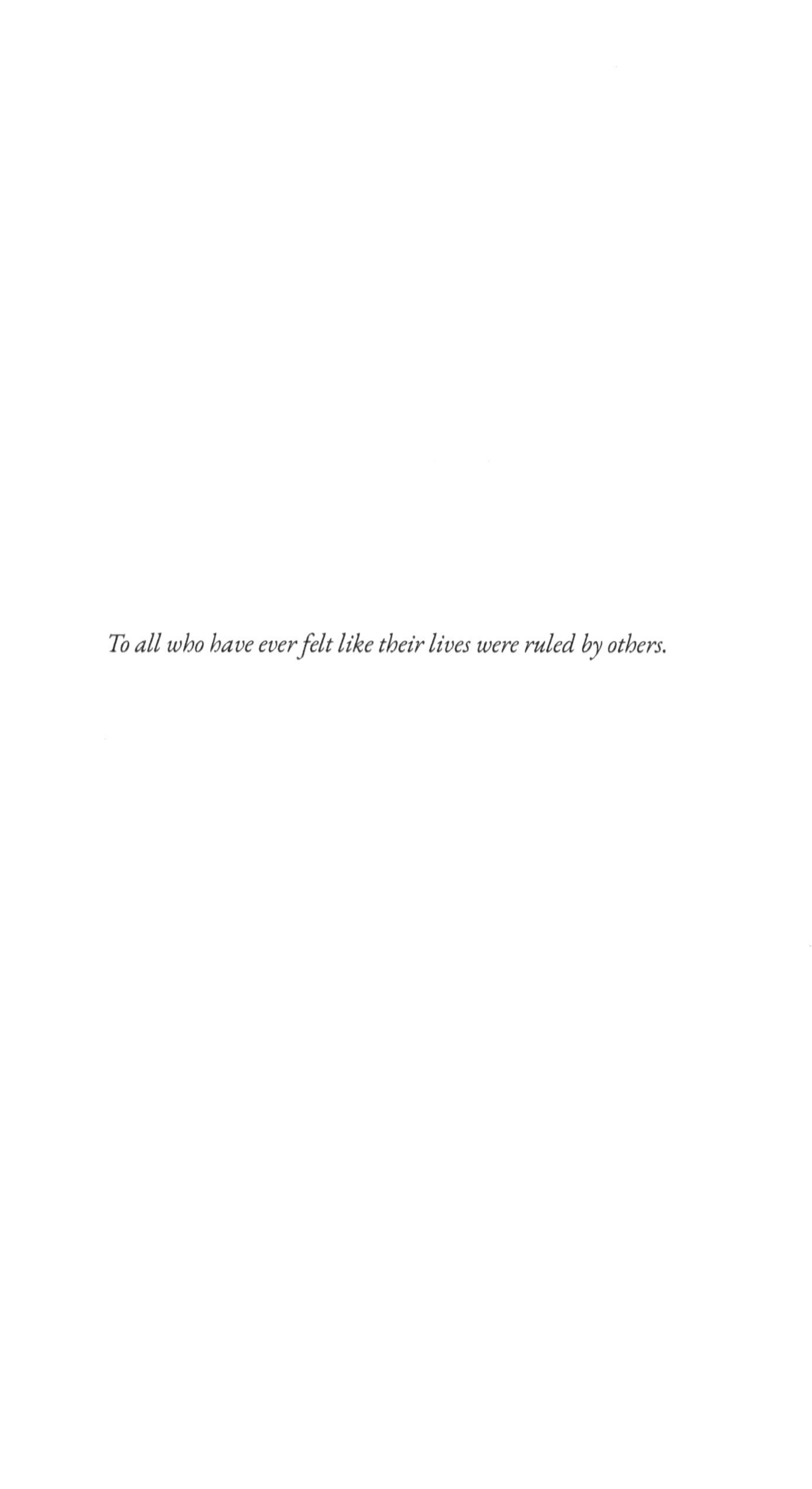
To all who have ever felt like their lives were ruled by others.

CHAPTER ONE

The Announcement

Alaceandra

*B*etrothed. *I am BETROTHED.* The thought fills me with terror, disgust and sadness as I stalk out into the sheets of rain covering Tikilium. The king—*my father*—announced his decree this morning. The morning of my twenty fourth birthday. The morning of my majority. Tears threaten my eyes, and I let them fall, the rain peppering my face with gentle kisses. *It is not supposed to be this way. I am supposed to have more time.* His declaration came without forewarning, leaving both me and the people of Tikilium shocked at the news. *Shocked but not surprised,* I think to myself, groaning. *There is nothing that man will not do for power. Using me as his chance to have an alliance between two of the most powerful kingdoms? I should have known.*

"Stop!" Sorin yells, yanking me from my thoughts as he runs in my direction.

Sorin has been my friend since childhood, my rock through diplomatic bullshit, my hero through every scrape and bruise I have ever had, but he cannot possibly get me out of this asinine plot of my father's. I do not wish upon him my father's wrath if he were to try, so it is only best if I leave him out of it. Be that as it may, I know that if I were to completely ignore him, he would never leave me be.

I pause, sigh, and quickly wipe at my tears before turning toward him. "What?"

"Can you just listen to me?" He looks at his hands, his breath puffing out of him. The rain is making his shirt stick to his chest drawing my eyes to the defined muscle hiding beneath. Sorin stands at six feet tall, dwarfing my five foot three stature. He has a shock of red hair and a dusting of freckles across his nose that I cannot help but find adorable. *Why must the man be so handsome and unreachable?* Father would never allow me to be with him. Although his family holds power in Tikilium, they are not royalty themselves, and the king would never allow his only heir to be with anyone he could not gain political power from. 'A waste of a chess piece,' he always said. *But Ptheryeth knows if given the chance...*

"Lace?" My eyes flit back to his. "Did you hear a word I said?"

"Um, no." I continue walking and hear him sigh from behind me.

"Wait up!" He catches my arm and a tingle of warmth washes over my system.

My shoulders slump. I have become soaked with rain and honestly, I am not in the mood to have it out with Sorin, especially when he is looking like *that. Not that it looks like I have much choice.* "Why should I?" I clench my hands, peering at him as water assaults my eyes. The stinging of my nails digging into my palms helps me to steel myself against the flood of emotions that come with this particular conversation. "I tried to tell you—"

"Hey guys?" Sam comes running from the same direction as Sorin. *Fuck me, not the both of them!*

Sam and Sorin are in the king's guard together. Sam has been assigned my protector ever since I turned eighteen. He is an attractive man, with short silver hair and a killer smile. Sam stands an inch or so taller than Sorin, but whereas Sorin is all muscle and hard lines, Sam has a sleeker physic. He is five years older than the both of us and quite the heartbreaker. *I often find myself wondering— no, wishing— that he would try with me, but he never has.*

"Hey," we both chime, conversation blessedly paused. A whoosh of air rushes out of me.

"Why...are you guys just standing in the rain?" Sam finally catches up to us, brows furrowed, chest heaving.

"Why were you running in it?" I laugh, defensive. He, too, is soaked with rain and showing off his gorgeous *and untouchable* body. I dig my nails more firmly into my palms to stave off the growing urge to run my fingers over the cloth of their shirts. Instead, I fix my gaze on Sam's eyes and cock a brow.

"Well..." A look passes between Sam and Sorin before Sam rocks back on his heels. "I saw Sorin here sprinting and," he rakes his fingers through his hair, "ya know, if your bud is running, you kinda want to know if it's from something or to something." He straightens and my eyes catch on the nipple ring barely contained within his shirt. I avert my gaze. "If it's from, well, why get left behind?"

I have always thought of Sam as an insanely intelligent person, but I know he tries to play it off as something on reserve. For instance, this current act of his. I know full well that Sam knows exactly why Sorin is here, but he is trying to feign ignorance in order to gain some kind of advantage in this conversation. Fortunately, our years of friendship allows me to see through this act of his most of the time. The people of Tikilium often dub him a 'Master of Disguise,' because if Sam wants to hide something, it will not be discovered unless he reveals it. This has made him an instrumental asset to my father. *Unfortunately for me, sexy and cunning has always been a weakness of mine and being surrounded by the both of them has led to many bouts of frustration on my end.* Although I do not know the full extent of the men's abilities, Tikilium claims them to be most formidable. I, though, have always known them as my friends, *or, at the moment, pains in my side.*

My gaze turns pleading. *Please, Sam, I do not want to be chided by the both of you, leave Sorin's schemes to another day.* I silently urge him to drop the subject.

"Sorry, Sam I didn't mean to worry you, I just wanted to catch up to Alaceandra," Sorin scratches the back of his head, his tone not enough to convince me Sam's presence here is not one planned by the two of them. "We need to talk," he gives me a pointed look, further proving my suspicions.

"Yeah…" I squint my eyes, "we do need to… eventually… but not now." My eyes stay on Sam, urging him to take my side in this.

"Yes, now, Lace, come on—"

I see the moment Sam breaks. "Guys!" Sam cuts in. "We are soaked, either we get an umbrella, or we go inside, if we get sick—" *Success!*

"Thanks for your concern, Sam, but we did not ask you to come out here—" Sorin bites back.

"Why are you being rude to Sam now?"

Sam sighs and kicks the ground, covering his shoe in mud, his brows furrowed in frustration. "Whether you did," a glance "or did not makes no difference. It's not like I can just let you all run off to Ptheryeth knows where. While you guys are my friends, you should also know I would get the brunt of the punishment if you guys get lost—or sick—because of some little disagreement."

"It's not little—" Sorin tries to interrupt.

"I know! But who Alaceandra marries is none of our concern." A pointed glance. "So, it is better if we treat it as little instead of badgering her over it. It's not like we can change the king's decision." He seems upset with himself over this thought but proceeds forward anyway.

My clothes are getting uncomfortably wet, and my hair is starting to stick to my skull. I rub my eyes. "Exactly, so can you guys just... go? I would like to be left alone."

Sam's eyes track the direction I am walking. Ahead there are no outbuildings, only trees, bushes and a variety of flowers. Truly, there is no real place I can feasibly get to off castle grounds without going through the woods first and, with the weather outside, I am not going in the woods. Which means I am walking in circles around the castle and, by the look in Sam's eyes, I can see he has just caught onto that. "Where are you even going Lace?"

A pause, then I shrug, pointing behind me. "That way."

"And that way is where to exactly?" Sam raises his eyebrows, but the question itself was one full of amusement. The tension of the moment briefly broken.

"I do not know, just that way. I want fresh air." *I thought Sam was on my side...*

"Okay fine, we won't talk about it, but I have suddenly decided I would also like to go that way as well." Sorin starts to walk towards me, his face filled with stubborn resolve. My belly flutters at the intensity with which he regards me, and I back up a step.

"Need I remind everyone it is still raining?" Sam grumbles.

"I like the rain, it's cleansing," I argue, snapping my eyes away from Sorin.

"You say that," Sam rolls his eyes "until you're coughing up a lung in bed and then guess who has to hear from her royal highness about her daughter's activities?"

"Yes, yes your life is so hard Sam," Sorin interjects "but we will be fine."

Sam groans. "Fine. Fine! But I'm coming too. Somebody has to get you guys back before the dinner bell rings and with the trouble you two get up to, I know I can't rely on you to get yourselves there."

"I did not ask for company…"

"Well, you're getting it," they both stand like statues, their faces tolerating no argument.

"Whatever…" I mutter, continuing my walk. They, of course, follow.

Once we have rounded the castle at least three times I cave. "What, Sorin? What did you want to talk about regarding my betrothal?"

He grits his teeth, casting his gaze towards Sam. "Later, Lace."

I think I feel my eyes bug out of my head. "What do you mean later? You were adamant not even twenty minutes ago and now that I am willing to talk about it you are no longer interested?"

He wipes a hand down his face and water droplets flick to the ground. "I have to go." Then he just… walks off.

I give Sam a *what the fuck* face and he shrugs. "Let's get you inside for dinner."

Reaching the castle entrance, we run into my mother, May, exiting my father's office with tears in her eyes. My mother's tears are unfortunately a regular occurrence when leaving my father's chambers for a variety of reasons. She taps my back as she walks by shooting me a look filled with pity. Before we can take another step forward, a blond also exits my father's office, fixing her hair. Her lipstick is smudged across her face and her dress is falling off of one of her shoulders. *Ah I see... mom walked in on another of father's conquests.* The blond sneers at me as she passes and my eyes track the woman down the hall, her hips sashaying as she struts around the corner.

I grab Sam's hand. "We better hurry before-"

"What are you doing out here?" *May I catch any breaks today?*

My father stands in the doorway glaring down at us. Or shall I say up? He is not a tall man, but what he lacks in stature he makes up for in brutality. He has one motto in life: All shall be punished. *Whether they have done something deserving of it or not.*

"What are you doing outside of your chambers?" His voice booms through the hall. From the corner of my eye, I watch as the servants scatter, leaving only barren stone walls in their wake.

"I was out walking with Sorin and Sam like usual."

"You are soaked."

"It was raining."

"Did you have one of my escorts with you? I do not see them." He searches the area but only finds empty stone halls.

"Escor— father you have never had me bring an escort before?"

"That was before. Now that you are betrothed and have reached majority, I cannot have you prancing about the gardens like a common who-"

"Father," I cut him off and the look he gives me would have meant my death if not for the fact that he needs me to marry this prince. I am his only heir so there would be no one else he could slot in to do it for me should I 'go missing,' much to his chagrin.

He takes a menacing step forward. "You will stop associating yourself with those men. Now. I cannot have word getting around about your so-called activities with them. If you slip up even once, I can promise you will not like the consequences." I should not be surprised by his demands. Engagements often mean tighter restrictions, but I find myself having to hold my tongue to not argue.

My relationship with Sam and Sorin has always been a point of contention. I am lucky he has allowed it for so long. He has spent countless hours spouting nonsense about how he will not let anyone's devotion to me ruin his kingdom and their proximity to me can only mean trouble. *Whatever that means.* So instead of dreaming of a more permanent relationship with the two of them, I have settled for an amazing friendship with mischievous men. At the end of the day, I am bound to the crown and my duty to my father, *even if he is an asshat.* Arguing this point will only land me in bigger shit than I am in already, especially if I try in the heat of his anger. I take the safe route. I choose not to respond in words but instead drop my gaze. *The sooner he thinks I give in, the better the chances he will give up on the conversation.*

He huffs a noise of satisfaction. "Go. Find Mandi. Now!" Sam starts to lead me to my chambers. "Leave the boy," he grits out.

Sam turns and bows to the king before starting to walk down another hall to my right, shooting me a little wink before he departs. I hold back a smile and make my way up to my room.

CHAPTER TWO
Oh Zyphel, Oh Zephel

Alaceandra

When I reach my room and shut the door behind me, I hear its lock click into place behind me and sigh. Technically he is not unwise to want to have his people watching over me, but to lock me in my room? *Seems excessive, but we are talking about King Nikoli.* Once a royal reaches their age of majority they are afforded a couple royal permissions for the first thirty days. The most troublesome one being that they are able to release those in their family's service should that servant wish to go. This is supposed to serve as a way for newly matured royals to thin out the servants and acquire new ones that will be loyal to them once they come into power, but instead it tends to cause derision amongst families. At least castle arrest is not a terribly severe punishment—and it could have been. My father is not a kind person, and he detests anyone seeing him as having little control over those in his charge. I know that if the people of Tikilium found the future princess drenched in the woods with two men, no matter the status, it would not be a good look for the royal family, but I have been adventuring with those two for years now. It is not like I am going to stop because my father decided now would be the perfect time to marry me off. I can deal with a little castle arrest.

I start to pace. Now that I have some time alone my brain cannot help but mull over that odd interaction with Sorin. He acted as if speaking to me was so urgent, but when I finally gave in, he just walks away? *It does not make sense, but what does it matter? Whatever he was going to say would not make a difference in the long run.* My future is not in my hands, at least in my current state. The only thing I truly have going for me is time. Ancient law states I am not to be wed before the nearest solstice, which is six months away, *but even that is uncertain.* Rumors are floating around that the other kingdom is pushing for the marriage to be sooner, but such a thing would prove disastrous for the reputations of both kingdoms and may even provoke war. This, of course, is not helped by my proclivities with Sorin and Sam. News travels fast in Tikilium, I would be surprised if someone did not report something already about my morning walk.

A caw sounds at my window, and I haul myself up to greet my elvisera, Addie. The giant bird-like race, elvisera, are used as a means of carrying letters and people where they need to go all through Ptheryeth. Usually the people of each kingdom's most elite are assigned one at birth, although their elvisera can change due to marriage, politics or the death of their birth-given companion. Addie has been with me as long as I can remember and she has delivered countless messages. Her most notable task has been to deliver letters to the continent's gossip and my best friend Philos.

I met Philos when we were thirteen and she had visited Tikilium for some music lessons. We became quick friends. Using her father's, the king of Areletos, connections she has been able to maintain contact with me ever since. My father allows this relationship, although I am not sure why. He has always kept a close eye on my dealings with others, preferring to keep me in the dark about all things outside of the walls of my bedroom, but for some reason has never enforced any kind of restrictions on our friendship. *I hope that does not change now that he has decided to watch me more closely.*

Addie drops the letter into my palm. The letter has yellow parchment and is adorned with pretty green flowers. *Areletos' colors!* Excitement flutters in my belly as I sit on the edge of my bed and watch Addie unfurl her wings and soar into the sky before unraveling the letter from my dear friend Philos:

~~~~~~

My dearest Alaceandra,

It has been much too long since we spoke, and from what I've heard you'll have much to tell me next time we do. You know how I <u>hate</u> to gossip, but you were found alone with two men in the rain? I would love to know the details. Also, you're engaged? Who is this gentleman and how did he come to be? You simply must come visit me before your betrothal. Bring Sorin with you as well! He is always so fun. I miss you dearly, Lace. I really do hope all is well. I hope you always know; you'll <u>always</u> have safe haven with me should this marriage not be favorable in any way. You know my father, always ready to pick a fight for a just cause and you also know how much he cares for you (and how much he hates your father).

Write back soon,

Philos

~~~~~~

I snort. *I guess the news has already made it across the continent.* Placing the parchment in my top drawer, I rub my face. Although I am grateful for Philos' support in my love life and against my father, this news does not bode well when it comes to my chances of him changing his mind about my associations with Sorin and Sam. *Maybe I can come up with a plan to get out of my betrothal before the solstice with the help of Philos? Then I would not even have to worry about this stupid marriage.* I sigh. *No, not likely.* I fall backwards onto my bed in exasperation. *Knock Knock.* I glance at the door, spotting my handmaiden. *Great, dinner is here.*

"Hi Lace, I hope you are holding up well." Mandi smiles at me, my food in her hand an offering. She wears a simple bronze colored dress lined in gold, marking her Tikilium heraldry.

"Hey, Mandi..." I lift my head up in greeting, before plopping it back down onto the bed in answer.

"Yeah... that's kind of how I thought it was going." She chuckles. "Here, I brought your favorite stew. I'll just leave it here." She places the food on my nightstand, then sits on the edge of my bed. "I know this situation is... unpleasant, but please just stay here until the king calms himself. I don't want him to make any rash decisions and any rebellion from him after your little... adventuring... won't end well for you." She raises an eyebrow. "Of course, you know this already..." She pokes my side, playfully. "But just to make sure..."

"Yeah, yeah, I will stay put." I swat at her.

"Good, see you tomorrow, Lace." She ruffles my hair and then walks towards the door.

"Wait, Mandi!"

She turns to me. "What is it?"

"This prince. The one I am to marry? What is his name?" My cheeks heat slightly with embarrassment.

Her face pales. "Oh." Her eyes dart from mine. "I do not know. No one does. Helomasi does not disclose such things."

My eyebrows furrow. *That is kind of rude, no?* "Why is that?"

"Some kind of custom. I do not know." She walks back over and pats my cheek. "Do not worry yourself over that for now. Just focus on staying out of trouble."

I sigh. "Fine."

"Good. Sweet dreams, Alaceandra."

"Sweet dreams."

I wave at her lazily as she exits my room and, of course, locks the door again sealing me back inside my boredom. I sniff the air and my stomach growls. *At least I am left here with yummy food.* I drag myself from my prone position on the bed and retrieve my stew from the nightstand before sitting back down and digging in. I am about halfway through my bowl when I hear a slight tapping on my window. At first, I ignore the noise, thinking it is a branch or maybe an animal but then it starts to get louder. "Maybe another letter?" I wonder aloud, walking over to my balcony.

Looking out, I spot a shock of bright red tresses. Sorin. *Of course, it is.* Opening the golden glass doors, I give Sorin an amused look.

"Oh Zyphel, oh Zephel, may your hair become vine! Long and thick and easy to climb!" He scream-whispers at me.

I roll my eyes. "What are you doing here? You are going to get us in trouble— again," I reply to him in much the same way. Trying to hide a smirk.

"We still need to talk."

"Now?" I frown.

"Yes, now, please it's important."

"I am not allowed to leave my quarters, especially with you. I am sure you know that." I look behind me and then back at him, anxiety settling into my chest.

"It'll be quick, I promise! They won't even know you're missing, and look! I brought Sonny!" He gestures behind him, and I peer out into the darkness to find my mare munching on some grass.

"Where are we going that we would need horseback?"

"It's a surprise, besides talking back and forth out here like this is much more likely to get us caught than a quick little talk out of your quarters."

I bite the inside of my cheek. He has a point. "Fine, but how will I get down? My door is locked." My chamber is on the top floor of the castle, which is the only reason my father even allows me to keep the balcony doors unlocked.

He smirks at me and touches the ground below my window. A long, velvety vine with lobed green leaves extends itself upwards and circles itself around my iron railing.

"You want me to climb down?" I look at him dumbfounded. I would rather not go sliding down vines at this hour, especially in my pajamas.

"Yup. Why? Don't think you can make it?"

I narrow my eyes at him. Not that he could see the expression very well in the low light. "No, I can do it." I start to descend the plant—which is surprisingly soft and yet not slippery—when the vine suddenly starts to grow in circumference. It is now free standing, no longer needing the support of my railing, and starts to wrap around my middle like a harness and gently sinks itself back into the ground. I wiggle a bit and glance at Sorin who looks hyper focused and on the verge of laughter. Once my feet touch the soil, all that is left of the plant is a big green stump-like form that transforms itself into a pumpkin. I glare at him.

Sorin smiles wide and flutters take over my core. Walking towards me, he extends his arms for a hug. "I knew you could do it, but do you know the trouble we would have been in if you fell? I thought this would be much safer."

I continue glaring at him and push at his arms. "Whatever. Where are we going?" His vines have caused my golden nightdress to be streaked with green. I wipe at the stain I know is forming and look at him impatiently.

"This way, my lady," he says teasingly and points towards Sonny.

We walk over to my favorite mare. I mount her and watch as he mounts the other horse, I missed standing next to her, an obsidian Clydesdale named Nightshade. Although mares usually are not one for male riding companions, Sonny and Nightshade, much like their riders, are unlikely friends. The journey into the woods starts as a gentle walk. I watch as Sorin seems to get more and more agitated as we continue on.

"Hey, are you—"

Sorin urges Nightshade into a trot then a gallop. I gasp, clutching onto Sonny for dear life. Sonny follows their lead increasing her own speed until she too is racing through the forest. After a couple minutes, we reach a little clearing.

"Slow down!" I shout towards Sorin. I am not dressed for riding so the saddle is chafing my thighs, making it hard to stay balanced. He comes to an abrupt halt, and I have to stop myself from falling forward as my horse follows suit. We both dismount. "Why the fuck were you going so—"

He rushes towards me, and I go to take a step back, but he catches me with a firm grip.

"Look Alaceandra, you can't go through with this marriage." He grips my shoulders, his tone desperate.

"Sorin..." I try to shy out of his grip, but he only holds me tighter.

"No, you don't understand. He wants to kill you—" A bird starts to caw in the distance and Sorin chokes a little on his words. The sentence seemed to almost take the wind from him and he releases me abruptly before almost falling against a tree.

I startle at his sudden weakness and rush over to him, but my head spins at his unfinished warning. "Who wants to kill me? The prince? Look he does seem to have prickish energy especially with the fact no one here apparently knows his name, but I do not think he is going to marry me just to…" My voice is nearly hysterical at this point and Sorin's head starts to droop as his skin turns even more pallid. My heart races as fear churns low in my gut. Throwing his warning out of my mind for the time being, I realize how idiotic I must look questioning him when he looks on the verge of passing out. "Hey, Sorin are you okay?"

He pulls a vile made of a black opaque glass from his pocket and gulps down the blue iridescent liquid inside. Color returns to his cheeks and he shoves himself back upright. The bird caws again. "I can't tell you anymore, just please trust me on this." He gasps out, voice hoarse. "Alaceandra please I—fuck!" We hear the pounding of hooves coming towards us, Sorin stomps in frustration. Grabbing my face, he places his forehead to mine. "I can help you more if I'm not here when they find you, okay? I have to go—"

"What?"

"I know, I know, but there is no time—" The sound of hoof beats in the distance grows louder. Sorin looks around. "You'll be fine, I'll find you later, okay? It needs to be this way." His eyes beg me to understand as he backs away from me. Sorin mounts his horse and disappears behind the trees just as my father's Clydesdale, Trymisyus, comes pounding through the forest in the other direction. My father's face is scarlet with fury.

"Alaceandra, what are you doing?"

"I, uh…" I look around. Great, a nightgown this time. I really know how to dress for the weather.

"Back to your quarters—now!" I start to grab Sonny. "No—you will be riding back with me. How dare you think to defy my orders. Do you think being at your majority means you have any power here? You are a stupid little girl. I will show you powerlessness." He pulls his horse next to me. I notice there is a small pumpkin in his hand and grit my teeth. *I guess we forgot to get rid of that.* My father follows my gaze and shoots me a look of disgust. Reaching down, he captures my arm in a punishing grip and yanks me up harshly onto his horse. Once I am seated, he throws the pumpkin to the forest floor causing it to break and coat the ground with pumpkin seeds. "You will be moving in with the prince tomorrow morning. I don't have the time to babysit you every day, but maybe your future husband will—no matter, just because the law won't allow him to marry you immediately doesn't mean I have to be stuck with your rebellion any longer, he can look after you until the wedding." He sneers at me once more before turning forward and urges the horse to walk. "I will, of course, be checking on your behavior in the meantime, but that doesn't mean I need to have your insolence under my roof." He then kicks the horse into a canter, ending the conversation.

I hold on for dear life and cringe. *Fuck.*

CHAPTER THREE

Goodbye

Alaceandra

In my quarters I pack a up a few of my belongings in a small bag. I look in the bag to account for all my important items. Diary? Check. Stationery and pens to write Philos? Check. My locket? Check. I sigh. I understand Mandi will ensure all my necessary items are accounted for but even still I am stressed. I am definitely not equipped to argue with my father on this matter, but I feel as if I am even less equipped to be married. Thus far my life has been admittedly sheltered. The only knowledge I have regarding married life has been from watching my parents. My father's predisposition for cruelty has not only resulted in a long line of infidelity and fear from the kingdom, but also a lifetime of brutal punishments for my mother. I hope that my future does not mirror theirs, although it seems unlikely. All kings are tyrants, are they not? Philos never mentioned her father's brutality but it is hard to imagine that there is any other way royalty could live outside of my family's habits. Admittedly, this is the way my father likes it. My naivety is one of the many ways he tries to pull the strings in my life. He warns me frequently if I try to wander outside of my station then the consequences of those actions will only result in disaster for those I hold close. While any damage he does to me does little to sway control in his direction, he knows harm coming to those I love keeps me in place.

Mandi walks in, her eyes brimming with tears. "The king requested I stay here."

I look up from my bag. "What?"

Mandi nods.

"Why?" I shake my head.

"I think his exact words were something along the lines of I would be of more use here or in his bedchamber than I could be in forming alliances with you."

I shudder.

"Don't worry, I'm sure it is more of a power play on his part to keep you in line. He will be sending someone else with you so you won't be alone, but..." Her eyes well up again "sorry—I- I'm just worried. I knew I should have kept a closer eye on you and you're not ready for—"

"No! Do not blame yourself. I gave you my word I would not leave and yet I did. The fault lies with me and not with you."

"Oh, darling. I only wish that were true..." she trails off and clenches her hands, bringing my attention to an object within them. "Well, we cannot stop the past, but maybe we can save ourselves some heartache in the future, eh?" She holds up a bracelet. The bracelet is a single silver band laced in an illegible red script; its center holds a scarlet gem of unknown origin. Mandi notices my questioning eyes. "It's for protection I should have given it to you sooner but—" she chokes on her next words, much the same way Sorin did in the woods yesterday. "—but" she begins again, taking a deep, calming breath "there is no time like now, right?" she holds out the bracelet to me in offering, as she had with the food the day before.

I offer my wrist to her, but do not ask questions about the bracelet, not wanting her to experience pain like Sorin did. I could maybe get answers from her another time. "Thank you," I whisper. "Do you know who he will be sending with me?"

She flinches. "Unfortunately, yes. He summoned Fadres and Credour last night."

"Who are they?"

"Ruthless murderers, really, and not for the protection of the kingdom either. Their corruption runs deep. The only loyalty they have is to your father as they were some of the men he brought in when he reached his age of majority. 'Birds of a Feather' as they say," she mutters. "Stay on your guard. I have yet to hear about those two getting up to anything honorable." My heart sinks.

Down the hall I hear my father hurling orders, among other things, at the servants. "We better—" I frown. "Or, I guess, I better get going then." I bite my lip to hold back emotion knowing at this distance father would hear my cries and take them as challenge, and as I am already in over my head when it comes to his anger, I best not make it worse on myself or anyone else. I look at Mandi and, on a whim, give her a deep curtsey in appreciation and then hurry from the room before she can garner a response.

As soon as I exit my quarters my father spots me. "Alaceandra? Are you trying to sneak away once again?" His gaze is filled with both unbridled excitement and fury and I freeze, nausea churning in my gut. Mandi appears behind me.

"Are you ready, Alaceandra?"

"You will not be escorting her; I obviously cannot trust your watch—"

She cuts in. "As she is still my charge until the time of her marriage, I will be looking after her, at the very least until she leaves this castle, my king."

I glance at her in surprise but am even further shocked by the determination shining on her face.

My father glances around to see if anyone was a witness to this particular rebellion and seeing as everyone else had made themselves scarce due to his previous tirade, he found no one. Gritting his teeth, he spoke "You are lucky no one else was around to hear you, you insufferable blight." He rubs his temples and then flicks his hand in our direction. "Fine. But if she is even a tenth of a second late to her elvisera you will live to regret it." Shooting another look of annoyance in our direction he storms off.

"You did not have to do that. I do not want him to trouble you, but nonetheless, I am grateful. Please try to keep yourself out of harm's way."

"Lace, I am afraid that is not possible when looking after one as special as you," she says this on a laugh, but not in a way meant to be offensive. Her words ring only of truth.

This struck a chord in me and made words come to my lips before I had the brain to think them. "Then I release you from your service." A breath whooshes out of Mandi in an instant, her eyes widen with shock. "Please once I leave the palace find a way to escape from this place. I hope one day, maybe, we can meet again but for now I only wish you safety. I cannot stand the thought of my father using you as a pawn in this twisted game of his. You and I both know your safety is tenuous at best if I am not within castle walls, especially with that stunt you just pulled so please—"

She puts up a hand. "I agree, I'll go. I know of a person who can take me to safety, but your father mustn't know of my release until things can get sorted. You might hear some unpleasantries come up in the press with my disappearance but I promise they are planned. Now, let's not draw anymore ire from the king, this plan will only work if you are not late." She shepherds me towards the front of the castle.

I feel relieved, but still antsy about the journey ahead of me. We walk quickly to the front gates, and even with our talking, still manage to arrive early to take flight. I walk up to my elvisera, Addie, primed for my departure. She is a magnificent creature. A seven-foot tall, winged bird covered in feathers of burnt auburn with a mouth and talons brushed with silver, I could not imagine beauty in a more glorious form. I bow my head in respect for the creature. Although these birds bring me many joys in the form of letters and sunset flights, I know their beauty is better appreciated elsewhere, away from my father's rough control. Addie looks me in the eye and tilts her head to the side as if studying me. I smile slightly and bow my head once more. A door slams open.

My father walks out rubbing his hands together and looks around expectantly. I wonder if he would have preferred our tardiness as when his eyes land in our direction he slumps his shoulders, as if in disappointment. He approaches. "Are you ready then?"

I look towards my toes and nod once. Biting my tongue in anger. Although my plan is in no way thought out, I have the beginnings of an idea. One that rides on my father thinking I am properly cowed by his banishment of me, so I must hold my tongue until I arrive to Helomasi, King Demetrius' kingdom, otherwise we all may be in danger. My father grabs my chin and raises my eyes to his.

"Behave," he commands. Although my eyes are now raised, I do not dare make eye contact, I have made this mistake before and know there is only danger lurking within his gaze.

"Yes, father," I reply as meekly as possible. At this point I am a ball of fury but cannot let it show. He squeezes my chin hard enough to ensure it will match the bruise now marring my arm and then drops it walking away. My hands feel warm as I mount my elvisera. I look around and spot Sorin and Sam. They notice my gaze but before they can say a word, I shake my head. I know they too cannot follow me on this journey and seeing as their influence has gotten me into this mess, I decide I must temporarily remove them from my life until I can get it back on track for their safety and for mine. My eyes start to water and I look away for a second to compose myself. When I glance back out to the crowd they have disappeared, in their place stand two men unfamiliar to me. These men approach and climb onto the elvisera on either side of me.

My father speaks to the gathering crowd, his leering eyes boring into me. "These men are two of my closest friends, Fadres and Credour. They will keep you company and be my eyes. Treat them well, daughter and they should keep you safe." He glances towards the two men. "You know your mission. Do it well." I have never met these men before in my life. Sure, maybe they did seem a little familiar in a passing way but none of my father's so-called friends have ever made me feel as if I wanted to be within a closed space with them, let alone rely on them to keep me safe. That coupled with Mandi's warning has my stomach filling with dread at the journey before me.

They nod towards him and then turn towards me, smirking. "Time to fly," one of them commands on a whisper. Motioning to our elvisera, we all take to the wind, and I try not to think about all those watching us on those castle walls, especially not Sorin or Sam and especially not Mandi.

CHAPTER FOUR
Welcome to Helomasi

Alaceandra

We arrive in Helomasi without much fanfare. The elvisera are very speedy creatures. They deliver us to the front gates of the castle, setting us gently in front of King Demetrius and my supposed betrothed. They both wear teal robes lined with pink floral accents. *Helomasi's colors.* I have never seen the prince before, but Mandi had once described him to me, although he is much more intimidating in person. A six-foot five man, he easily towers over those surrounding him, including his father. His gray-green eyes pierce anything they touch. He has a silky inky braid spilling over his left shoulder and an aura about him that reeks of arrogance and authority. I sigh, not looking forward to this encounter.

"Welcome to Helomasi, Alaceandra," King Demetrius smiles, but there is something ominous about it. The welcome did not seem very genuine. Goosebumps break out across my arms.

Sliding down the elvisera's wing, I gain footing on the cobble stone walkway. The air smells of spring. Floral blooms and clean linen mix in my nostrils along with an undertone of *something*. *What is that?* I take in a deep breath and pause. The flowers almost seem to be masking a staleness in the air, but glancing around I cannot see where the disturbing scent originates. I wrinkle my nose and admire the surrounding trees. The leaves are showing out in brilliant bursts of reds and pinks and little winged creatures flutter around their branches. I smile at the sight. Returning my eyes to the men in front of me, I dip in a slight curtsy to acknowledge the king's welcome. "Thank you." When I come up from my curtsy, more people have appeared around the king and prince.

The king motions to them and then looks to me. "They will be escorting you to your new chambers. Please try not to cause any trouble. Your father, as well as other parties, have informed me of your mischievous tendencies of which will not be tolerated in my kingdom." With that he turns his back to me and makes his way back into the castle.

I look around, steeling myself when Fadres and Credour appear at my back. "Let's get going," Fadres says in a low tone and grabs my elbow to steer me towards the castle. A servant curtsies and leads the way into the castle.

We walk in and I pull my elbow out of Fadres' grip, he gives me a disapproving stare. "I am fine, thank you."

The woman leading us finally arrives to my new quarters. "The prince requested you reside here until the details of your marriage are secured. The prince is in the room next to you. Men you will be in the other wing of the--"

"No." Credour interrupts. His voice sends a shiver of unease through me. "Please find us quarters in this room here." He points to the room on the other side of my new quarters. "We will accept nothing else. We are here to guard Alaceandra, and we cannot do so from the other end of the castle."

The woman purses her lips. "Sir, I do not assign the rooms."

"Well then find the person who does. We will either be in that room or sleeping on her floor." Fadres enters a staring contest with the woman.

"I do not think that is neces-" I start to interrupt.

"Quiet, Alaceandra." Fadres chides. I bristle at the ease in which Fadres says my name, holding back the urge to lash out at the strange man.

The woman sighs.

"One moment." She grabs a small comms device from a leaf on the wall and speaks in low tones into it. *Odd.* Returning it to its place she turns to us. "Although this situation is most unproper, the king said he will allow you to quarter next to Alaceandra for the time being. In exchange, once she moves into the prince's quarters, he requests you be dismissed from the premises. A young woman being so close to two men would not be the start to a successful union especially in the eyes of our subjects, do you agree to these terms?"

"For now," Credour responds firmly.

"Fine. These quarters should be ready within the next half hour, until then feel free to explore the gardens. They can be found on the main floor at the end of the left hall." She turns in a flourish and walks back the way she came, looking much too busy to continue hanging around us.

"So..." I start.

"Come," says Credour. He walks in the direction of the gardens and Fadres herds me with them. I finger the blade hidden in my skirts ready to fight them if they get too handsy with me. It is a small black blade that Sam had given me on my twentieth birthday. Its handle is wrapped in leather and has little symbols carved into it. He told me never to unsheathe the blade unless it was an emergency. I could not bear to leave it behind, especially with Mandi's warnings still ringing in my ears.

We make it outside and Fadres throws a hand up. I flinch and shrink away from him.

Fadres laughs. "Don't worry, Lace. I'm just disabling any surveillance magic or devices they might have out here. Since they think little of our magic usage, I knew they would not be hard to disable."

I look at him, puzzled. "Your voice sounds familiar and yet I do not know of you, nor have I ever met either of you in my lifetime. Why is this?"

"You haven't figured it out, yet?" Credour chuckles his voice transforming into a very familiar sultry sound. I glare at them, confused.

Fadres rolls his eyes and waves a hand. In a blink their forms morph into Sorin and Sam's. I squeal and Fadres—now Sam—covers my mouth. "Lace!" Sam whisper yells at me. On a chuckle he continues "I only disabled the enhanced listening tools; I did not cloak the gardens; we still need to be quiet."

Credour—now Sorin— ruffles my hair a bit. "Did you really think we would let you go without any kind of protection?"

"I mean technically I did have protection."

Sorin wrinkles his nose. "Those jerks?" He says referring to the forms they were just inhabiting. "They would not have been much protection. Sam and I went down to the pubs the night before your send off and caught them doing some... let's say unsavory... things to some of the women within them. There was no way in all of the kingdoms of Ptheryeth we were going to let them anywhere near you alone, especially as your only form of protection." Sorin and Sam shared a disturbed look.

"Are the women okay?"

"Physically, yes," Sam offered. "Mentally? We don't know, but we did make sure Fadres and Credour would never touch anyone ever again..."

"How can you be so sure?" I wonder aloud, upset by the turn in conversation.

"Kind of hard to touch anyone from beyond the grave," Sorin states, flippantly.

"You killed them?" I say in shock.

"We did what we had to," Sam remarks, looking a little troubled.

"Wait." I hold up a hand. Both men turn towards me. I point at Sorin, accusatory. "Last time I saw you, you were hauling ass away from me, abandoning me to my father's anger out in the woods, and now you are here claiming to be my protector and a martyr to others?"

"I know. I know! I will explain, but I told you if I was with you when your father caught you, I would be of no help later. I would not have been able to be here now if he had caught me then."

"I would not have been here now if it were not for our outing then," I bite back.

"I know you think that but there is more at play now then what meets the eye—"

"More riddles..."

"Lace, I would tell you without them if I could, I promise, but even now my tongue is spel—" he chokes on that word and grits his teeth. "Look more information is to come, but Sam and I will have to remain in disguise until we can sort out a couple more details. We only revealed ourselves to you so you would know you were not without allies here, but you must not let anyone know of our identities."

I grunt in frustration. "Fine. I guess I am happy you both are here, even if you are being quite strange about everything..."

Sorin smiles gently at me. "Thank you, Lace."

"You are not out of hot water yet, Sorin, I am still very upset with you."

"I understand."

"Good."

Sam smiles widely. "Now that that is out of the way." He pulls us into a huge hug, and I release tension I did not realize I had. I love Sam's hugs. "I am happy we are together again," Sam says this almost inaudibly, his face buried in my hair. Baby elvisera are alight in my belly having them so close and I allow myself to luxuriate in the feeling. Sorin is usually the touchy one of the two, a fact of which I adore, but it is always a treat when Sam initiates. I inhale deeply, breathing in both of their scents, but do my best to be quiet. For the first time since Sorin left me in the clearing, I can feel myself start to relax. Once he releases us, he nods his head as if he is agreeing to some internal thought. "Alaceandra you should be able to see through our forms now that I have revealed ourselves to you. Please be sure you continue to call us Credour and Fadres in public. We do not want to cast further suspicion on ourselves by dropping the disguise now. Too many have seen us with you." I nod. "Good. We should head back to our rooms. We do not want people to come looking for us." Regrettably, I agree. Sorin and Sam re-cloak themselves back into Fadres and Credour's forms and we all head back into the castle and the madness that awaits us.

CHAPTER FIVE
Spyware and Spiders

Alaceandra

T he woman who greeted us finds us again in the hallway. "Oh! Great timing, your rooms are all finished." She looks a little frazzled and oddly guilty. She runs her fingers through her hair. "Do you remember where to go?" She directs the question at Fadres. He nods. "Good, well then if you'll excuse me." She walks past us and then turns down another hall, disappearing from view. A moment later a man strolls down the hall, also looking a tad bit disoriented. He gives a smirk before disappearing down the same hall as the woman.

"That was strange," I mumble to myself looking after them.

"Definitely weird," Credour echoes.

"Well..." Fadres trails off.

"Yep," I finish the thought. Whatever she has going on, at least at the moment, is not our problem. *Maybe Philos will have some insight on this kingdom's rumors...* I promise myself I will inquire about it after finding my own footing here in Helomasi.

We make our way back to our rooms.

"Lace," Credour stops me before I enter.

"Yes?"

"Do remember we are right next door. Tikilium rule no longer holds sway here, which is helpful to us in the sense we no longer have to watch out for the king's wrath and manipulations, but that does not mean the danger here is not present. Fear unknown can be more sinister than that that is learned. It can also be a door to a better future for us all. Let us hope for the latter. Please be careful and do not underestimate your captors...or our willingness to knock down a wall." He gives me a wry smile.

"Noted," I reply, returning a small smile. They walk into their rooms, and I enter mine, now thoroughly exhausted. The first thing that catches my attention is the bed. Not only due to my state of exhaustion but also due to its magnitude. It has to take up a third of the huge room and is set up on a marble pedestal step as if it is a holy offering. The bed has four posts and is draped in pale pink silks. Teal sheets hug the mattress and a thick fluffy comforter sits folded at the bottom of the bed. To my left is a large dark wood wardrobe and a door I presume leads to a closet. To my right sits another door, this one open, leading to a bathroom. I take a step inside and gape at the large porcelain clawfoot tub. My quarters in Tikilium were nothing to turn a nose up at but these accommodations were almost ridiculous. Not necessarily in monetary grandeur but in size. It looked as if this room was made for giants.

As I am taking all this in my body decides this is the perfect time to force a yawn to overtake it. I welcome this, remembering my earlier exhaustion. I can wonder at the political play being made here later. The night was made for sleep, and I am not one to turn my back on that. No, tonight I will enjoy the beauty of the bed and try not to drown in its linens. I make my way over to it and plop my aching body onto the soft mattress before sprawling out. Looking upward I notice the fairy lights adorning the ceiling and the vines winding themselves around the room's interior. *Those are probably riddled with spyware... and spiders.* I think absentmindedly before sleep overtakes me.

CHAPTER SIX

Strange Gardens

Alaceandra

I awake the next morning feeling drained. Physically, the flight to Helomasi was arduous; but it is the emotional burden of the last few days that have me truly exhausted. I am grateful for Sorin and Sam's being here, but I had already started coming to terms with the fact I may never see them again. I am still reeling from the grief of the situation and the surprise of their secretive plans. Although I know I should be elated they came along, I cannot help also being somewhat upset they did so without telling me. I hate feeling completely in the dark, but with a future so uncertain, I at least hoped my best friends would loop me in on their schemes. *It is comforting they are here though.* I admit to myself. *Maybe we will just need to have a discussion on keeping secrets.* At the very least Sorin seems to be keeping some important things from me and I do not know how to feel about it. *I will get it out of him somehow.*

Luckily, no spiders were found tickling my face this morning, only sunlight. A loud caw of an elvisera startles me. I blink open sleepy eyes and smile at the beautiful creature taking up the expanse of the large pink bay window at the front of my lodging.

"Yes, yes. You are mighty... and loud... what are you doing outside my window at this hour?" It was late in the morning by the look of the sun, but still far too early for any letters from Areletos.

The elvisera drops a letter on my floor and then, with another loud caw flies off, leaving the window open. I rub my eyes and coax my aching limbs to move. They comply, although stubbornly. I make my way to the front of the room and bend down to grab the letter. Unfortunately, the sun's brightness does very little to dampen the frigid temperatures outside, and I am not dressed nearly enough to withstand the weather for long. I shiver as a breeze whips through the room. Snatching the letter, I close the window, then stop in my tracks. "Not dressed..." I look down at myself to see I am in a white slip dress, something I had decidedly not fit myself with before my exhaustion took me last night. I cross my arms, uncomfortable. *I really hope none of the king's men changed my clothing.* "I knew this room was not secure..." I groan to myself. There is nothing that can be done about this now. I plop back onto the bed and look at the letter in my hand.

"Just great..." I mumble looking at the dagger embossed in the seal. A letter from my father.

~~~~~~

Daughter,

I have eyes everywhere, just because you are out of my house does not mean you are out of my grasp. Do your duty, or else you will find yourself in a prison much worse than your gilded cage. I see you, but so do they. Do
~~~~~~

not make yourself a leaking faucet. Your purpose will soon be revealed to you.

Your King

~~~~~~

I crumble the paper. I knew the room was filled with spy ware. *How annoying.* "So much for a new beginning." I mutter. A knock sounds on my door, and I sit up. "Announce yourself," I yell, hoping it is the new and improved Fadres and Credour.

"Miss, I have come with your attire for today..." a meek voice calls out from the other side of the door. I get up from my bed and pad over to the door, opening it only a crack. A girl a little younger than me peers through the door, her arms laden with clothes. I open the door wider.

"Thank you," I nod at her and scoop the clothes from her arms. She nods back. *Maybe she can be my first ally.* I smile to myself. *Would she be willing to give me more insight on the prince? Like maybe his name.* I blush a little bit at the thought of having to ask someone what the name of my betrothed is but brush off the embarrassment. I drop the clothes on my bed and open my mouth to ask, but when I turn around, it is to my bedroom door slamming. I sigh at the sound of footsteps quickly departing. My shoulders slump in disappointment. *Hopefully she is assigned to me, it would be nice to have another female around, even if she does seem a little skittish. Probably best not to rush people for information though.* Ptheryeth knows if I only have men to confide in, I will go absolutely insane.

I change quickly, hoping to maybe get a chance to sneak around the castle or at the very least explore the garden further. The shy handmaiden gifted me with a white dress embroidered with little pink flowers up my spine and delicate green ivy flowing down the sleeves. Although embroidered, the dress is as soft as a cloud. It barely feels like I am wearing
~~~~~~

anything. My favorite feature is the dress' leg holes that allow me to move around freely without having to worry about a stray breeze or too casual of a sit exposing me. They did not have dresses like this in Tikilium and I find myself grateful for the change.

I leave my room with soft footfalls, taking care to pass by the boys' room with extra caution. Although I know they are here to help guide me, I find sneaking about is best done alone. If I was found wandering the halls with them... the picture might not land me in a suitable position with this kingdom's monarchs. I need to be as unassuming as possible in order to have any cards to play here, especially if father has anyone watching me.

I find myself once again in the gardens. I know there are listening devices here, but I cannot help but be drawn to the place. Cameras were not mentioned so hopefully if I can stay quiet enough no one will know of my being here. Although, I have only just reached my age of majority, I am still unsure of what abilities I possess. I should feel a spiritual call any day now, but alas my spirit alludes me. Usually, Pthereyians get their powers in their childhood, but that was not the case for me, much to my father's dismay. Therefore, I cannot quiet the sounds I make or the devices listening to them.

The expansive garden is a breathtaking sanctuary, filled with majestic trees, delicate pink leaves, and exquisite blossoms I've never encountered before. It is easy for me to be swept up in its beauty. I depend on the lush ground to quiet my steps as I wander further. Luckily, nothing cracks under my weight and I am able to make it to a large clearing. Small winged creatures flutter away as I get closer. Their wings are iridescent and shimmer in the sunlight. It is there I realize I am not alone in my wandering. The prince sits with his back against one of the large trees. His eyes are closed and the winged creatures are dancing around his form.

He looks so peaceful. His inky black hair is adorning his shoulders in waves and, for a moment, I marvel at his beauty. I come back to my senses in a rush and position myself behind a tree, before taking a slow, quiet breath. I hope he has not noticed me yet, although it will be hard to escape him now I am aware of his position. It is much easier to be quiet alone than in the presence of another, especially when the consequences of being caught could be disastrous.

As I go to take a step away from the prince, I hear his voice ring out "I know you are there, Alaceandra. I've known since you entered. Why don't you join me?"

Fuck. Of course, he did. I lick my lips and take a small step away from the tree still wondering if I can escape.

He chuckles a deep, elegant sound and I hear a rustle from his direction. "Alaceandra, you are behind the tree. There is no reason to hide from me, this is my garden, you know. When I am connected to it, I see all. Now, come. No use hiding from your betrothed." He says the word betrothed with a little bitterness and I wonder at the tone. Maybe he is not as enthused about our arrangement as father made him out to be. That would suit me best, I suppose, but I cannot help being a little offended by the notion. *Well, no point in being miffed over a blessing.*

I purse my lips before making my way over to the prince. His eyes are still closed, but he has now crossed his legs, his fingers dance across the ground as he waits for me to approach. I do, cautiously. There is no getting out of it now. When I get within touching distance his eyes open. They flash a pretty lavender color before fading back to their grey green and he smiles.

"Nice to meet you without your escorts," he says, wryly.

I choke back a snort. "Yeah…" I mumble "same goes for you." I cock my hip out, doing my best to project confidence.

He snorts. "Fair, I seldom am without my own."

I nod awkwardly. *Why have I not left yet?* I am standing in front of him and am starting to get uncomfortable by his gaze raking over my form. Covertly, I look for the best escape route. Returning my gaze back to his, I eye him warily. He meets my gaze, tracking me with intensity. I start to edge away from him, but quick as lightning he snatches my hand and pulls me to him causing me to ungracefully fall into his lap. *What the fuck?* I scramble away, once again grateful for the leg holes in this dress. Once I feel like I am safely away from his grabby hands, I sit across from the prince, warily. "What...why did you do that?"

He chuckles again. "Why do you keep trying to leave? You've not been focused on this entire conversation. Need to get back to those men of yours?"

I bristle at his insinuation. "What, no," I say, maybe a little too quickly. "We have only just started talking, I was just taking in the scenery." *I really hope my new dress is not now covered in dirt.* I look down to check for any spots of dirt, but also to break eye contact, and am stunned when the dress is completely unmarred.

"Right... That's why you were eyeing the tree line like it was your only salvation." He rolls his eyes but then lets out a chuckle causing my stomach to flutter with excitement. I bite my inner cheek willing my hormonal body to behave. The prince was an attractive man, I could admit that, but his arrogance left something to be desired. "You are cute when taken off guard, it's too bad..." he trails off, his chuckles melting into a frown.

"Too bad?" I snap my gaze away from my dress and back again to the prince's eyes. I hate feeling toyed with. He is making me feel unbalanced, which is frustrating. If he has this much power over my emotions after one conversation, that can only mean bad things for my future.

"Too bad you are merely a pawn, although I will enjoy playing with you." He smirks. His eyes suggesting there was a lot more meaning behind those words than anything purely political.

I wrinkle my brow and squeeze my legs together trying to stay collected. "Playing with me?" I squeak and then become annoyed with my pitch. Ignoring any double entendres that can possibly be associated with that phrasing, I clear my throat. "As if you are not a pawn as well?"

"Pawns do as they are told and believe what they are told... I have other plans."

"And you assume I do not?"

"Do you?" I cannot help but feel like there is an underlying condescension to his tone.

"Maybe I do, but that is for me to know and you to find out," I bite back at him.

"Oh, I hope to." He smiles again.

He stands offering me a hand. I take it, hesitantly. Once I stand, he traces his fingers over my arm, before pulling me forward and placing a gentle kiss on my forehead. I inhale a quick breath, my body tightening at the contact, and I internally scold myself for being unable to maintain control. This encounter alone proves he is not to be mistaken as trustworthy. His arrogance and aggressive manipulation of my body should surely make me disgusted with his touch. *So why the fuck am I so turned on?*

His body tenses at something and he once again leans back against the giant tree behind him, closing his eyes. I look at him quizzically.

"Here come your men," he states before I hear hurried footsteps approach.

CHAPTER SEVEN
Where is She?

Sorin

Panic cannot begin to describe how I felt when Lace was not in her room this morning. I had convinced Sam we should let her sleep in a bit longer than might have been necessary. She looked so exhausted before going to bed last night. I figured with her world being turned upside down and the plans her father has for her, maybe a little more sleep in these early days might be helpful. Even the strongest warriors need extra sleep sometimes. I regretted this decision as soon as we found the room empty.

Normally, we are not ones to burst into Lace's quarters. Knock on a window in the middle of the night? Sure. Steal her away when we have no business doing so? Sure. Never a break in— we are gentlemen after all. The circumstances we have found ourselves in, though, are not of the ordinary. I can't trust a single soul here and although her father is something to be feared, I have the protection of my lineage there. I am the youngest child of the Ilksbrough family. One of the oldest noble lineages in Tikilium. We are the sole providers of high-quality grapes in Ptheryeth. My own father always had the saying: *Where there is alcohol, there is coin to be made.* Hence why I still have my head. *The king does love his wine.* Here, though? I have no such protections. Not that I truly care about them. Those who get in the way of my mission here will find themselves dead. Along with anyone who dares harm my Lace. The thing about those protections is with them comes restriction. I am now free of both of those things.

"The door!" Sam points to the door to the garden. It is cracked just slightly; someone must have forgotten to close it completely.

"Let's hope Alaceandra is the one who forgot to shut it..." I mumble, her full name foreign on my tongue. It has been ages since I've called her by her full name, but you never know who is listening. Sam nods although the cracked door is not a great hint at her whereabouts it is the best clue we have. She could not have wandered too far. Her bed was still slightly warm when we checked it earlier. We approach the door. "We need to have a talk with her about wandering by herself," I grumble, making my way back into this cursed garden.

Sam nods his agreement, keeping quiet. The grounds feel much different today. The magic laced within it is unsettling and rubs against my aura in an aggressive manner that makes me want to throw something. Nature is supposed to bring me peace but instead this energy does its best to amplify my ire. I pinch the bridge of my nose and huff out a breath, trying to keep myself calm. I will not find Lace if I cannot control myself.

Sam tilts his head up at a noise. "I hear her; she's in the center of the garden."

I storm over, not caring whether I damage any greenery in my way. Although it hurts me to pain nature, right now I could not care less. I will pay my respects to the mother later and ask for forgiveness, for now I must get to Lace.

"Here come your men." I hear a voice drawl in the distance. As I part the trees with Sam I come upon a clearing. On the edge of it I see what looks to be the prince leaning against a tree and a red-faced Lace across from him, shooting him a confused look. If he has done something to her, I will deal with him accordingly. For now, though, my priority is Lace.

CHAPTER EIGHT
Mysterious Gift

Alaceandra

Fadres and Credour come crashing through the trees into the clearing. They look quite frazzled, until their eyes lock on me. Relief fills their expressions, that is until they spot Prince no-name. Credour speaks first.

"Alaceandra, are you okay?"

I go to respond but am interrupted by the prince "Of course she is," he states in exasperation. "How could she not be? She's with me."

"We are unsure of your intentions, sir," responds Fadres. "We are tasked with keeping her safe."

"My intentions?" The prince huffs. "They are of no concern to you."

"To the contrary, actually, they are very much a concern of ours," Credour bites back. "Alaceandra, come here please..."

I start to walk in their direction, but the prince pulls me to a stop. "Alaceandra, feel free to visit here whenever you wish, I look forward to speaking with you further. For now, I will finish my meditations in peace." Releasing me, he smiles dangerously. His eyes are still closed, and his body is still relaxed against the tree. He crosses his arms, directing his voice towards Fadres and Credour. "But men, if you continue destroying my gardens, I will not hesitate to let them destroy you."

Credour scowls. "Is that a threa-"

"Our apologies," chimes Fadres.

I chose at that moment to scurry over to them, and we began to make our way, carefully, out of the garden. Before we successfully exit, I hear the prince's voice on a whisper of wind "I'll be waiting..."

I cross the threshold and cringe. All I have accomplished during this meeting is angering Sorin and Sam and ensuring the prince's interest in me is piqued. To make matters worse, I still have no insight into what is next for me.

"Sooooooo..." starts Fadres.

"You really scared us, Lace." Credour looks frustrated but the worry in his eyes is clear.

"You do not need to worry about me, I was just exploring." I place a gentle hand on Credour.

"With tree prince over there?"

"Well, no, not intentionally."

"Then...." Fadres prods.

"I stumbled upon him. I wanted to leave the garden, but he had already sensed my presence. They are *his* gardens..." I emphasize. Credour shoots me a look of alarm and understanding before grunting.

A thought hits me. "Wait... Do you think it is possible to hear through plants?" If he could sense everything in the garden maybe he would have heard our conversation yesterday."

"It's possible but unlikely he would have overheard our conversation yesterday," Fadres supplies, answering my full question before I can ask it. "The shield I put up should have blocked that. He would have felt our presence in the garden though." I guess he had the same thought.

I look at him a bit unsure "Are you sure there is no chance he knows your identities?"

Fadres pipes up again. "I wouldn't say no chance... there is always a slim chance of anything... but it is unlikely."

"Okay... good." I pick at my nail.

Credour grasps the hand I am picking at and uses it to twirl me around. "Nice dress, where did this come from?" He compliments me with a smile. I giggle appreciating the subject change.

"Thank you, a sweet handmaiden gave it to me this morning."

"Oh, so they have already assigned you with staff?"

"It seems so. I am hoping to befriend them," I smile.

A look of worry crosses over his features for a split second, before he gives me a gentle look. "Be careful, although I am happy they are treating you appropriately, you don't know if everyone truly means you well."

"I know..." I shiver, thinking back to father's letter this morning.

Fadres looks at me curiously. "Are you okay?"

"Yes. It's just a little... chilly in here is all." I rub my arms for added effect, glancing around. I am not sure why I do not tell Credour or Fadres about my father's little message this morning. Although I trust them implicitly, I am paranoid about the eyes my father alluded to.

"Come, let's go find you a cloak, we can discuss this later." I nod.

Credour and Fadres escort me back to my room, but as they go to enter with me, I stop them.

"Wait out here, it would be odd if you followed me inside." I smile at them, reassuringly.

Credour rolls his eyes. "Fine, fine. We will be right here, but no sneaking off."

I nod my acceptance of these terms.

He mumbles to himself and leans against the wall. Before I can close the door Fadres stops me and gives me a quick hug. "We really were worried, please be quick." He grins at me and casts a nervous eye towards Credour. "For everyone's sake." He chuckles in response to Credour's glare.

"I will, I promise. I just need to find a cloak. That room is massive."

He nods at me then releases my arms and leans on the other side of the door from Credour. "We will be right here."

I give him a thumbs up and then walk into my room, closing the door behind me. I rest my hands on my hips wondering where to start my search. I actually have not done much exploring of this room other than, of course, the bed. I glance over at the bed in question, exhaustion sneaking its way into my limbs. *I could use a bit of a nap.*

I notice something lying on my bed and I walk over to inspect the material. There lies a cloak. One that matched the dress perfectly. It has the same white fabric, a hood, and it is hemmed with the same flowers and vines. Although beautiful, I was a bit disturbed by its presence. There is no other way to take its appearance other than a sign we are being surveilled. The only question now is, who is watching? King Demetrius? My Father? The prince? I bite my nail. *Let us just hope this particular stalker has good intentions.*

Nausea churns my stomach as another thought hits me, this gift serves as another message as well. This room is not a safe space for me. Not only due to the almost confirmed spyware littering the ceiling disguising itself as vines, but the fact I have no idea who has access to my room. A rustling on the other side of the door, causes me to jump. I calm myself remembering Sorin and Sam are still awaiting me outside, quickly I throw on the cloak and rush back to the door. *I need to get back.*

CHAPTER NINE
Faraway Allies

Alaceandra

Despite the prince's invitation, over the next couple of weeks, I steer clear of the gardens. I still spot the prince in the halls around the castle, but we do not find ourselves alone, and for that I am grateful. He made me feel so off balanced and I am not sure what to make of him. Instead, I find refuge in a little library doing all I can to learn about Helomasi. Hard as I try, the texts are bereft of any information regarding the kingdom or its history. I found only two things of interest. One was the mention that Helomasians use smaller elvisera for mail carrying, as they are much speedier than their larger counterparts, which I found to be quite odd, as I have never heard of a smaller elviserian race. The other was a singular sentence in one of the children's books. It mentioned some sort of plague that had wreaked havoc on parts of the land eons ago:

Those who are naughty best be careful of the plague, for once darkness finds you, you can never be saved.

As creepy as that line was, it only led to a dead end. When I tried to ask some of the servants about it, they refused to give me a straight answer on the matter, citing some chore or task that they must get back to before making a hasty retreat. Once word got around that I had been asking questions the servants started avoiding me all together. I found food deposited on my bed along with my garments only after I had left my chambers and the halls strangely empty when I walked around. I am sure that they are probably still there on the outskirts watching me, but they are doing a great job of making themselves scarce. It is frustrating to know so little about the new place I am living, but it is quickly looking like that cannot be helped. *This is definitely starting to feel like I have just hopped prison cells.* My father also enjoyed keeping me woefully in the dark about information regarding Tikilium and the surrounding kingdoms, and I hate that this new king is acting similarly.

Sighing I pick up a pen, writing out a letter to Philos. *She is sure to have more information than anyone on these matters.* The watchfulness of this kingdom has me on edge. I have only let my elvisera, Addie, carry my letters to Philos instead of their smaller elvisera, which the king did provide for me about a week ago. Although Addie's size means the letters get back and forth a bit slower, I do not mind. It is better to have a carrier I can trust than a speedy one that might spill my secrets. Plus, Tikilium did not have such small elvisera, rather we used our full-sized elvisera to serve both the function of mail and travel carrying. I worry about the origin of the smaller ones and fear they might even be the babies of the magnificent creatures being put to work too early. I bite the edge of my pen, before shaking the thought away for the time being and continuing my letter to my dear friend.

~~~~~~

Philos,
~~~~~~

It has been so nice to be around Sam and Sorin over the past couple of weeks, although I do miss the freedoms, I had with them in Tikilium. They are supposed to be my guards here in Helomasi. Logically, I know that once I marry the prince that will be over entirely and moreover, I would not have had them anyway had they not had this plot to disguise themselves as Fadres and Credour, but still. Having them so close and yet so out of reach has been difficult. I have found that the crush I have on both of them that I have been trying for so long to bury has only gained in intensity by their constant nearness (yes, I admit it. Hush your teasing!!). At least in Tikilium their constant distance from missions made it easier for me to ignore these feelings, but now... I do not know. Any of your sage wisdom would be welcome here.

*Moreover, there **is** the issue of the prince of Helomasi. He is.... complicated. We have only met once and yet I find that my thoughts get tangled up between the three of them in the middle of the night (you would be proud of me admitting so). Should I go back and see him? Would I survive losing Sam and Sorin? I do not think so and yet what choices do I have?*

Speaking of! What all have you heard of Helomasi? I should have asked you sooner, but I figured I would be able to learn more of this kingdom organically. That is not proving the case unfortunately.... I did read a children's book mentioning some kind of plague here as well... have you heard of it? The book is called Fables of Helomasi: Children of the Sun. Also, do you have tiny elvisera in your land? They tend to be yellow and fly quite quickly due to their size, but I find them quite unnerving. I never thought to ask the question before, but I have not seen these creatures so small in Tikilium. Any information would be welcome at this stage.

I miss you dearly,

Alaceandra

p.s. I do hope this letter gets to you. I am having my elvisera burn any letter close to interception by others. If you do not receive a letter in a while, please do not think I am ignoring you. It only means our means of communication has been interfered with. I will be sure to write out a code for you in the future... just in case you never see this one. Love you so much!

~~~~~~

I fold the letter into a nondescript envelope and call Addie to me. She comes with a loud caw, and I giggle at her antics. I lay my head against hers conveying my need for privacy with the letter and her returning emotions tell me she understands her duty. Kissing her nose, I give her the letter and with one last look she flies off, her speed gaining until she is just a speck in the sky. I smile and lay back onto my bed, closing my eyes for the night.
~~~~~~

CHAPTER TEN
Secret Messages

Alaceandra

I am standing outside my door staring at my disguised Fadres and Credour. It is weird to see the boys in these forms knowing it is them. I am starting to see some of their idiosyncrasies peek through the surface. Sam always chews on the bottom of his lip when he is nervous or worried about something. Sorin always jiggles his leg when he is feeling on edge. It is adorable and something about seeing them be them, even in their disguises, brings me much-needed comfort.

"So..." I begin, mischief alight in my voice. "What are we getting into today?"

Sam looks up and seeing my good mood releases his lip and smiles at me. I squirm a little, his smile evoking all kinds of forbidden feelings. "I don't know. What are you thinking?"

"Well... it seems like a waste to only know the landscape of the castle and the gardens... maybe we can explore the grounds today?"

Sam's eyes twinkle a little mischief speaking through his serious expression. *I love that look.* "I know a route we can take."

Sorin, catching on to our excitement, chimes in. "I know how we can go undetected."

"Sounds like a plan." My body vibrates with excitement. "Come on, then," I say to Sam and Sorin "lead the way."

Sam guides us through the hallways of the castle while Sorin trails us ensuring we are undetectable as we make our way outside. We come across a large teal bookcase teeming with various literature about the botanicals in the area. Sam pulls a book wrapped in blue leather labeled: *Pink Lolcasis.* With a soft click the bookcase swings open into a long hall with a light just peeking out on the other side of it. We walk into the hallway and Sorin shuts the bookcase behind him. It is dark and a tad bit creepy in here, with the only light being at the end of the hall.

"How did you know this was here?" I ask Sam.

"I accidentally stumbled upon it when looking for some reading material. I wasn't in here long but I was looking forward to showing it to you. Thanks for the excuse to do so." He throws me a wink.

"We should be careful who we use this around." Sorin touches one of the black stones lining the passage.

"We will," I supply.

We finally make it to the end of the long hall and find ourselves behind a large red bush. We squat and move around it to peer out. I gasp. The world around us is not lush with pink and red blooms and teal foliage but instead is covered in hard rock. The stones are black with red rivulets running through them as dark as blood. I do not remember this landscape when flying here, but maybe something has changed since I arrived. I really have not seen much of outside. The staff steering me mostly to my room or about the castle. The stones are strangely mesmerizing. I did not know Helomasi had lands like these, not that I was informed much about Helomasi lands before arriving, but I am eager to explore them.

"The coast is clear." Sorin's voice jerks my eyes away for a split second. As a unit we come out from the bush and approach the rocks. I brush my fingers across one and notice how warm they are. The rock responds to my touch, emitting a soft light.

"Whoa," I say in awe.

"What did you do?" Sorin asks.

"Nothing I just touched it."

Sorin runs a hand across a stone opposite of mine, but nothing happens. "Sam, try touching this." Sorin points to a rock. Sam places his palm against the stone, but again nothing happens.

"Weird," I say. "Maybe it was a fluke?" I skate my fingers across the stone next to the one I just touched and that one also starts to emit a faint red glow. Suddenly the light from the two stones starts traveling over the other stones further down the path. Right before the light is too far to see it pauses. "Should we... follow the light?"

"I don't know..." Mutters Sam, looking a little uncomfortable.

"For once I agree with Sam." Sorin scratches his head. "We don't know where this might lead us."

My shoulders drop, but my curiosity is piqued. I really want to see where the rocks are leading me. "Are you not curious?"

Sorin looks at the dancing lights again, distrustfully. "No, Lace. We don't know if it's an elaborate trap or who might be watching us right now. I think we should leave the weird floaty lights alone."

Sam's eyes widen. "Yes... exactly." Sam looks at Sorin like he's gained a new head. It is not often the boys agree, especially when it comes to matters pertaining to adventure over safety. Sorin really must have a bad feeling about this path.

I push out a breath, disappointed, I was really hoping for an adventure today. "Okay, I guess you are right."

Sorin notices my disappointment and lightly rubs one of my shoulders. "Hey," he soothes "we can check it out later. We have not really covered our tracks here. If someone comes looking for us, I want to make sure we are where we need to be for now."

I wrinkle my nose at him playfully, but smile. "Fine."

"Aaaand," he drags out, "I might have seen a certain elvisera delivering a certain princess some mail earlier."

My eyes light up in excitement. "Really?" He nods. "Well then what are we waiting for?" I bounce lightly on my toes.

Sam chuckles warmly. "Come on, then." We make our way back through the passageway and into the hall undetected.

I rush through the halls back to my room with the men on my heels, just keeping enough decorum as to not downright sprint. When we arrive to my room Sam and Sorin depart. I give them both a quick nod before wrenching open my door to find my beautiful elvisera sniffing at one of the definitely bugged vines in my room. When she spots me, she flies gently into the air causing the room to stir with the wind as I approach her. She deposits a pretty letter into my hand, and I pet her gently before she soars back into the sky and out of sight.

I glance at the letter and realize it is from Philos. A slight squeal escapes my lungs, and I settle into my bed to read it:

~~~~~~

My dearest Lace,

Never plead for something irrevocably yours, now and always. You know I am never one for politics, so I trust your judgment, but do know you will always have safety here. I also agree, there is much more at play than what seems. So, ensure you keep a <u>keen</u> eye on what's in front of you.
~~~~~~

You've been quite the topic as of late. Apparently, you are rooming next door to not one but three men?! I'm so proud you've finally taken my advice to be more... exploratory <3. I want __all__ the details, my dear. __Caps__ off to you!

Please write me back soon, you know how much I enjoy details!! I'm practically starved, though your last letter was most illuminating.

All my love,

Philos

p.s. So i hear your old maid mandi has been busy! How could you let someone like that around you for so long? Earnestly, the situation is quite concerning!

I heard from crena that she's run from tikilium, leaving rubble and ash in trail behind her. She destroyed nearly half your father's estate after turning into some sort of "scaly she-devil."

She apparently also stole something of value. Although rumors are quite muddled as to what. Fidelity is so hard to come by now-a-days. Even from the best of staff.

What a fiasco! I also heard the queen has left with her! Though i'm not sure i believe that. Her highness has always been so enamored with your father. Maybe mandi has been a bad influence on her? Either way, enough gossip for one note...

~~~~~~

I squint at the paper. The handwriting is definitely Philos' but there is something definitely off about the wording she used. Philos never has any good thing to say about my father, moreover she would never say anything negative regarding Mandi. She knows how much she means to me and has only ever spoken highly of her. I press my eyebrows together in confusion fiddling with the side of the pages. I really hope Mandi is okay. I have never seen her turn into a "she beast" of any kind and she was always a gentle soul I could talk to whenever I was home, but more than
~~~~~~

anything she was my friend and I really hope if anything is true about this letter, it is that she is out of my father's grasp.

A tear falls and lands on the page smearing the ink slightly. The sight of it catches my eye and I tilt my head then read the letter again and notice the underlined words. Then I blink. "Keen all caps?" I whisper to myself with a smile. No wonder this letter is so weird. There is a secret message within it! I find something to write with and start to circle the capitalized words. Then bite my lip in confusion. Maybe the message is in the p.s.? There does not seem to be any pattern in the letter itself. Only losing steam slightly I forge on and start to circle the capitalized letters in the postscript. S...H... E I... S S...A...F... E W...I...T...H...M... E. She who is she? I stare at the letters, then the tears rush back to my eyes full force as I realize their meaning. Mandi! The subject of the letter. Mandi is safe and with Philos? Was Philos the connection Mandi had? My mind is reeling but the only thing I can focus on is the fact she is safe for now and maybe... maybe soon I can see her again. I hug the letter to my chest in gratitude.

My smile drops as a thought hits me. The letter being coded is worrying. It must mean our communications are indeed being interfered with otherwise she would have told me outright. She had yet to answer my letter about the boys and Helomasi, maybe she never received it? Did it go up in ash? If so, why would she feel the need to code her thoughts? Is something happening in Araletos? So many questions, but no answers. I drag in a ragged breath and then call my elvisera back with a breathy whistle. When she makes her way up back to my balcony, I lay my head against hers to convey what I want her to do. With a nudge at my hand, I open it, and she blows out a small stream of fire, turning the beloved letter to ashes. I smile and pet her in gratitude before she once again departs, leaving me to my thoughts and the ashes to the wind. *At least Mandi is safe.*

CHAPTER ELEVEN

Important Matters

Alaceandra

Some time passes before a knock sounds on my door. I have been puzzling over a way to let Philos know I have received her message without giving away what the message is or how to do it without interception. I miss my friend. Although the company of Sorin and Sam is nice, there is no better comfort than in the arms of your best girl especially one as informed as she. She has been the one who has guided me through all of my crisis whether they be political, trivial or social over the years. Although she prefers women herself, she has even been good at providing a rational or an empathetic ear to my troubles surrounding my feelings for Sorin and Sam. She is the one who pointed out my crushes on them early on and even though she has teased me about it ever since, her levity when it comes to intense situations has always been a dear comfort to me. I would really appreciate her views on my current situation here in Helomasi or any insights she may have about the kingdom and truthfully it would also be nice if she could provide some clarity as to my growing infatuation with the prince.

He is both an asshole and annoyingly intriguing. He elects to cast me secretive looks whenever we cross paths, ensuring Sorin and Sam are not watching. I cannot help but be curious as to what those glances mean. I also wonder what he might have told me had Sorin and Sam not interrupted in the gardens. Would he have shared with me more of his secret plans to go against our fathers? I guess it is good to know that he has other plans than to play pawn in our parents' game, but his still seeing me as a pawn even within his own plans does not bode well for me. He is a puzzle, and I cannot help but want to solve him, let us hope I do not lose pieces of myself in the process.

As I muse at what I assume Philos would say to the clusterfuck my life has turned into, another knock echoes through the room. Sighing aloud I hoist myself from my bed and pad over to the door. I start to reach out before thinking better of it. "Announce yourself" I yell at the door. No one responds. I crack the door slightly, peering through in curiosity and finding a note at the foot of my door, I snatch it up.

~~~~~~

Please meet me in the gardens in the morning before breakfast. Alone. There are important matters to discuss.

~~~~~~

I look around. The gardens? *Maybe the Prince wrote this?* I furrow my brow at the note. It had to be. Those are the prince's gardens, who else would want to meet me within them? I look around and notice a servant walking away from my room, his movements stiff and jerky. As he starts to turn the corner his eyes meet mine and I quickly duck back into my room. My heart is pumping a thousand miles a minute. *Something was wrong with that man.* His eyes were bloodshot and unseeing. His face unnaturally pallid. *What was he doing outside my room?* I crumble the paper. *Hopefully this meeting with the prince will provide me some answers.* I try to push the man from my thoughts. Walking back over to my bed, I lay down. As soon as my head hits the pillow, I fall asleep.

CHAPTER TWELVE
Risky Choices

Alaceandra

I wake up early the next morning, sweating. I had nightmares the entire night before but cannot recall their contents, which is strange. I dream vividly every night and usually can recall at least bits of every dream I have, but this morning the memories have escaped me, leaving me with a sour feeling in my stomach. Shaking my body to get rid of the awful feeling, I throw off my covers, and I stumble out of bed before my body convinces me to sleep for any longer.

Padding over to the bathroom, I complete my morning routine. Staring into the mirror, I sigh. It is hard to navigate a place that I have no knowledge of to begin with, but couple that with being avoided at every corner by staff, and being watched by a stranger who is supposedly your future husband? *This is starting to feel impossible.* If that were not the least of my problems, there is still the mystery of the lights and red glowing rock. I am dying to continue to investigate it, but I understand

Sam and Sorin's hesitation. Diving headfirst into the unknown does not always prove beneficial, especially when you are already in dangerous waters. Despite this, I cannot help but be so curious, I know there is only so long I can go until I lose my resolve to be safe. It has gotten me in trouble on numerous occasions and a person does not change overnight. Truly, I am happy that there is mystery to solve. At least now I feel as if I can have some purpose here outside of my father's plans. Those lights were unlike anything I had ever seen before.

I bite back tears. I thought that, maybe, if I were able to get away from Tikilium and my father, I could explore more of the world. Get to know more about the kingdoms surrounding me and maybe even have a chance to visit Philos. If these last couple weeks are any indication of what my life will be like here... then maybe my father is right. *'You are just another chess piece,'* my father's voice invades my thoughts. *'A pawn will always be a pawn, no matter whose hand it is in. Know your place. Submit to it. Curiosity will only lead to your death in the end.'*

I slam my hairbrush onto the sink. *No. No!* I will take control of my future if it is the last thing I do. *Starting with this note.* I snatch the piece of paper from the counter.

Stalking out of the bathroom's warm embrace, I find clothes have been laid out for me once again this morning and my bed has been made. Today there is a light-yellow dress. It has the same silky texture as the dress the day before along with leg holes and pockets. This one also has a vine design around its hem, although this design is a lot more subtle and delicate than the day before. I quickly get dressed and then let out a short huff of breath. I find a piece of paper and scribble down a note thanking my handmaiden for the beautiful selection and leave it on my bed. While I have paper and pen, I also scribble out a note to my pretend

Fadres and Credour letting them know they can find me in the garden if they need me.

Shoving the prince's note into my pocket, I resolve myself to the fact that I will have to once again face the prince alone. I set my shoulders back and leave my room.

CHAPTER THIRTEEN

Endearments and Endangerment

Alaceandra

A s I reach the red, wrought iron doors leading to the garden, I notice the space is looking suspiciously dark. The sun is nowhere in sight and shadows are cast along the stony floor sending chills down my spine. Pushing open the heavy, ornate metal cautiously, I peek my head out. Nothing immediately jumps out at me, but a shiver runs down my spine. The gardens did not feel so foreboding when I was with Sam and Sorin, nor with the prince. The oppressive tension in the air is ringing all kinds of alarm bells in my head. *I could have sworn I saw the sun beaming through the castle windows on my way here.*

"I definitely should not go in there," I mutter to myself. "This is how people die..." I stare into the dark garden, but something within me will not allow me to walk away. Taking another longing look behind me, I walk into the dark landscape. Each step I take causes the dread to build within my gut until it becomes downright unbearable. *Fuck this...* I am about to turn tail and run when something slams into me. Screaming, I fall to the ground. An image gets blasted into my mind of the rocks outside of the castle walls, but instead of them just glowing, they blink between black, white and red. The image shifts to a rock covered in dirt with strange lettering etched into it I cannot quite make out through the haze of the vision. I reach for it, but it disappears beneath my fingertips. As abruptly as the vision came is as abruptly as it disappears, and my mind is basked in darkness. I flutter my eyes open again, groaning, and squint at the sun now beaming above me. I am no longer at the entrance of the gardens, but instead in the clearing I was in when I met the prince last. Something moves in the wood line. I jump up and try to maintain my balance as I brace myself for another attack. I scan the area for a weapon. A stick lays several paces in front of me, and I lunge for it, holding it up to ward off whatever entity is watching me.

As I take a breath in, I realize the air is much lighter than it was when I first entered. "How long was I out?" I mutter aloud. *Or was I even out at all?* Feeling more and more paranoid of my surroundings, I raise my voice to yell at the figure watching me. "Who are you?" There is a slight tremble in my voice.

A soft chuckle sounds from the figure, the voice familiar. *Is that... the prince?* I squint into the darkness and see a flash of his lavender eyes.

"What are you doing here?" I ask. He walks into the clearing, his eyes returning to their normal color.

"I was just checking on you, little dove, you rushed out of the gardens so quickly earlier after your watch dogs came, and I have not seen you in these gardens since. Now I find you in the middle of my clearing. Truly I can ask you the same question."

Dropping the stick to the ground, I pause, "Little Dove?" I wipe my hands of dirt.

He smirks "Well, aren't you supposed to be a symbol of peace for our fathers? It only suits."

"I did not think we were in a pet name phase."

He shrugs. "If it fits..."

I narrow my eyes at him. "You were the one who invited me here. Or do you not remember the note you left me, your highness?"

He throws me a confused look and then frowns. "See that is not a good pet name..."

I smirk. "Does it not fit?"

"No, it doesn't. It is extremely uncreative and you would not be the only one who addresses me as such. Therefore, it would lose any uniquity. If you are to try again, give it some thought first." He waves a hand at me and leans against a tree with a cocky smirk.

I purse my lips. "Okay well I am not sure I will take you up on that, but thanks for the offer..."

"Afraid of challenges I see."

I quirk a brow at him. "I never said I was afraid."

"You didn't have to."

"What is that supposed to mean?"

"Well," He walks over to me and lifts up a finger to trace the side of my face. My stomach flutters at the contact. "For one, you've been avoiding this place like the plague." He caresses my neck next. A shiver invades my body, and he smirks. "For two, you've been here two months and have barely left your room, save to eat and run to the library with the guard dogs." His hand finishes by tracing down my arm. "You seem to love hiding away from your future here in your nest of blankets and the safety of your past." His wondering hand travels back to my chin lifting my eyes to his. "That does not seem like someone who luxuriates in a challenge to me." *Get away from him, Lace!*

I will my body to pull away from him. My nipples are pebbled, and I know my face is flushed. I clear my throat. "You seem to know a lot for someone who has been doing just as much sneaking about." My voice is embarrassingly breathy, and I curse myself for it.

"Not sneaking, observing, little dove. I need to know the intricacies of my pieces properly before I can play them."

I scoff, backing away from him further. "You are an ass." I start to walk off, trying to shake off his effect on me.

"Flying off so soon?" He tilts his head, watching me.

"Well, if there is nothing else, I would prefer not to spend my morning toyed with."

"Who said there wasn't?"

I huff. "Look, it is obvious all you are here to do is aggravate me and quite frankly this morning has been far too odd to deal with anymore of your riddles." Which in all honesty is kind of a lie, I am enjoying the verbal sparring match a little too much, but I do not want to get too comfortable and have it bite me in the ass later. *I know we are about to get married and everything but maybe it can be more like a roommate situation rather than anything romantic, most kings have many lovers, right? It could be easy for us to forget we are even married, other than I guess any public appearances...* My body tightens, making its disapproval at that thought known. *Yeah, with the way he touches me? That is so not happening.* I am jerked from my thoughts when the prince catches my wrist. I jerk back. *How does he move so silently?*

He crosses his arms and stares at me expectantly.

"Ugh, fine tell me what you want." He smiles. "But hands to yourself." I add in a rush. His smile only grows wider. *We have not known each other long enough to be touching as much as we have as it is...* "Besides," I continue with a jolt of apprehension. "I do not even know your name; everyone just refers to you as prince or the king's son. Touch is a familiarity reserved for those known and trusted not strangers, even if they are your betrothed..."

He smiles at me wryly. "Names have power here, Dove. It is not an accident my name is not known to many but," his grin turns teasing. "Once I have found you have spread your wings, I will give you a hint."

"I do not have wings to spread," I grit out.

"It is a metaphor, little dove."

I roll my eyes. I cannot help feeling like I am presenting myself as the pawn he continuously accuses me of by playing this game, but curiosity scratches at me. "Only a hint?"

"Only a hint." He confirms.

"What kind?"

"You'll see."

"I do not trust you."

"Oh, you shouldn't," he confirms.

I bite my bottom lip. "Will it at least be a good hint."

"Of course, there is no fun in the game if the reward is too minimal."

I think for a moment but ultimately decide to agree. "Fine, you have a deal."

He claps. "Great!" He sits down taking his signature place leaning against the big tree in the center of the field and then holds out a hand to invite me to sit next to him. I do, reluctantly. "Now what note were you speaking of?"

I jerk my head to look at him. "Umm the one you wrote me... asking me to meet you here early this morning... alone?"

His brows furrow. "I did not write you any such note."

My spine straightens. "What do you mean?"

"I did not write anything to you, Dove. I was surprised when I felt your presence in the gardens this morning, so I came to investigate, but this was not something I had planned on earlier."

"Huh."

"Huh indeed, but don't worry I will look into this, do you still have the note?"

"I do." I pull it from the little hidden pocket in my dress and uncrumple the paper.

"Thank you," he says, taking the note from me. As he does, his hand brushes mine ever so gently and a shiver runs over my body. He smirks.

"What?" I ask.

"Oh nothing, Alaceandra. I will let you play your games for now."

"I have no games."

His brows furrow once again. He is going to wrinkle that handsome face of his if he keeps this up. "Sure, you don't"

"I do not," I say firmly.

He chuckles softly but then seems to drop it. "It's actually not a bad thing I found you here exactly. I did need to ask you something."

For some reason, elvisera choose that moment to flutter inside my abdomen. "Yes?"

"Please join me for lunch tomorrow."

"Um, sorry what?"

He chuckles. "Lunch? The midday meal? Please join me for it... tomorrow." He spells it out for me like I am a moron. *Asshole.*

"Yes, I understand what lunch is. You are just..."

"Just?"

"Confusing!" I say in a burst. "You go from calling me a pawn to giving me pet names and asking me on dates."

"Ah, I see, you misunderstand, the lunch is a requirement of the king, we will not be alone."

"Oh..." My shoulders slump.

He tilts his head at me. "Unless you want--"

"No," I cut him off, my cheeks burning. "Understood, I will see you then."

He laughs then stands. "Yes. As lovely as this surprise rendezvous has been, I unfortunately have matters to tend to before this afternoon."

"Right," I say and scramble to my feet as to not be sitting alone. "I also should check back in."

"Ah yes, with your guard dogs?"

I roll my eyes. "I wish you would stop calling them that, but yes."

He laughs a full laugh this time, leaving the echo of its jingle in my ears.

I cannot help but feel a bit... disappointed at his quick departure. I know I should not get too comfortable, he said it himself and truthfully I do not know what I was expecting. There is more at play than at least I am aware of, and I really need to remember that. Wiping my hands on my dress I start walking towards the exit of the gardens. He follows, pointing out any difficult to see branches along the way. Once we reach the entrance we start to go our separate ways when he stops me.

"Also, Dove?" I stop, before chiding myself for responding to his silly nickname. "Do remember we have appearances we must keep up. It is not beneficial to go against our father's plans quite yet." *Yet?*

The defiance laced in his words gives me pause. Such defiance hints at some broader plan I am not in the loop of and it aggravates me to know he will leave me in the dark, but I grit my teeth and nod. *So much for taking control.*

"One more thing." I once again halt my progress. "Our fathers aren't the only ones with plans for you. You would do well to remember that." A devilish smirk enters his gaze. "See you at lunch." He turns and walks off. I huff out a breath and watch him leave for a second. *I need more answers. I cannot continue like this.* My mind wanders back to the vision I saw earlier.

I make it to my room quickly and shut my door. Leaning against it, I take a breath, questions filling my head. *What the hell does he even mean? Is there another enemy I need to be wary of? Is it him? What plans could he possibly have for me?* "Nothing good," I whisper aloud, biting my lip with worry. "Definitely nothing good." I walk back over to my bed, close my eyes and throw myself into it. It had been a very long morning; I could stress myself about all this later today... after a nap. "For now?" I mumble to myself and snuggle under my blankets. "I am going to bed."

CHAPTER FOURTEEN
Lunch

Alaceandra

The afternoon comes sooner than I would like. I wake up to the soft closing of my chambers, the handmaiden once again eluding my questions. *I am sick of being avoided.* Frustrated, I continued getting ready knowing the boys will not wait too long before wanting to speak with me, seeing as I had been unavailable all morning. I wash and dress for the evening. This time styling a pretty dark blue gown laced up the sides, cinching in my waist. Briefly I wonder how I was going to get this off later. The intricacy of the gown, although beautiful did make for a challenge to put on. I glance in the mirror. "It sure is pretty though" I smile at myself before going to my desk to write a couple more brief letters to Philos.

Sam and Sorin come and retrieve me from my room, and we find ourselves in the library hidden in a little nook of the castle. After the sound barrier is in place and our conversations can be hidden away from any prying ears, I start a line of questioning before they can. We are lying on some pillows on the floor, and it reminds me of laying out in the grassy fields of Tikilium as a child.

"So…" I start "How have you guys been faring?"

"Okay," Sorin replies, fiddling with the hem of my skirt. "Most tend to stay away from us. It seems like servants and guards alike here are pretty much ghosts to each other and those they serve."

"Yes," Sam chimes in. "I wonder if there is any significance to that or if it is only a custom here. I know in Tikilium most stayed out of sight as to not endure the king's wrath but we still all talked with each other for the most part. It is the silence among staff here that is cause for concern."

"Hmmm…" my brows knit in concentration. "That is weird… maybe it is all the surveillance here?" I question, motioning to the general area around us. "Kind of hard to bitch about royals who can hear your every word."

"True," Sorin agrees. "Except it's not just a lack of conversation concerning the royal family, but a lack of conversation in general… it's disconcerting." He blows out his breath and then his hand brushes over mine. He picks it up and starts massaging it between both of his absentmindedly. "How are you doing? Has the prince made contact since the gardens?"

"Um… about that."

Sam and Sorin tense around me and sit up to look at me. Sorin does not drop my hand but instead clutches it gently in his and tugs at me to make me sit up and look at them. "Lace?"

"He… might have talked with me briefly this morning…" I bite my bottom lip gently. Sam's eyes drop to it before his brows knit together, eyes snapping back up to mine.

"When?" Sam picks up Sorin's line of questioning.

"Just a couple of hours ago."

"Really?" Sorin chimes back in. "We were awake we didn't hear you leave... we even passed by the gardens... I thought you were just sleeping in today"

"Weird. I left you both a note. I had assumed you saw it."

"No." Sorin looks worried. "What did you guys talk about? Did he try to touch you again?" Sorin's grip on my hand tightens slightly.

I look away from him. *Yes, but do they really need to know that?* "He has a new nickname for me." I elect for a change in subject.

Sam snorts. "What's that?"

"Dove."

"Dove?"

"Yes 'Dove'. Apparently because I am supposed to 'bring peace to the kingdoms' or whatever." I put peace to the kingdom in air quotes. "It was odd. He also still refuses to let me know his name." *How am I to marry someone if I have no idea what they are even to be called?*

Sam snorts. "Peace, my ass, keeping up with you is like trying to keep up with stampeding elephants, damn near impossible and frequently life threatening."

"Hey!" I push at Sam, not expecting the outburst from him, but also slightly offended.

"What?" He says. "I love it. It makes life interesting, Lace. All I was saying was I would not really describe you as a peaceful person."

"I can be peaceful..." I argue, although I do not know why.

"Sure, you *can*." He boops my nose, then catches my hand, rubbing it in a soothing motion. "When you are sleeping maybe." He jokes, squeezing my hand before letting go and leaning back. "No, but really Lace if you were all calm waters and smooth logic, you wouldn't be you or have the spirit you do. How boring would that be?" He glances at me, a gentle look on his face. "That is not to say you are not wicked smart—you are. All I am saying is the passion and vigor in which you take on life has never screamed straight lines and 'don't rock the boat' mentality."

I stick my tongue out at him. *He always has the strangest compliments.* "I guess."

"Also," Sorin chimes in. "Who else would get our boy Sam here out of his shell if not for you getting him to go on all these wild adventures." He claps Sam on the arm earning him a glare.

"I would say he is pretty good at getting into things himself," I laugh, "because as I remember it, I do not think I ever extend an invitation to you all to come on these adventures with me..."

"Yes but you love it." They both say.

"Not untrue..." I smile, picking at a nail. Then I frown. "I have to tell you both something."

They turn serious. "What is it Lace?" Sorin asks.

I recount my experience in the gardens this morning and the creepy image which popped in my head. Sam pales and Sorin's grip on my hand tightens again this time almost to the point of pain. I pull my hand away gently and take a breath. I do not mention the weird man in the hall. Although the thought of him gives me the creeps I do not think adding another mystery to this conversation would make matters any better.

"I think I need to explore the rocks and soon. There must be a reason the image of them shot into my mind. There is something I need to find, I think."

"Wait," Sam cuts in. "You want to listen to what the eerie energy is telling you? I don't think it is a good idea, Lace. It could be a trap."

I blow my breath out in frustration. "True, but it could also just be a message... and what am I supposed to do, run from it? I do not think this will just go away." *I know it will not. Something wants me to follow these rocks so much so that it is willing to invade my mind to convince me. Something like that does not give up easily.*

"How do you know? You haven't even tried to ignore it. Look, Lace, I know you love adventure and Sorin and I would follow you anywhere, but we have no idea the intentions of the people here or the power they might hold. We should give it more time before we start traipsing about the property and winding up into trouble. The king already warned you he would not turn a blind eye to you and being he isn't your father we don't know the punishments that might be in store for you if you make too much trouble."

"I know." I hang my head. "But we do not have much time, at least without the watch of the entire kingdom as the prince's wife. If I am doing this, it needs to be now."

Sam looks to Sorin for support, but Sorin is conveniently not looking in his direction. He grunts in frustration, but then a small smile enters his expression. "I had to give the speech, just in case you would change your mind, but..." He looks to me once more with a hopeful look on his face. I purse my lips together and he sighs. Shoulders slumped he continues "... when are we going?"

My mood immediately brightens, and I let out a small squeal, throwing my arms around Sam. He holds me tightly, sticking his nose into my hair as if he was trying to breathe me in. "Thank you." I whisper.

"Don't say thank you yet," Sam mutters, still holding me, his chin resting on the top of my head. "I don't think this is a good idea, I just know if I don't go with you, you'll concoct a more dangerous plan to go alone, and I like that idea even less." He ends our embrace by tickling my sides slightly.

I giggle pushing away from him. "I would never." I gasp out in fake outrage. Sam throws me an unbelieving look and Sorin laughs out loud, finally giving up his pretense of not being a part of the conversation.

He sobers and then steadies his eyes on me. "If we do go you have to stay with us. No running off." I nod. "Good. It should be this week. Once the marriage arrangements start ramping up-" he rolls his eyes and huffs "-you'll have less time alone, making this a lot more difficult."

I nod again. "I have thought about that, and I agree, the sooner the better... maybe we can sneak off tomorrow? Would that give everyone enough time to prepare?"

"So soon?" Sam groans slightly.

"I think so." Sorin responds. "But we will have to go near nightfall. I'll have to grab a couple of things."

"Sounds good. Until then I think we should just focus on getting through this lunch. Since the king will be in attendance, we have no idea what plans or challenges he or anyone else attending may put us through, or if they are testing us in any way. I hate to think this kingdom would have bad intentions, especially so early on but if father has taught me anything it is we cannot always trust those in power, especially kings."

Sam stands and brushes off his pants before giving me a hand up. "You are very wise, Lace. I could not have said it better myself." He brushes his fingers over my knuckles softly, causing my arms to break out slightly in goosebumps, before dropping it. "That being said we should go now, or else we will be late in our attendance."

"He's right." Sorin pipes up lazily pushing himself from the floor.

Lunch begins with little fanfare. Credour, Fadres and I sit towards the head of the table. Credour and Fadres are across from me, while the prince sits to my left. King Demetrius places himself at the head of the table. It appears we are at one of the smaller tables in the castle. There are only three more seats to mine and Credour's left remaining unoccupied along with a singular chair at the other end of the table. I wonder to myself where the queen of this kingdom is, or even if there is one. Lamenting over not knowing yet another piece of maybe crucial information, my finger starts to trace over the bracelet Mandi gave me. Something about this motion calms me and I breathe deeply as a humming sensation overtakes me. I let out a small sigh trying to come back to those around me, tension leaving my limbs. King Demetrius is chewing slowly and watching the table. His eyes trace over everyone in attendance until they land on me. Fadres and Credour look tense, while the prince on the other hand is smoothing out the napkin in his lap. His posture reading as relaxed, but his fingers twitch almost imperceptibly under the table, giving away a more nervous demeanor. Once the king finishes chewing, he clears his throat.

"Alaceandra."

My gaze shoots up to his. "Yes, King Demetrius?"

"How have you been enjoying the castle?"

"It has been lovely, thank you for allowing me to stay here until the marriage."

"Of course," the king smiles, but there is an edge of something in his eyes I cannot place. "It was what was best for both kingdoms."

I nod, because I do not really know how to respond and pick at my plate. Ptheryeth is large with many different species of birds and plants. Since Tikilium and Helomasi are so far from each other, the cuisine varies quite distinctly. Mandi informed me that it is custom for princesses to bring along some of their own foods to their betrothed's kingdom, so I have been dining on that bounty since I have arrived. Unfortunately, that means I have yet to encounter Helomasi's dishes. The food in front of me looks, for lack of a better term, slimy and unappetizing. I pick at my plate, hesitant to try it. I do not want to offend anyone, but no one but the king seems to have even touched their meals, making me unsure if I should either. The king, of course, notices this.

"Is the food not to your liking Alaceandra?" The king inquires in a tone feigning concern.

"I am sure it is very good, King Demetrius. I am just finding myself quite nauseated this morning, likely due to the change in climate here in Helomasi, my apologies." I lie, not wanting to insult the king.

Annoyance flickers over the king's expression, before smoothing back over to gentleness. "All's well..." He mutters, wiping his mouth, his plate now empty. He claps. "Now that we are all here. I have gathered you two to talk about your impending nuptials, there will be servants at the castle over the coming days to start measuring you Alaceandra so we can start fitting you into your gown. I was thinking we would hold the ceremony in a month's time."

The prince chokes "A month, father? But the law--"

The king glares at the prince. "Yes, is that a problem?" The king grasps onto something beneath the table and the prince sucks in a breath and looks down at his hands, gripping the napkin in his lap tightly. "I did not think so..." Releasing the object the king once again turns his attention onto me. "Now Alaceandra--"

Fadres cuts him off, "Our king will want to know of this advancement in timeline. The law clearly states she must meet her age of majority plus six months' time before being wed. It has only been two months since she has reached majority. I do not think he will be pleased."

"It does not matter whether it will please him or not." The king turns his glaring eyes to Fadres. "The minute she stepped into these walls she became my kingdom's property and problem. If I find out Tikilium's king hears of this before I inform him, there will be consequences. I know you all do not want to be responsible for hurtling Ptheryeth into an early war, now, will you?"

"No disrespect, but our duty is with Alaceandra and to King Nikoli not to you, your majesty." Credour bites out. "We are tasked with keeping her safe."

The king grits his teeth. "Well, a war will not be very safe now, will it? So, consider keeping this a secret a part of your duty, unless you would rather serve from the motherland. They do say there is a lot to see within the great beyond." Condescension drips from King Demetrius' tone and he laughs to himself.

"Are you threatening us?" Credour says between clenched teeth.

An army of men in teal armor appear from the corners of the room, fire glowing in their palms, their eyes trained on Credour. "No, young knight. Consider this a warning. You are all being watched closely by my men and although you may think you are hiding from me with your tricks." His eyes sharpen on my two men. "I will not allow for such insolence in my kingdom, you all will fall into line on my time, not your own."

Fadres' eyes turn calculating at this and he gently nudges Credour to back off. I feel a gentle touch to my thigh, and I jump, before noticing it is only the prince. He gives me a firm but soft squeeze before returning his hand back to his napkin in his lap. I take this opportunity to calm myself tracing my fingers back over Mandi's bracelet.

Finally, Fadres breaks the tension. "Of course, your majesty. Please excuse Credour he is still learning and sometimes his devotion gets in front of his sense. We will trust your judgment in this, besides our kingdoms are to be joined soon." He smiles pleasantly. "You are correct we do not want war on our doorsteps anytime soon, we hope this hastened marriage will bring both our kingdoms peace sooner." He bows his head slightly to King Demetrius in a show of respect, then glances towards Credour who copies the gesture.

"My apologies. Fadres is correct, I am being narrow-minded. We will be sure to keep this information to ourselves until told otherwise. Please excuse my outburst."

The king stares hard at the two men before taking a breath and putting on a pleasant smile. He claps again and the men wielding death in the form of fire sink back into the shadows of the room. "Wonderful, I knew we would all be in agreement. Well, I have things to do. Although this meal has been grand." He looks to me. "We should do it again soon. Until then, Alaceandra as I was saying servants will be coming for your fittings over the next couple of days starting right now. Your handmaiden awaits you, do not leave her to linger too long." He stands and turns to go. "Please do remember, children, you are always being monitored. Do not make me regret keeping you alive." He exits, leaving his soldiers to watch us from the shadows.

I shiver remembering my father's note had that same menacing sentiment. The room slips into a tense silence before Credour stands. "Let us go, Alaceandra." Credour commands before walking over to lead me from the room.

Fadres follows on our heels, and we walk swiftly to the little library. Credour shoots his eyes over the room, finding some new plants decorating the small space. He grabs them and sets them outside the room in a little closet across the hall before walking back in, shutting the door and closing his eyes. When he looks up his eyes burn a dark gold and he looks almost in pain.

Alarmed, I rushed over to him. Taking his head in my palms, I whisper to Sam, "Is it safe to speak?"

Sam nods.

"Sorin are you okay?" He stares into my eyes and brings me to him in an almost crushing embrace. I hold onto him tightly. I have never seen my friend so distraught.

"I just... I thought we had more time." He breathes the words, his voice shaking with emotion.

"What do you mean?"

Sam comes behind me and places his hand over Sorin's. "Before the marriage, Lace."

"I did too..." I trail off then sigh, still in Sorin's arms. "We still have a month." I say trying to stay positive. "And truly what is the difference? In the grand scheme of things, I will still be married off to the prince and..." I bite my lip, sadness taking over the sarcasm in my tone. "And you all will have to go."

"We would never leave you, Lace." Sorin declares.

"You might not have a choice." I whisper, a tear slipping down my cheek. Finally separating from him to look at them both, I see we are all now standing in a tight circle.

Sam wipes the tear from my cheek and fits a finger under my chin guiding my eyes to his. "There is always a choice, Lace."

Sorin grabs my hand, squeezing it in his. "And we will always choose you."

I nod at them. I believe they want to always be there for me, but I just do not know how they are going to pull it off this time. Or how I will for that matter. I set my shoulders back and raise my chin a little. "I should probably get back to my room. I do not want the king looking for me."

Sam grimaces. "Let's meet by the bookcases at midnight. I am sure the fittings will last you well through dinner."

I pout. "Ugh, hopefully there will be food at some point. Adventuring on an empty stomach is awful."

That finally pulls a small smile from Sorin, breaking the rest of the tension in the room. "I will be sure to grab you something to snack on just in case, my little adventurer."

I roll my eyes and smile at him. "Thank you kindly." I say with a hint of sassiness before dipping into a slight curtsy, when I rise Sorin and Sam pull me into a hug pressing their own quick kiss to my forehead. Sorin has not kissed me since we were kids, for obvious reasons, and Sam's affection has not been near as blatant in the past. Elvisera flutter in my stomach at the display. I wonder at their timing, but feel gratitude nonetheless. The sensation of being in their arms grounds me and I take the moment to steel myself for the path ahead. With one last squeeze, I release them with a shy smile before departing back to my quarters. There I find many women laden with fabrics, measuring tapes and sharp looking pins and groan softly. *This is going to be a long afternoon.*

CHAPTER FIFTEEN
Misconceptions

The Prince

I pace my room. This is all going to shit. Not only has the king moved up the wedding date allowing me far less time, but Alaceandra is nothing like I thought she would be. My fault for underestimating the women of Tikilium but when father spoke of them, he always described them as weak and easily swayed. He claimed Tikilium only gained power due to age old fears and they have grown soft since the wars, which is why he was marrying me off to the daughter of the king. I don't know why in all the lands of Ptheryeth I would trust his judgment on anything, especially women, but here I am.

Helomasi used to be a force, taking over half of Ptheryeth, but due to a plague overtaking our lands to the south, we now only maintain less than a quarter of our kingdom. The dead lands are quickly encroaching on our territory and eventually we will fall prey to them. That is, unless we can find a cure to fix the lands or more lands to flee to. My father, in all his righteousness proclaimed he will not be one to flee, instead he plans to take the rest of the kingdoms by force, but he needs more land and forces to start a war hence the alliance. *Or at least that is what he always said. I know there is more to his plans with King Nikoli's daughter than he is sharing with me.* I read a prophecy once before, one about a girl who can bring death and destruction to the lands of Ptheryeth or peace depending on how she is nurtured by those around her. If I am correct in my assumptions, Alaceandra is at the center of it. *She has to be. It is out of the ordinary for a woman her age to not have powers yet. Their delay must mean that there is more at stake for her.* Which means, depending on how the cards fall, she could bring the ruin of us all and yet— I run my fingers through my hair—and yet it seems she is ignorant of all this.

I, myself, have always been more interested in curing the land. The feeling of nature around me has always been a solace in my whirlwind of thoughts. I would have gone mad if I did not find my powers so early on in childhood. I moved my first strands of grass at ten years old, heard the first conversation whispered to me through the wind only a couple months after, and I have fallen in love with every shade and color the world provided me since. I thought it would be the only thing that would ever quiet my thoughts. That was until I met the little dove. When she is around the world sinks into a low buzz, the castle's conversations, misdeeds and schemes become only background music to her voice's delicate symphony. When we touch my mind empties. It is the most peace I have ever felt and yet, I know I will lose it. I hate her for it. I hate that she has shown me peace that I cannot maintain. I hate the fact that she cannot live in this world if she chooses the wrong choice when the time comes. I hate, maybe most of all, that I know my father needs her to choose wrong.

I walk by my reflection and let out a disappointed huff. *I must get close to her and manipulate her into showing me her abilities so that I can know for sure if she is the one the prophecy speaks of. I must torture myself with knowing that whatever peace she may bring me may need to disappear forever should my father succeed and I will be at the center of it, but* "Can I really manipulate an innocent? Am I destined to be no better than my father?" I whisper. I quickly jerk my head away and massage my temples. The racing of my mind is getting out of control and far too loud. I allow my mind to picture her beautiful, delicate face. Her long eyelashes and captivating eyes. I am launched back into the memory of lunch today. How terrified she looked at my father's promises of death to her guards and how helpless I was to help her. I wonder about her real relationship to them. They seem to be much closer than any guard to lady relationship I have ever come across. The thought does not bother me. I know they are a much better option for her if she were to have them, especially with what I have planned. *Will they help or hinder me? They must have cards up their own sleeves, but what are they?* Since they have arrived, I have been watching the trio more than I have ever watched anyone. The more I see of them the more I want to know.

I sit on a large chair, fingers clawing into my hair. If only I could have stood up to my father so I would never have to see that look on her face again, but I cannot. Not now. The king's control over me makes me want to vomit. With one tiny squeeze of his fist around that sculpture he keeps in his pocket, I am filled with such an overwhelming pain I can barely breathe. The only way to get away from this control is distance but my father is quick to ensure the servants always keep me on castle grounds. Therefore, all I can do is plan, and wait for the perfect opportunity. Until then... I rub the back of my neck... I need to talk to Alaceandra. If not only to patch up the damage lunch has done, but also, to quiet my mind.

I check the time. It is a little past midnight. *Has so much time already passed?* I take out a pen and some paper and write her a note asking to speak with her tomorrow morning before breakfast. Tucking the piece of paper into my pocket, I head next door. *I hope she has not quite drifted off to sleep yet.* I open my door quietly to knock on Alaceandra's door when I spot some movement from the corner of my eye.

Is that...? It is. Alaceandra and those two guards. What were their names? Fa...dris? And Cre...door? Something like that. They are sticking to the sides of the walls and travelling up the hall. I follow slowly behind them. Using a small bit of magic, I test the air, then smile- impressed. It seems one of them is advanced enough in their magic they can block the sound from the spy ware, but I do not sense anything hiding them from the spyglass. *They must not know it is present.* Curious, I urge the wind to cover the spyglass with the pink blossoms I have had a servant conveniently place beside each camera. Since the spyglasses can only observe, not record, no one should become suspicious of the leaves fluttering. It should only look as if a stray breeze caused the petals to rustle and block the glasses for a couple of seconds.

They make it to a bookcase, which they pull a blue book from causing the whole structure to pop open. My eyes widen. *How was I not aware of this passage?* I melt into the opening along with them before the bookcase closes with a soft sound. Fadres turns back, glancing down the stone corridor and I do my best to hide against the walls. After a moment, he turns back and they continue making their way down the damp path. I conceal myself within the bush guarding this passage's entrance, recognizing the dead lands on the other side. Alaceandra approaches the rocks and I stare in wonder as they light up with a soft red glow when she places her hand against one of the stones. They come to light in a row leading them down a pathway. They follow the lights and I follow them, sticking closely to the shadows and covering our tracks so we are not spotted by any of the spies on the perimeter of the property. *What are they planning?* I know very well the danger lying within the dead lands. The creatures living there are unruly, murderous and very loyal to their newfound king. The portal rarely allows newcomers through, and when it does it often leads to their death. *Or that is what we have always assumed. No one has ever made it back from being sucked into the dead lands.* Unfortunately, the rocks path seems to go directly to the deadly opening in the rocks.

The portal has shown itself. I start to reveal myself to the trio, hoping to warn them away from the void leading to the dark kingdom, when Alaceandra walks forward to reach for something near the entrance. A whooshing noise comes from the rocks and suddenly she is sucked into the void. Credour shouts and races after her their fingers brushing before he too is pushed into the opening, the rocks glow a deeper red as they enter. Fadres, the furthest away from the portal entrance, goes racing after them and finds himself jerked towards the entrance but the rocks are not glowing red, instead a white light permeates. He resists the pull, grabbing hold of a boulder to stay grounded. *Fuck, I should not have hesitated so long.* There is no telling where in the dark lands one may end up. The only guarantee it gives is those who enter the portal together will find one another.

Seeing as Credour and Alaceandra were making contact upon entering I am confident Alaceandra will at least have one of her guard dogs, but the other one looks to be entering on his own. *This can be the opportunity to free myself from my father. Alaceandra's protector is almost sure to die in the dead lands without guidance.* Fadres' hand slips on the boulder and he is hurtled towards the portal entrance. I run towards the cavern and throw myself through, my hand barely making contact with

Fadres' ankle before it fully disappears. I sense him go limp from the force of the magic choking the air around us. Although we are being thrown to Ptheryeth knows where, I smile because I know we will at least for a time be free. I will find out if Alaceandra is the prophecy's subject and the meaning that holds for her future. If in the meantime she can quiet the endless hum of my mind? I smile again letting the portals magic sweep over me. That is fine by me. Wherever she leads me, I will, of course, follow.

CHAPTER SIXTEEN
A Whole New World

Alaceandra

I awake with a start; my head is pounding. *Where am I?* Using both hands to press into my temples, I try not to puke. Assessing my surroundings, I realize the ground I was sitting on was rough and sand-like in texture. The atmosphere is cold, not necessarily in temperature, but due to an ominous chill swirling itself through the air. Groaning, I crack open my eyes and look around. The last thing I remembered was my bracelet glowing as I reached for a red object sitting on the edge of a rock and then… nothing. I shake my head trying to knock the grogginess out of my body and sit up. *I must have been… transported somewhere. I do not recognize these lands.* My palms begin to sweat. I am alone. Worse than that, the area around me is covered in decay. Skeletal trees weep red sap and cast spindly shadows across the ground. The bushes surrounding me are blackened, their leaves barely hanging on to brittle branches. The area smells of something freshly burned.

Before I can fully gain my bearings, I hear a noise in the distance coming in my direction. Rolling to my feet I quickly throw myself behind one of the bigger trees before the voices can materialize into people. *Fuck. If Sam and Sorin are not with me, where did they go? Why am I alone here?* I continue looking around, but father never told me much about the other kingdoms, making locating myself impossible. I tuck myself against a tree when I feel something dig into my thigh. Pulling up my skirts, I let out a sigh of relief. *Sam's dagger!* I strapped it to my thigh before departing on this adventure. *Thank Ptheryeth it is still with me. Let us just hope I will not have to use it.* I huddle more into myself pulling the bits of the dress closer to my body. The voices are now uncomfortably close. I listen in on the conversation.

"... more than that boy."

"I agree, I think I sensed four new energies."

"Wow so many?"

"I know the portal does not usually allow so many through, I wonder it's plans."

"No matter, they cannot come to fruition. We need to capture them before they can cause too much trouble for the king."

"Yes, but maybe we have some fun with these intruders before handing them over, we haven't gotten to play in so long."

"Of course, the king only said we needed to find them and bring them to him. He never specified the condition they needed to be in. If they just happened to have died before making it to him well... there *are* lots of dangerous creatures out here." They both laugh at this.

Okay... maybe I will need to use this dagger after all. Steeling myself for an altercation, I unsheathe the weapon and slowly move to a crouch. They are being thorough in their search, which means it is only a matter of time before I am found. Not that it is hard. The skeletal trees and bushes do not provide much in the form of coverage. They only need to pass my location in order to spot me.

"Let's ensure we do bring them back to the camp though first, hmm? Maybe the boy will be more apt to talk if we can find some of his comrades."

The boy? I wonder who they are speaking of. Also, a portal? I assume is what dropped me here, but seeing as, at most, there was only three of us at its entrance, maybe they are speaking of something else? As I am pondering this, I notice the men have stopped talking. Looking up I see there is the edge of a boot at the base of my tree. *Fuck they have noticed me.* I quickly hurl my body at the booted body stabbing my dagger into its thigh along with my body weight.

The burly giant grunts and tries to grab for me. Using the leverage of my dagger in the man's thigh, I push away from the man and roll out of the way. He screams in pain and stumbles back. Sending a mental thank you to Sorin for urging me to sharpen the blade before our departure I stand up and ready myself for my next move. My eyes zero in on the dagger still embedded in the man's thigh and I cringe. *Probably not going to get that back... fuck what do I do without a weapon?*

"Looks to me like we are in the presence of royalty," the man I stabbed grunts out, blood pouring between his fingers as he clutches at the dagger.

"Seems like we are," a voice says from behind me. *Cocky of him to speak so close*, I think to myself, ducking and spinning out of his reach. The men both now stand in front of me ready to pounce on me, their faces filled with malice. I do the only logical thing I can think of, I run hard and fast in the other direction, clutching the front of my dress for dear life. I have no idea their level of skill and, from their conversation, what they plan on doing to me, so I do not want to chance my nonexistent hand-to-hand combat skills in a fight. Weaving in and out of the trees I hear the other man laugh.

"I love a chase. The king is going to be so happy with this find!" he calls out, far closer than expected. Picking up the pace, I turn towards a more densely covered path in the forest, hoping to lose the two men in the brush, but as I continue to weave through the forest to try to gain distance, I feel a tug against the back of my dress. Crashing to the ground, I gasp for breath. My dress got caught on one of the branches of a lifeless bush. Panicking, I yank at the gown. *Looks like I will need new clothing once I find safety. I wish I could cut the end of this fucking dress off.* I mentally chide myself for leaving the stupid dagger in the man's thigh. After what seems like a millennia, it yanks free, but it is too late. The uninjured man takes hold of me, holding a cloth tight to my face. Wriggling violently, I kick out with my legs and throw us into one of the prickly bushes, but he holds me firmly.

Hissing in pain, his grip tightens as he pulls me closer to him. Chuckling in my ear, he whispers, "I am going to have so much fun with you." That is the last thing I hear before I pass out.

CHAPTER SEVENTEEN

Caught

Sorin

I wake up chained to a wall. This is, unfortunately, not the first time this has happened to me, but nevertheless it is not my favorite place to come into life in the morning. I take stock of my body first, making sure I keep up the façade of unconsciousness. I seem to have some bruising and a massive headache forming but nothing life threatening. *Where am I?* I do not think I am still in Helomasi. The last thing I remember is grabbing Lace to try to pull her from getting sucked into inky blackness and then... nothing. *Lace!* I strain my ears to pick up the sounds around me, but I don't sense her energy. *Did the void separate us? We are definitely in some enemy territory, but where?* I hold back a shudder *They better not have Lace chained up... or worse. Their deaths would not be quick.* Pushing the thought from my brain I consider my situation. I need to escape it quickly and find Lace, then I can worry about punishing whoever has me.

Briefly, I also allow myself to worry for Sam. I know he must have followed us; it would be unlike him not to. He can handle himself frankly better than I can, but this territory is more unknown to us than the lands of Helomasi. I grit my teeth. Either way I will find him after I have recovered Lace, and we will all make it out of this death pit. I am sure of it.

Taking a breath, I try and see if I can connect with the soil, if I can grow a strong vine maybe I can get myself out of these shackles. I feel the ground beneath my feet, and yet my connection to it seems to be blocked. Stitching my brows together, I try to see how strong this blocker is. I throw my magic at the ground and start to push hard, but before I can gain much headway my body shakes violently with exhaustion. Alarmed I stop and try to gain some strength back. Cracking my eyes open I take in my surroundings. I am in a dark cellar of a room, my body thrown against a wall, my feet are barely standing on a dirt floor. I am covered in bruises and small cuts but otherwise seem whole. Most of all I seem to be alone. There are no guards on the other side of the pillars holding me captive. *How silly of them*, I think to myself. *They must think me weak to leave me without a watch.* This can be used to my advantage. They must have captured me while I was unconscious after my transport here and as I am not bearing any clothing denoting my status, it would make sense that they think I am someone without skill. That gives me the opportunity to take them off guard, but for that I need energy. Sighing I slump back into the wall. I will take the next couple hours to rest and make my escape once the light has disappeared from my prison. *For now, sleep.*

CHAPTER EIGHTEEN
Touch Her And...

Sorin

I awaken to a loud thump. Staying as still as possible, I covertly survey the room. Across from me, guards are chaining someone else to the wall opposite mine. Their bodies are blocking the form, but the hair on its head seems familiar. Finally, they move out the way with a snicker and I bite my tongue.

A cold shiver runs down my spine with the revelation of who is now chained opposite me. *Lace.* She looks to be in good shape, but her clothes are dirty, and her dress is torn on the bottom. I will burn this place to the ground if that is what it takes to get her out of here and once I'm done, I will do whatever needs to be done to rid myself of King Nikoli's spell. I can't stand the thought of keeping things from her and watching her suffer the consequences of this ignorance. These battles are becoming too big for me to protect her from on my own and I won't let the bastard force a wedge between us any longer. *We need to get out of here.*

Another man walks in and slaps one of the other men on the back.

"Who do we have here?"

"Not sure, exactly, but she looks to be royalty." The other man straightens up.

"Good. The king will be pleased." He smiles and inspects Lace's form. His eyes narrow on a scratch along her cheek. "Make sure to not hurt the girl yet. We don't want to earn the king's wrath when we present her to him."

One of the other men makes a noise of disappointment in his throat. "But she stabbed Thyris! You should have seen the figh-"

"I said not yet. We know how quickly the king tires of these women, but we don't know what trouble she brings to our doors, and you know well the punishments that will befall you if you try to touch her too early."

He growls. In a flash the man has a dagger to both the goons' throats. "Don't test me."

The growling man grits his teeth. "Yes, sir."

The dagger man pulls away. "Out," he commands and the growling man leaves, stomping like a child.

The growling man will die first then. I decide, before zoning back into the conversation.

Dagger man and the other goon still stand next to Lace.

"Who is the other?" Dagger man asks lazily gesturing over to me.

"Not sure, but it seems he came around the same time as the girl. He seems to be some kind of commoner, but we are unsure from which lands."

"Interesting, has he awoken yet?"

"No, sir. We have not heard anything from the room since we placed him here"

"Good let me know if there are any changes. Dismissed."

The goon leaves. Dagger man walks back over to Lace and traces the cut on her face. I tense ready to cause a commotion if he tries to hurt her but when he lifts his finger her face is healed. Dropping his shoulders, Dagger man leaves the room, closing the prison door.

That was odd, what are their plans for her? On the bright side, I now know where she is and that, at the moment, she is unharmed. Unfortunately, her being here will make our escape much more complicated. *No matter. I can't let these assholes take her to their king.*

Upon examination it seems I have slept off whatever exhaustion had overtaken me. I once again attempt to push through whatever is blocking my magick from reaching the soil and jolt as I break through. Growing a thin long vine, I have it wrap around the shackles and pick the lock on the cuffs until they release me. Being extra careful as to not make noise, I have the vine slowly lower the cuffs to the ground. I massage my shoulders and stretch my fingers. *Let's hope no one comes to check on us soon.* They haven't so far, but it is only a matter of time, especially with how hostile that guard was towards Lace. *No chance he won't come back as soon as he can to enact some sort of revenge.*

I glance around the space to see if I can find any obvious listening devices. Spotting nothing brings me little comfort. *I doubt they are smart enough to hide the devices but that must mean they have some other means of listening into this room, especially with no guards outside.* It is not safe to move quite yet so I send a vine over to Lace and have it wrap around her feet to ease her weight off of her arms. Now all there is to do is wait for her to wake up.

CHAPTER NINETEEN
Prophecies

Alaceandra

I am in pain. Opening my eyes to darkness, I try to blink the grogginess away. I either just had the worst fucking dream of my life or I am in a lot of danger. Taking a quick inventory of my body, it seems like it is doing okay. I am disoriented. It is not usually this dark when I wake up in the morning. Further, there seems to be something soft and tickly under my feet. More importantly, my shoulders are aching. I go to rub one, but my hands are shackled above me. Holding back impending panic, I blink in rapid succession to try to make my eyes adjust quicker to the darkness. Sorin comes into focus across the room. My eyes widen and I start to call out to him. A vine rushes up and covers my mouth. Sorin puts a finger to his lips and then mouths, "Not now. Stay still." The feeling under my feet recedes causing the ache in my shoulders to increase.

Confused, I nod, trusting him but still very unsure of everything going on around me.

Once my body slackens against my restraints, the vine around my mouth releases me and recedes back into the soil beneath us. A large door swings open and in walks a guard.

"Oh, I see the little princess is awake?"

I cringe away from the intruder, my body swinging slightly. He keeps his eyes firmly on me as he stalks in my direction paying no mind to Sorin behind him. He is covered in a thin sheen of sweat and dirt and the look he gives me turns my stomach. I curse the chains holding me and glare at the man, struggling against them. He reaches up and rubs a bit of my hair between his fingers. I flinch at the contact.

"Oh, the murderess is afraid of me?" He chuckles and licks his lips then grabs a hold of my neck. An involuntary whimper escapes me. I only now recognize him as one of the men who had captured me earlier. *Shit.* "You should be. You killed my friend, you bitch," he growls in my face, his grip tightening. A small, choked sound escapes me. "You will be repaying that debt with this body of yours. A body for a body, seems fair, no?" He smiles. "I do not give a fuck what Sydon says, I can't let you get away with killing, now can I? Who would have known that dagger of yours had a slow acting poison, if we would have caught it..." His face screws up and he grits his teeth. "No matter, I have many potions around the corner that will make you willing should we need it. We can keep you relatively unharmed for the kings use with those, but I won't have to use any of them if you behave. You will, won't you? Knowing what you have done? The king doesn't even have to know about this little meeting, does he?" His voice is now filled with an unhinged excitement, and I feel his other hand tracing up my belly making its way to my breast. I try to struggle but his hand around my throat only tightens further. I try to gasp for air but nothing happens. My chest tightens painfully as fear takes hold. *I cannot breathe.* "Maybe the little commoner over there will wake up to enjoy the show before he dies. Wouldn't that be nice?" I have the opportunity to flick my eyes over to the very much awake Sorin, his face red with fury, before the guard blocks my view, his body pressing closer to mine. I try not to gag as the stench of death and rot overwhelms my senses and my head goes light with lack of oxygen. I close my eyes against the sensations and try not to panic. *Sorin! This would be a great time to help!* My mind screams as I start to black out. Just when I feel the tip of the guard's fingers reach my breast, I am suddenly released. A crunching noise fills the space, and I snap my eyes open and suck in air, coughing at the tickle in my throat each inhale summons.

A huge vine lays wrapped around the guard's ankle. A guard who is now sprawled on the floor, his head canted at an unnatural angle. Sorin stands above him. We make eye contact. The vine snakes its way towards me and up to where my hands are chained above me. After a second the lock clicks softly and the tension is released. Dropping my shoulders I watch as the vine gently lays the cuffs to the ground before transforming into a bundle of grapes. I stare at Sorin, mouth agape.

"Did—" he shakes his head at me and puts a finger to his lips. On light feet Sorin makes his way over to me barely making a sound as he crosses the small room. His clothing is blood-stained, and he has little bruises dotting his skin. My brows furrow when he gets close to me, and I reach towards a bruise on his face, but he catches my hand and shakes his head again. Giving my hand a gentle kiss, he rests his head against mine and takes a deep breath. I am shaking, my body still filled with adrenaline from the encounter with the now deceased man at our feet. Sorin lifts his head and traces his finger over the marks that are sure to be forming on my throat, his brow knit with worry.

Where is Sam? Pulling away from Sorin, I search the room, but do not spot him. I figured that if they captured both me and Sorin, they would have caught him too, but he is not here. *I hope that means he was not captured like the two of us.* I bite my lip. *But...what other dangers does this land hold? What if he is meeting a worse fate than us? What if--?* I cut my train of thought off. *He must be* okay; *he has to be okay.*

Sorin squeezes my hand once again and nods towards the door. *Right. I will speak to him about this after we have escaped.* I tilt my head at him in a "well now what?" move. He smiles once again, a cute dimple appearing on his face before he pulls me down into a crouch, his hand still holding mine. He scoops up the grapes placing them in his lap and popping one in his mouth before offering me one. I take it and eat it. Luckily, the remnants of Sorin's magick have always proved tasty, but I cannot help but be a little annoyed with him at the moment. *Why did he wait so long to save me?* He shoves the rest of the grapes in his pocket and then leads me to the prison door. He pulls out a leaf which I assume was on the vine he made earlier, then looks outside the bars of the cell. Seeing no one he shoves his hand through the bars and expertly picks the lock with the leaf's stem.

I stare at him again. *First, the skill in which he killed that guard and now master lockpicking skills? Why-- How does Sorin know how to do all this?* Biting my lip to keep the questions from spewing out, I follow Sorin as he drags me out of the cell doors and around a corner before dipping us into another room. My jaw drops. The room is filled with different bottles and vials of liquids. Sorin, less amazed, sweeps his eyes across the room before grabbing a couple of vials and storing them in his pockets. He grabs my hand once again and pulls me from the room. My eyes are now the size of saucers, but I am trying my best to keep my shit together.

Shouts erupt from behind us. *They probably found their guard.* Sorin squeezes my hand and pushes forward at a pace I can barely keep up with. *Stupid dress.* I cannot wait to tear the bottom off as soon as we are out of here. We round another corner and find ourselves confronted with a huge door reading:

"Warning! Beware Those Who Enter. Once Truths Have Been Revealed, Fate Cannot Be Undone."

"The dark lands," Sorin whispers. "If that is where we are, then that means that behind this door..." He pushes it open, but hovers at the entrance. There is a huge stone at the center of the room. I can tell there is writing on the stone, but I cannot quite make it out. The sight of it is oddly familiar, but I cannot place where I have seen it before. *Was this in one of Helomasi's texts? No. It could not have been. Then where have I seen it?* Glancing at Sorin, he seems to be almost entranced. A look of determination flits across his face. Abruptly, Sorin pulls us into the room to the stone and starts wiping off the dust with his shirt, finally revealing the engraving written on it.

Before her twenty-fifth birthday is upon her, this shall come to pass. Catastrophe will strike those who wish to mar her skin. Demoni shall roam the land in which she once called home. Every creature shall know her name. Fear will strike those with the most might. Giants will pass away. Hark, you who do not wish to hear this warning! Ignorance will not save you from her bloody fists! Justice will soon rule this land again. Kindle her fire, make it worth her while and maybe her flames will not scorch those she loved so fiercely (though her flames are strong and grow hotter with her age, do not worry about their effect on you, they will not last too long—do not be afraid of her or yourself in this journey—we are counting on you to show her the true way to salvation, a way not lined with bodies, loss, and despair, but instead alight with the truth of the meaning behind her sparks—you are the only one who can achieve this, S, you are our only hope, please bring her back to us).

"Look, Sorin," I manage to whisper, pointing at the mark of blood at the bottom of the stone that is all too familiar to me. *A dagger.* Not only is it a dagger but it is my family crest's dagger. My hands are shaking, and my body has gone cold. *Oh fuck, who in my family could this be referring to?* Despite my father's best intentions, I am his only heir. There is no one else under the age of twenty-five in our lineage. *It cannot be.* My hands go clammy, and my heart starts to race.

"Quiet!" the guard on the other side of the corridor shouts at the other guards—*they are on to us.*

"Rely on me to get us out of here?" Sorin holds my hands together.

I take a deep breath, and close my eyes, nodding at Sorin. Utilizing a sharp rock lying next to the huge stone, he runs at the guards rounding the corner and swiftly incapacitates them, before pouring something over their bodies. Victorious in this quest, he runs back over to me and grabs my hand pulling me towards the entrance of what I now can see was a cave.

"What if they find us?"

"Xanthosoma potion, it'll at least stave them off so we can find another place to hide." Yellow potion bottles appear from his pockets, and he smirks at me. Zipping them up into the safety of his bag he grabs my hand once again and off we run back to the safety of the spindly woods.

CHAPTER TWENTY
Fire

Alaceandra

Enraged screams echo behind us as we escape into the dark forest surrounding the cave. My stupid dress snags viciously on the brambles reaching out for us as we run. I hold it close to my body but find the loss of arm movement is only making my running slower than the dress was. Sorin stops us with a hand and looks around.

Finding another little cave we can hide in; he grabs my arm and pulls me inside it. The cave is much longer than it looks on the outside, curving slightly to the left. A little divot sits in the center where we can both just barely fit laying down. The curve hides us from the casual passerby, but would not protect against any sounds we made, as it is relatively shallow. *It will need to work for now. If only Sam was here. He could use his noise cancellation skills to ensure we remained completely undetected.* I slant my eyes over to Sorin. I cannot help but find myself impressed by his display of skills over the past couple hours. We both are sitting next to each other in the cave. Me, totally out of breath, my body thrumming with adrenaline, chest heaving from the effort of keeping up with him. Him, not only looking stupidly handsome with sweat glistening softly across his forehead, but also not even slightly phased by all that just took place.

"I am learning about a lot of... interesting talents of yours lately... should I be concerned?" I blurt out.

He laughs but sobers when he realizes I am not joking. "Of course not, Lace. Is that even a question?"

"Maybe..." I wrinkle my nose at him. A quiet moment spans between us before I ask in a small voice. "Why did it take you so long to save me back there?"

He frowns at me. "I was trying to save you from the moment the guard walked in, Lace. I thought you saw my vine closing in when you glanced at me."

I look away. "I did not. I just saw you staring at me and that guard. I was not sure how far you were going to let him go." My voice catches.

He grasps my face in his palms. "I'm sorry. I was working as fast as I possibly could without alerting him or any of the other guards who might have been nearby. It killed me to watch him touch you and I wish I could have made his death much more slow and painful." He grits his teeth. "I never meant to make you think I was just going to watch that monster touch you."

"Maybe we should have a little signal for next time. I can still feel the asshole's fingers against my breast." I cross my arms.

"Agreed," Sorin grunts.

I start to readjust my sitting position when my foot catches in a small hole in my dress causing pain to shoot through my leg. I cry out in frustration and then hold out a hand to Sorin. "May I see that rock?"

Sorin narrows his eyes at me. "Um... yeah."

Grasping the rock tightly in my hand I finger the edge to test its sharpness. *Sharp enough.* I start violently hacking away at the length of the dress aiming for it to fall just above my knee.

"What are you doing?!" Sorin reaches for the rock.

"This fucking dress got me caught in the first place." I laugh out loud, my voice a touch hysterical. I was having maybe too much fun. I admire my work, before looking up at Sorin. "It is far too long for exploring and running from madmen in the woods." I hack away more of the restrictive fabric. "I do not want it to cause more trouble in the future." I pause. "Now, can you please help me with the back?"

He eyes me, before snorting out a laugh of defeat. "Sure." I spin around in my seated position pulling the dress from underneath me.

Taking the rock, Sorin continues cutting my dress. Once he sets the rock aside, I spin back around, throwing the extra fabric away from me. A wild smile curves my lips. I catch as Sorin's eyes latch onto the scrapes and bruises along my legs and arms before his eyes finally land on my face, troubled. "Are you okay, Lace?"

I stare at him. *Might as well tell the truth.* "No, definitely not," I say, fingering the frayed edge of my dress. "Honestly? I feel like I am one more disaster away from a mental breakdown." I take a breath, trying not to laugh hysterically once again. "And on top of that? I feel like everyone knows a lot more about what is happening around me than I do myself." I watch his face for a reaction. "Including you who seems to be entirely unsurprised by the huge foreboding rock back there." I hitch a thumb back to where we came. I know I am about to break down and cry, so I quickly turn away from him, trying to keep my composure.

Blowing out a breath of frustration he gently grabs my face to look in my eyes, his thumb tracing over my cheek. "Lace, look I—" He looks pained. "It's eating me up inside that I can't tell you all I know, and I promise I will make things clearer to you when I can but for the time being I just really need you to trust I am doing my best to not only protect you but to keep us both alive. If I were to reveal everything too soon, I couldn't—" He chokes on his next sentence.

I try to pull away from him, but his grip, although still gentle, firmly holds me in place. I bite my lip. "I know. It is just—a lot." Giving up for now, I lean into his palm slightly, the feel of it against my face causing longing to bubble up inside me. I have always found it so difficult to stay upset with Sorin. Whenever he touches me, my body seems to short-circuit the heat of the room racking up a thousand degrees warmer, making it hard for me to focus on whatever I was upset about in the first place.

Truthfully, I prefer not to be upset with him, especially after everything he has done for me, but I just hate being so fucking confused about everything: my next move, my purpose now we are fuck knows where, Sorin, Sam, the prince. Everything that I have ever known or will know is out of my hands or hidden behind some riddle. I just want to be able to control one thing. Sorin's eyes flick to my lips and a spark lights within me. My nipples are hard, and the adrenaline is making my head rush, twisting my anger into forbidden thoughts. I chew my lip a little harder trying to distract myself.

Completely oblivious to my inner struggle, Sorin softens, speaking to me in a tone full of reverence. "Lace, if it is the last thing I do, I will get us through this and make it up to you. I swear." His eyes catch on my bitten lip, and he pulls it free from my teeth. A soft noise escapes me, and I watch his eyes dilate and as he rubs a finger over my swollen lip. We sit, staring at each other as time seems to still, the air in the space seeming to become alight with some foreign energy. I feel myself slowly start to close the space between us, until we are a hair away, breathing in the other's next breath.

"Lace?" Sorin whispers, his lips barely brushing against mine.

I glance up at him and then back down to his lips, one of my hands finding its place on his thigh. Energy crackles through my palm. Maybe it is the stress of the situation, maybe it is being stuffed in a tiny cave, but either way, I am not letting this opportunity go—not this time. "Fuck it." I whisper, more to myself than to him.

Before I could over think the action, I press my lips to Sorin's, a move he meets with the same force, and I am lost. Drowning in the feeling of his lips moving on mine, I thread my fingers into his hair, pulling him in. He responds by lifting me onto his lap, our breaths filling the quiet of the enclosed space, his hands roughly grabbing my hips. Breathless and dizzy, my body aches for more. I grind myself into Sorin's leg, trying to soothe the growing need inside me.

With a tortured groan, Sorin lets go with one hand to entangle his fingers in my hair, using the leverage to tilt my head deepening the kiss. My skin heats further as my arms continue to trace the planes of Sorin's chest before vines weave themselves over my body, encircling my waist and arms like a harness. Gasping I pull away for a moment. The greenery sprouted from behind Sorin, its tendrils feel like a soft rope against my skin, holding me firmly in place. Sorin pulls me back into him and I moan as the vines start to squeeze and massage my body with a gentle force hitching my desire and turning my thoughts to mush. My newly shortened dress allows Sorin more intimate access to my thighs, which he takes advantage of his hands wandering to squeeze them, while his vines do their work massaging my breasts. Overwhelmed, I pull away from Sorin's lips for air. He starts trailing kisses down my neck and I whimper, opening my eyes to watch him. Something flickers in the corner of my vision, and I freeze.

The entire cave is alight, the rocks around us glowing molten red. I blink rapidly. *Not only red but on fire. The rocks are on fucking fire. Are we under attack?* I jump from Sorin's lap and pick up the sharp rock we used earlier, glancing around the corner to watch the entrance of the cave. Sorin still has yet to move from his seated position but worry coats his expression. "Lace? Everything alright?" His voice is breathy, and he clears it before slowly standing. His gaze turns watchful, but more towards me than any intruder. Even in my alarm, my body is screaming at me to go back to him and finish what we started. I will it to calm down, but it chooses to do the opposite, my heart racing as the flames start to grow.

"The- the cave?" I splutter. My mouth refuses to form the words to tell him the obvious so instead I just stare at him dumbfounded. My panic is making way for confusion as he does not seem to notice the roaring flames surrounding us. *Does he not see what I see?*

"What about it?"

I start to move towards the cave entrance, but pause at his question, my eyes connecting with his.

As we continue this stare down, I start to calm and strangely so does the fire licking the cave walls. "Oh fuck." I jump, startled by the sudden extinguishing of the flames around us. Looking around at the cave walls I see no evidence it was even there in the first place. I walk over to the wall and touch its smooth surface. No scorch marks, no heat, nothing. I shake my head in disbelief. *Did kissing Sorin cause me to hallucinate or was this wall not on fucking fire two seconds ago?* Sorin's head is now tilted, a smirk of amusement plastered to his face as he watches me. For some reason this makes me feel insanely embarrassed about the whole thing and out of instinct I do the thing drilled into me from birth, I start to apologize.

"Sorry I do not know what came over me I—"

Sorin barks out an amazed laugh, which causes me to jump. "Sorry Lace, I—that was...wow." He is looking at me with a weird expression now I cannot place.

I close my eyes. *Shit, I am totally about to cry, am I not?* The last few minutes have been a roller coaster of emotions I would like to depart from. *Please keep your cool, you do not want to prolong this cluster fuck by sobbing in front of the man you just lost your first kiss to!*

Sorin sees my face drop and straightens. "No no no, Lace. You misunderstand." He walks over to my position near the entrance of the cave and coaxes me to the back of it, urging me to sit. I do and he starts to stroke my hand slowly pulling me back towards him. His pull is gentle, like I am a fragile treasure he does not want to break. The carefulness of this maneuver frustrates me, especially after the primal heat of earlier, but I relent, if only so I can hide my face in his chest.

Sorin has always felt safe to me. No matter what the situation, if he is around things just get better. No matter what adventure we went on, or situation we ended up in, he has always been consistently there for me. Consistently in a great mood. Consistently my rock. He allowed me to roam free and enjoy Tikilium despite my father's wishes. He was the shoulder I could cry on whenever things went to shit. I have always adored the care he has for me. His gentleness and dependability have always been my guiding light, but what if I have depended on him too much? Or worse, what if these feelings I have for him, feelings I have now acted upon, ruin any chance of friendship we may have in the future? My capture along with the fact that I would have no idea what to do should we have actually been in any danger has me nervous. *If something were to happen to him, would I be able to survive it? Survive life without him in it? I do not think so.*

"In all the lands of Ptheryeth I never thought I would get an opportunity to kiss you. That was amazing, Lace." His face fills with that expression again bringing me back to the present. "You're amazing, Lace." He tucks a tendril of escaped hair behind my ear. "But..." he scratches the back of his head. He is definitely fidgeting. "I apologize if I went too far with it. I didn't mean to freak you out." He whispers this, seemingly worried and continues stroking the top of my head.

I release a small laugh into Sorin's chest.

"What?" he asks, laughter tinging the edges of his voice.

"You did not go too far, if anything I—"

He lets out a huge burst of laughter. "You did not have huge vines shoot out of the ground to hold me down, although..." he chuckles. "What I am saying is, I should have eased us into it. I apologize if I overwhelmed you."

"You are fine. Truly... maybe... maybe we can do it again sometime?"

His hand stills on my hair, and he glances down at me, his eyes hooded with desire. "Yeah?"

"Yes." I try and stamp down the blush starting on my cheeks but finding that impossible I once again bury my face in his chest. Chuckling warmly, he continues stroking my hair softly.

In the peaceful silence, I think back to the firelit cave and decide to chalk it up to a crazy hallucination, at least for now. Sorin does his best to maneuver his big body and mine to the floor of the cave, snuggling me into the crevice of his arm and half on top of him. The position looks more awkward than comfortable for him, but he does not seem to mind too much. He lets out a content breath. I snuggle deeper into him, taking this moment to enjoy some peace and privacy.

"The cave should be safe for now. Rest. I will wake us early next morning to start the search for Sam."

I nod my head into him, and he throws an arm around me. The noises of the night filter through the cave. *This was probably the craziest day of my entire life* I think to myself before I am lulled into a deep sleep.

CHAPTER TWENTY-ONE
Sleeping Beauty

Sorin

L ace is so beautiful, but when she sleeps? The stress of the day falls away and peacefulness radiates from her form. She is the only thing making this cramped cave bearable. I hold her in the crook of my arm, her soft breaths echoing in my ear, her plush, soft pink lips open just a fraction. *So fucking perfect.* She shifts, nuzzling deeper into my hold and I hold back a groan. It feels amazing having her like this. To be touching her. Her betrothal had me almost giving up on the thought of being this close to Lace but by fate or temporary insanity here we are. *I cannot lose her now.* I squeeze her a little closer.

My mind cannot help but wander back to earlier. Her soft ass in my hands. Her scent filling the room as she ground against my leg. My vines encircling her beautiful breasts. *She felt so fucking good.* My cock twitches, begging to be released and relieved of its frustration. I let my head fall back against the cave floor. Staring at the cave ceiling for a minute, I convince myself to let my eyes fall shut. If her powers did not choose that moment to show themselves, I know we would have gone much further. In a fucked way, I'm kind of glad for the cockblock. It was too much too fast, and she deserves to have her first time on a bed or, at the very least, not in a cave of all places. She's so vulnerable right now and who's to say her decisions aren't being motivated by the fucking near death experience we just shared rather than her actual feelings towards me.

I pinch the bridge of my nose with the arm Lace is not currently using as a pillow. I can't fuck this up. I have been in love with Lace for as long as I have known her. I vowed I would always protect her, would die for her if it came to it and that had nothing to do with her royal status. Not long after that I met Sam. Sam had already been a part of the king's guard then and he convinced me to join him as well. I used this as an opportunity to learn how to protect Lace with more than my status but with my body as well. I became a master assassin, my vines allowing me to sneak into small places and kill quietly and effectively. Once Sam was assigned to Lace he informed me he had a calling when it came to Lace and it only made sense to include him in my vow. If I break Lace's heart, not only would I not be able to forgive myself, but Sam would kick my ass. *As he should.* My eyebrows furrow. *I hope he is okay.* Knowing Sam is out there alone in this place has me worried. I know he can handle it. He is the one who trained me, but still lone missions are much more difficult, and neither of us know what danger this place holds.

Opening my eyes again, I glance back over at the stunning creature in my arms. It feels wrong to be pursuing Lace without talking to him. I twirl a piece of her hair in my fingers. I hope Lace's upbringing will not close her mind to being with the both of us. We agreed we would both offer ourselves to her if given the chance. If she wanted us both? We were not opposed to the idea. Sam is already closer to me than anyone and sharing a woman is not out of our realm of experience. We promised each other we would make it work. Lace deserves all those her soul sings for. If her prophecy holds any truth at all she will need an army to stand by her, and who better than those completely devoted? We refuse to limit her, especially when such limitations could lead to death. I shudder at the thought and allow myself to think of other things.

Her soft breasts pressing into my side have another image blasting into my mind. An image of her between Sam and me. I can almost hear her pleading whimpers and feel her soft skin, my vines holding and caressing her while Sam teases her with his tongue. My cock once again tightens against the restraints of my pants and I sigh, adjusting myself. As exciting as the thought would be, it is definitely too early for it to be a consideration. I don't even know the depth of her feelings with me, let alone with Sam and I don't want to scare her off or inadvertently push her to do something she would not be comfortable with based on my own desires.

Then there is the issue of her betrothed. I grit my teeth. King Nikoli's ambitions are always fucking up my plans. Obviously, Sam and I knew the king would use his daughter in a political marriage, but we thought he would have given her a bit more time and, at the very least, explain her own fate to her. In that time, we were going to confess to her our true feelings and let her decide whether she wanted to mark us as hers. *Instead, I get my tongue cursed against revealing the kings' plans or any mention of Lace's fate.*

If the prince can put aside his own agenda and assist in her rise to power, then I will let there be no reservations in Lace having another suitor. *Even if I do not trust the man.* The power she holds needs people to channel through. I fear the outcome if she is left to harbor it on her own. If Sam and I play our cards right, everyone can be happy. If not, we may cause the beginning of her ruin. *Or her ours.* I can only hope everything works out without much bloodshed.

Releasing myself from the spell of those thoughts, I bring my gaze back to the corner of the cave, zeroing in on the noises around us. The cave will be safe tonight, I will make sure of it. Lace needs rest if we are going to begin our search for Sam tomorrow, especially without being caught. Turning on my side, I hold her closer and rest my chin on her head. Using what is left of my energy I encase the cave with half-dead vines. They will alert me if they are touched. Satisfied at our makeshift alarm system, I drift into a light, dreamless sleep.

CHAPTER TWENTY-TWO
Closer Please

Alaceandra

Waking up, my body is warm and languid. I snuggle into the heater to my left and sigh happily, fighting and losing against sleep trying to pull me back into its depths. Before I can surrender completely to my familiar friend, my heat source starts to chuckle, startling me back to reality. I groan and blink my eyes open. My body stills. I am staring into a very naked, muscular chest. A shirt that smells suspiciously of Sorin is draped over me. Still half asleep, I shiver as I feel Sorin start to stroke my hair lazily. Snuggling deeper into what I now remember to be Sorin, I start to slowly trace the lines of his chest, committing them to memory. Life has been fucking insane lately and I cannot help but want to ensure I do not forget this moment in the safety of Sorin's embrace. *It may be your last.* My finger pauses over a scar curving up the side of his chest. It is raised slightly but definitely not new. Before I can examine it further, a voice brings my attention upwards.

"Having fun, Firefly?" Sorin is staring down at me, a small smile touching his features.

My eyes dart up to his before falling back on his chest, my cheeks flushing pink. "Sorry, I have not noticed this scar before. When did you get it?"

He glances down at the scar.

I frown. "It looks brutal," I whisper tracing over a particularly jagged line.

He shrugs. "I got into a scuffle during what was supposed to be a training mission your father sent me on a few years back." He runs his fingers through my hair, causing goosebumps to race along my skin. "It's a souvenir. I am fine though, promise. You should have seen the other guys." He winks at me. "I think it was around mid-year? When I was gone for a moon cycle."

"After our adventure to the borders?"

He nods.

I shift away from him. "Why am I only now hearing about this mission? Mother told me you were visiting another village... I thought maybe you wanted to take time away because..." *because we almost crossed a line.* We ran into some guards right before we made it out to the bordering lands. When we ran away, Sam, Sorin and I ended up sandwiched between each other at the bottom of a hole hiding from my father's men for hours. I had just turned nineteen and the men had started acting distant around me. I was excited to be alone with them. Sam had been more and more obsessed with some assignment, and Sorin had been training hard in the king's guard. This was the one adventure they both agreed I could go on and we ended up almost caught. Being bored and cooped up in that hole started out innocently enough. We talked. We waited. Only this time the conversation did not stay on king-mandated topics. This time I pushed our conversation to more heated subjects. Their hands wandered as their bodies pressed against either side of me. Thinking back now, I realize this could have been the time that my crush became reality. Where I could have finally explored these two men without society or familial duties getting in the way. No one would have known, but before anything could truly happen, a bell rang in the distance announcing it was time for dinner, jolting us out of whatever spell we had been under. I quickly crawled out of the hole, using light-hearted jokes and feigning ignorance of the whole situation until we had arrived home.

It was awkward between us after and when I heard he had left I was terrified it had something to do with me. To make matters worse, Sam had also gone back to being withdrawn, refocusing on whatever assignment he had taken a break from. When Sorin returned, he acted as if nothing had ever happened. Sam had finished his assignment, and we continued as normal. As if we had never been trapped in that hole in the first place. *Which honestly had not made me feel any better.* I always wondered what would have happened that day. If that stupid bell had not rung. If I had never climbed out. I am not sure if it is better now knowing he was out risking his life and almost dying instead of avoiding me or not. I let out a long breath. "Well, it does not matter now, but I always thought the timing of your departure was... odd."

He quirks an eyebrow and then scoffs. He nudges my chin up to look at his. "I did not choose to leave, Lace. Your father sent Sam and I on many missions after that day. This one was just the beginning. Once he knows you are useful..." He gives me a knowing look. "I was tasked with chasing a group who had infiltrated our southern border. They um... apparently had intel the princess liked to venture around the borders and decided to make a move." He smirks, before his face turns serious. "They dressed as Tikilium guards and had followed soldiers back to the castle.

After poisoning the crops in the King's Garden, they made their escape. If it wasn't for the queen's sister nearly dying from the ingestion of the plant, it might have ended up on your plate. The king sent me out to... take care of the men, but the mission was much more difficult than what I had been briefed on. I should never have been on it, especially not alone, but—"

"What? Alone? You had only started training a year prior—"

"Like I said, I should not have been alone. I think the king wanted to teach me a lesson."

Guilt slams into me. "That was all my fault." Horror fills my tone.

His eyes harden and a faraway look steals away his focus. "No, it was not, Lace. If anything, it was mine for..." he chokes and then lets out a frustrated noise before sighing. "Please... just don't blame yourself."

I stare at him but decide not to push it, simply nodding at him. "Can I ask one more question?"

"Depends."

"Was the queen's sister okay?" *How have I not heard of an aunt before?*

His smile turns beaming. The light returning to his eyes. "Yes! Luckily the healer had encountered the poison before and knew how to handle it. It was a bit touch and go, but she ended up just fine. You should know. It was Mandi."

My mouth drops open. "Mandi?" Horror, guilt and betrayal swirl in my gut. *Why was I never informed of this? We had grown so close over these last few years. How is that something you can hide for so long?* My palms are sweating and I do my best to retain my outward composure.

"Yes."

I cannot help but thank Ptheryeth she is okay, but *fuck*. My stomach drops. Mandi is my aunt, not just a dear friend. *Why she had served as my handmaiden all these years, instead of as part of the royal court? Will*

I ever find out now that she has escaped the castle? If she of all people could retain such a secret for so long, what else could I be missing? Question after question invade my head as I sit with this new information. Right before I feel like I am about to be thrown into a panic attack, Sorin interrupts my thoughts.

Sorin stretches. "As much as I wish we can stay in this little cocoon forever, we need to get going. We do not know how much progress the people who captured us have made since we escaped. We are safest if we keep moving. How are you feeling?"

I force a smile. "Better. I slept well."

"Good." He unravels himself from me and stands, offering me a hand up. I take it and stand. "Let's get going, it'll be harder to find Sam once the sun goes down." He touches the cave wall and focuses, before leading me outside.

I turn around and look at the place we took refuge the night before. It is now covered with vines and branches, its exterior camouflaged in the world around it. I give it a little pat before setting off with Sorin.

We walk for a while through the dead limbs of the forest. I have decided to tuck Mandi's secret into the recesses of my brain for now. I have far too much to figure out and at the very least I should confront her about this revelation before making any final decisions. *Hopefully I will get the chance to do that soon.*

My dress is now, thankfully, swirling around my thighs rather than snagging on branches surrounding us. The gentle brushing of the fabric against me causes my body to flush with the memory of Sorin's hands on my thighs the night before. I try to sneak a glance at Sorin, only to make eye contact. *Shit, he totally knows I am blushing.* I trip over a stray stick, and he laughs. *How embarrassing.*

"Sooooo...." He slowly starts. *Here it comes.*

"So?" I brace myself.

"Looks like someone's come into her powers."

My eyes widen and I stop in my tracks. "Powers?"

"Of course," he laughs, grabbing my hand and pulling me forward to continue "The cave on fire last night? It was kind of hard to miss."

My eyes are saucers at this point. "I thought I was going crazy; you did not react and—" I process what he just said. "Wait, that was me?"

He gives me a confused smile. "Of course, Firefly, who else would have done it?"

I narrow my eyes at him. "So now you too then?"

He tilts his head. "What?"

"With the pet names! This is the second time you have called me that!"

"What?" He snorts. "It's cute! You made the whole cave glow!"

I toss my head back in frustration. "Whatever... you would think Lace would be enough."

His laughter lessens. "You'll always be my Lace." I soften slightly. "But.... now as it so happens you are also a firefly. A glowing light that is so fun to chase."

I huff and roll my eyes, but a smile peeks through. "I thought we were under attack."

He squeezes my hand. "Nope. Someone just got a little too excited."

"You are one to talk."

"I am." He scratches the back of his head.

"I should probably be more in control of my powers before we do that again then, so that I refrain from setting our surroundings ablaze..." *If he wants to kiss me again after all of that.* Elvisera start to do cartwheels in my belly as I let the unspoken question hang in the air.

A sparkle enters his gaze. He pulls me to a stop and presses a soft kiss to my forehead. "That would probably be a good idea." He answers my unspoken question and I try not to jump for joy. "I think it is important we enjoy our time here as much as possible and ensure we can find a good way to control that power of yours while we do it, as dangerous as this place is it could be the perfect opportunity for you to train these abilities of yours." We continue walking.

I smile to myself, feeling more confident as we continue. "While we are talking about training... I think it might be good if I could learn some extra skills. I know we went on a couple adventures back in Tikilium but none where I really have had to wield a weapon. Nor any I have felt truly in danger during. When the men found me in the woods I could only do so much before running was my only option. I do not want to feel that way again. A couple fake sword fights with Sam and you only can really get me so far it seems." I let out a self-deprecating laugh. Tension dropping from my shoulders.

"Hey, from what I heard you did pretty well for yourself. Looks like you even had your first kill out there." Sorin tries to soothe me, but the reminder I killed someone does not bring me as much comfort as it probably should. I have seen a lot of death in my life, but never have I been so closely associated with it. "As much as I want to say there will never be another instance such as that again, I realize there are no reassurances here. If we are caught off guard again... I do not want you captured. I can't stand the thought..." I run a thumb along the top of his hand. "We will start training once we are far enough away from their camp. I am hopeful after a couple days' journey we might be far enough away that we can buy ourselves time. Maybe find resources and shelter too." He runs his thumb over my hand in response. "On one condition though, Firefly."

"What is the condition?"

"If there is a chance you can run, you take it. Do not let any training convince you fighting is better than running. No matter what, getting away from the enemy is the best option."

"But what if--"

"The. Best. Option. Lace." He says firmly. "No matter what."

I bite my lip and nod. Then decide to pivot the subject. "What about Sam? How are we going to find him?"

"We can search during the day. For now, let's try to only worry about finding shelter and food. It is going to get dark soon." My face falls and he squeezes my hand, continuing in a gentle tone. "He is a priority to me, but I suspect it might take a couple of days to track him. This place is filled with death, and I don't want to join the decor." He attempts to move a blackened branch from our path, causing it to splinter and fall from its tree. Letting go of my hand, he gracefully climbs over the fallen branch and then reaches to hoist me over it as well.

"I could have done that myself." I mumble.

"I am sure you could, but the branch screams splinters and it is too big for you to climb without having to touch all over it."

I roll my eyes, my body warming at the spots he had just held me. "Touche." He continues to walk ahead of me, not reaching for my hand again and something inside of me cries at the loss. I watch him as I try to delicately weave through shrubbery. That kiss yesterday *was* mind-altering. It is no wonder that it triggered my powers. *And his vines?* My mind keeps racing back to the moment over and over again and I cannot help but want to see how far we can go, powers be damned. *He is one of your best friends.* I remind myself. *Yes, but that is only because there was no opportunity for something more. Not with my father's eyes constantly on us, or the kingdom's judgment. Although the setting is not ideal, this could be that opportunity— the only opportunity I get to explore whatever this thing is between us. Be honest with yourself, Alaceandra, can you truly be okay with never knowing?* I slant my eyes towards Sorin and watch as he maneuvers around a large rock. *No, I do not think I can.* Taking another chance, I reach for his hand and grab it.

He looks back at me, his eyes glittering with mischief.

"Shush." I say pre-emptively. "We should find somewhere to sleep."

He smiles gently, his large hand wrapping around mine. "You got it, Firefly."

CHAPTER TWENTY-THREE
Water is for Bathing... Right?

Alaceandra

We walk for what seems like forever, Sorin helping me over any big pieces of debris in our paths, until night starts to fall. Sorin starts scouting the woods looking for shelter. The land, luckily, is dotted with caves. Over the next few days, we find shelter in them and survive from the fruits of Sorin's magick, some small animals we come across and little streams of water. Although most of the land seems to be dead or decaying, the water sources have not caused us any sickness. Sorin runs it through a makeshift filter before we drink it, and I assume that has been helping. There also seems to be a notable lack of population here. It looks like where we landed upon arrival was just an unfortunate stint of bad luck. We have not seen anyone roaming the lands with us. Sorin has been on high alert, constantly scanning our surroundings and pausing at any noises we encounter, but I can tell it is starting to take a toll on him.

As light makes its bed on the horizon marking a week of being in these desolate lands with no signs of Sam, we come upon a huge river. "Here." Sorin scoops water into a makeshift cup, running it through some kind of filter he made from the fabric of my dress, before adding a drop of something from one of the potion bottles and offering it to me. I take a sip, noting a delicate floral flavor.

"Drink slowly," he warns for the umpteenth time, "You don't want to get sick."

I nod, taking in slower gulps of the liquid before passing it back to him. He drinks and then gathers more, before setting the bottle down on the bank. I sit down and notice just how filthy I am. "Do you think it might be alright if I bathed here?" I ask Sorin.

He quirks a brow. "Dirt getting to you?"

"A little."

He nods. "Sure, I'll keep watch."

I blush. "You should probably also rinse off." His dimple appears. Making a show of sniffing himself, he contorts his face dramatically. I laugh.

"Someone needs to keep watch."

"We can watch each other's backs; besides we have not seen anyone this whole journey."

"Are you just trying to get me naked, Firefly? Who knew little Lace could be so--"

I splash water at him, and he splutters. My face is on fire. "Stop teasing who knows when we will see water again, we should make the best of it."

Sorin

I laugh at Lace's antics, but pull my shirt off, and smile as a little squeak escapes my Firefly. I am glad we are getting an opportunity to find some kind of relaxation and fun. These last couple of days searching for Sam have been hard. We have not been able to get much rest, and we have had to fight against the sharp and abundant woods just to make it to our next destination. I decided it might be best to walk towards the mountains as they are something unmoving in the distance and have a clear direction. We have searched along the way for Sam, making sure to keep close to each other so we do not lose each other in the monotony of the dead lands. Once night starts to fall, I scout for an area we can sleep in and cover it in vines so that I can be alerted if anyone gets near our encampment. Then I leave Lace in the cave while I hunt for some kind of food in the woods, which although bereft of people, is full of tiny creatures. Although they are unfamiliar to me and a little gamey, they taste better than no meat at all, so I am grateful for their abundance. I come back and start a fire and skin and cook our meat before letting Lace know that it is safe to come out. We both eat and I create a fruit vine to satisfy our desires for sweetness. Lace's favorite so far has been the raspberries. She was so cute when she tasted them, her face brightening with delight as she downed as many as she could. I have grown those vines the most over the last couple of days just so that I could see her smile when they appeared. After we have consumed our fruits, we retire for the night and continue again the next day. *Lace has been amazing through it all.* She has not complained. Taking each day on with an admirable newfound determination. Not many people would be able to be thrown into the dark lands and still have a smile on their face the next day, but Lace is not many people. Her dirt covered radiance has been my inspiration to keep going and not allow the impossibility of getting out of this situation get to me. I want to say the situation has brought us closer than we ever had been, but I am afraid that may be all in my head. We have not kissed again, but she has been holding my hand through our travels and lingering in my arms every morning. *Probably because you are warm, dingus.* I hold back a snort.

She has gained a bit of muscle. I did not think that her form could be any more attractive than it already was, but seeing her softness take shape has been a beautiful sight. It means that when we finally do find Sam and we can get her training underway, she will struggle less in the beginning, her body already primed for work where it was not before. I do worry about how this change will affect her mentally. This visit to the dark lands has gained us more time, but once we find safety we will have to utilize it wisely. Sam is going to want to train her relentlessly once we find him and truthfully, she will need his rigorous exercises for the coming days ahead of her. *I hope she embraces it as much as she has embraced looking for Sam.*

As I continue to undress, I smile at her as she crouches behind a tree to do the same. I have never seen Lace without some kind of clothing covering her and nor she I. *How will this all play out?* I have my hopes, but I would hate myself if I pushed her in that direction. *She needs to be the one to choose.* For now, I will take her lead and focus on getting the grime of the forest off of us.

Alaceandra

"Are you getting in or are you just going to hide behind that tree?" Sorin calls out.

"Sorry!" I call back pulling the rest of the clothing from my body before jumping into the river. The water is cool but not unpleasant against my skin. I dip completely under before resurfacing. Clearing the water from my eyes, I open them only to find Sorin's ass in clear view. *Holy shit.* I blink extra hard and try not to ogle, but the man's ass is better than mine. I do a little self-conscious peek at my butt before wrinkling my nose in slight jealousy.

"You like the view?" he asks, pulling me back to myself.

"I...um..." I stumble over my words causing him to let out a low chuckle.

He gives me a little wiggle before calling out to me again. "One of the bottles I took from the caves should act as a decent soap. I would like to give it to you. All good if I turn around?"

"Um...." I sink lower into the water. "Sure." The chilliness of the water is making me break out in goosebumps. *Well, that along with being in such close proximity to a naked Sorin.*

He sinks into the water before doing a little swim to get to me. I do not know what to do with my hands. Should I cover myself? It seems only proper; the water is mostly clear, and it would not be hard for him to see my entire body if he gets close enough to me. *Calm down,*

Alaceandra. So, what if he sees you naked? I give myself a small pep talk. *He has probably seen many women without clothing before.* A sour taste fills my mouth at that thought. He approaches through the water and hands me a bottle and a strip of my dress. I watch Sorin as I slowly grab the bottle from his hands. His eyes are heated, curious but not roving. He looks to be observing my actions as much as I am his.

Breaking eye contact, I dump some of the liquid on the cloth, I hand it back over to him. He smiles and takes it from me before pouring some over his own cloth. I rub the cloth together in my hands and smile as the liquid sudds up. Turning away, I watch the trees and begin scrubbing my body with the liquid. It has both an earthy and floral scent to it. I diligently scrub away all the dirt and grime that has built up on my skin over the past couple days. It is refreshing. The feeling of being filthy was starting to grate on me. I touch my hair, dreading the knots I know are taking over.

"This is a long shot but, did you happen to grab anything that would detangle?" I call over my shoulder.

"You're in luck." I hear some splashing which I assume is Sorin grabbing the item from the shore before I hear him start to make his way back over to me. I keep my back turned until he is right behind me. When I spin around to retrieve whatever he brought over I notice Sorin has two things in his hands. "I think this might work to loosen the knots, but I made this to help." He hands me a brush-like object made of a spiky vine Sorin trimmed the tips off to make the edges blunt.

"Thank you." I smile at him and take them, tracing my fingers gently over his. Sorin smells of the same soapy substance, but there is an undertone to it which is distinctly him. I cannot help but let my eyes drag down his form. The water reaches his belly button. Its slight murkiness stops my gaze from wandering too far, but I can just make out the impression of his quickly growing erection before I snap my gaze back up to his. He is looking down at me, his eyes darkening. My body heats at the attention. *Act casual, Lace. This is normal.* Giving Sorin a soft smile I tilt my head to the side to dip into the water. Putting the brush between my knees, I shake a little bit of the new potion on my hands and massage it into my scalp. It bubbles up and fills the air with a sweet lavender scent. I repeat the process until my hair is coated with the potion, then I hand it back to Sorin, who repeats the process on himself before tossing the little bottle back onto shore.

As I start to rake through my ends, I wince in pain. *Ugh why are there so many knots!* This brushing and wincing continues on for a couple of minutes before Sorin, who has finished a quick wash of his own hair, comes over to me and gently takes the brush-like tool from my hands.

"You look like you're torturing yourself with this." He chuckles. "Let me." I relinquish the tool to him, huffing.

"I know how to brush my own hair."

"I am sure you do." He smiles. "But I am not sure your strands have ever been put through as much as they have in the last couple of days. I just thought it might be nice to have the help of someone who can see the tangles." With that, he starts to massage the tangled strands in his hands, loosening them, before using the brush-like tool to smooth out the rest of the knot. His ministrations are soothing, and I let my eyes flutter closed as he works.

When he finally finishes, he tosses the tool away. Delving his fingers back into my tresses, he gives me a scalp massage. I moan at the feeling, my scalp sore from all the extra weight of the knots I had not even realized I had been carrying over the last couple of days. Sorin let out a low noise in response and a tingling starts in my limbs. Sorin's naked form is very close to my back; his body warmth radiating through the water as his fingers make delightful patterns along my scalp. Slowly he guides me to wash away what is left of the potion, before squeezing out some of the moisture. Once he is satisfied with his work, he weaves my hair into a long braid and places his hands on my shoulders.

"There that should hold up for a bit."

I turn to him. My body brushing his in the water. "When did you learn to do that?"

He smiles before brushing his hand over my face. "Maybe three years ago? It is not uncommon for soldiers to have longer hair. When we were out on missions I became the designated braider."

I giggle. And his smile grows to a grin.

"You're killing me, Firefly."

"How am I doing that?"

He shakes his head. "It is taking everything in me right now not to kiss those pretty lips of yours again."

"Oh." My heart skips a beat. *Is he joking?* "Well... I mean... I am not opposed..."

"No?" His voice is husky as he closes the space between us until my breasts are firmly against him.

I stare up at him, a little breathless. "Yes... I mean we are out in the middle of the water; it is not like I can set anything on fire and—"

The only warning I get is his hand tightening on my braid before his lips are once again crashing against mine. My body instantly relaxes against his and I let out a little noise of surprise before wrapping my arms around him. He nips my lower lip for entry and I open to him, our tongues dancing. I feel like I have just been stuck in an oven, my breath coming out of me in embarrassing pants. I squeeze my legs together feeling myself get slick with arousal even in the water. I try to glance down when I feel something press against my belly, but he holds me fast against him. His vines creep their way along my skin, wrapping around me and flicking their leaves over my nipples. I gasp as Sorin lifts me in his arms. Wrapping my legs around him, his erection now pressing against my ass, and I pull away to look at Sorin, my eyes filled with question.

He gives me a shake of his head before pulling me back to his lips. I run my finger through his hair. His lips quickly find their way down my neck pressing soft kisses that send shivers through me. When he gets to the hollow between my neck and shoulder, he sucks it into his mouth. I let out a tortured moan, the sensation causing my entire body to shake. He chuckles darkly and continues working his way down my body. I flutter my eyes open to watch him. Instead, I catch sight of tiny flames licking the waves around us. Sorin's mouth latches onto my nipple and my eyes shoot back to his devouring gaze as his teeth scrape my sensitive flesh. Soothing the sting with his tongue, he moves to my other breast to enact the same torture.

My body is aching for something unknown to me. I pull Sorin from my breast and nip the skin below his ear. He lets out a groan and kisses my lips roughly, his hands kneading into the flesh of my ass. I reach down to grasp his impossibly hard cock in my hand and gently squeeze. I look at him with wide eyes as he pulls me from the water, taking long strides to shore and laying me down on the bank.

He takes a moment to fully look at my body. My breasts are heaving, their size engorged by the vines wrapping around them. My pussy is out on display, my wetness painfully apparent in the sunshine. I start to try to cover myself, but this only earns me a disapproving look from Sorin and a tightening of the vines on my limbs. Satisfied by his inspection of my body, he kneels between my legs and oh so slowly starts to kiss and lick his way down. My hands fly to his hair as a moan rips its way free when he nips and soothes my hip before his vines lift my ass off the ground.

Sorin soon replaces the air with his hands as he grasps my ass and finally makes his way to my core.

He pauses there for a moment and glances at our surroundings. "Firefly, look around."

I rip my gaze from him and glance around at my surroundings. Everything is ablaze, soft flames of white, gold, blues and oranges dance in the breeze and yet nothing burns. It is almost as if the fire skating along every surface, but never fully penetrating to cause damage. My eyes widen at the sight, but I do not have too long to think about it before Sorin's mouth is latching on to my pussy. Everything stills. I cry out, my face beat red at the thought of him being down there.

"What are you—"

"Relax, Firefly. Look at what you have created."

I whimper and try to breathe. His tongue starts to make lazy circles over my clit and the intensity has me wanting to, all at once, pull away from him and pull him closer. I rake my fingers through his hair and drop my head back. He starts to explore slowly at first, his tongue taking control of my body masterfully. An ache starts to form in my belly. As it winds tighter and tighter my breath starts to come out in short gasps. Noticing the uptick in my breathing, Sorin renews his efforts. Paying closer attention to the spots that make my hands tighten on his back and my moans louder. It feels like torture and heaven all at once. My body aches to reach some unimagined place I am just out of range of, and I grow frustrated by its aloofness. Uncaring of my actions, I yank Sorin's head tighter to my body and grind gently against his face. He lets out an animalistic groan and traces his fingers up and down my opening before sliding a single finger inside me and curving it up to reach a magical place. Screaming Sorin's name I feel liquid rush from me as my body shatters into a million pieces.

"Holy shit," Sorin whispers, staring at me in amazement. I look at him in confusion before a devious glint fills his eyes.

He stares at me as his finger continues to stroke itself in and out of my pussy, his thumb creating delicious circles on my clit.

"Come on, Firefly... you can do it again."

Panicked, I shake my head. "No, I—"

He pauses. "Do you not want to?"

I consider this for a second. "I do I just—" I manage to whimper out.

He continues his movements. "Just what, Firefly?"

"It is impossible," I whimper, my mind already splitting into a million different directions, making it hard to focus on any one thing.

"I think it is very possible. Look at you, already grinding on my finger. Does that feel good, Lace?"

I nod, a jerky motion.

"Good girl." Sorin applies a little more pressure with his thumb and continues pumping his finger in and out of my pussy. I squirm at the sensation. "Do you think you can take another finger?"

My voice is wavering. "I think so."

He gives me a satisfied smile before slowly working another finger in. The stretch is not unpleasant. If anything, the sting is mixing deliciously with the pleasure, making me want more. Sorin's thumb works skillfully over my clit while his thick fingers pump in and out of me until I am alight once again. My vision blurring with the intensity of my orgasm. When I am finally able to breathe again, Sorin gives me the biggest smile and allows his hand to softly caress my belly.

His cock is on full display. It stands proudly between his legs and *holy fuck it is big. Like, definitely not going to get anywhere in me, big.* I turn wide eyes to Sorin.

He chuckles. "Don't worry, Firefly. We won't go on that adventure today." He runs a hand up and down his length, watching my eyes as they flicker with heat. He lets out a pained groan. "Let's get you rinsed off again." He stands and offers me a hand.

I take a minute before accepting it. He deftly swings me into his arms bridal style before walking us into the water. Guiding me so that I am floating on my back, he washes me with a cloth and some more of the cleansing potion he must have grabbed while we were on shore.

"So beautiful," he whispers, mostly to himself.

"You are not too shabby yourself," I remark back. I feel languid and giddy.

He smiles. "You think?" He cups water into his palms and gently rinses me.

"Of course, Sorin."

He finishes washing me in companionable silence. I close my eyes and enjoy it. He looks lost in his thoughts. Once he finishes bathing me, he helps me back onto land and uses his shirt to dry me off. We dress and he ties the shirt to one of his belt loops.

"I don't know about you, Firefly, but I am really glad you convinced me to bathe." A wry smile is plastered to his handsome face.

A loud shout of a laugh escapes me. "Me too... although to be fair it did not take you much convincing," I say, taking him in out of the corner of my eye. His cock is still at attention, its impression straining against the restriction of his pants, but he does not press anything further. In a sense I am glad, because I have no idea how I am going to take all of... him... inside me, but disappointment twinges in the bottom of my belly all the same.

He follows my gaze and snorts. "Come on, Firefly. We still need to find a place to stay tonight. And as..." he smirks, "hot as it is to watch the world go up in flames when I have you beneath me, I don't think it is very sustainable for our surroundings." He winks. Scooping my hand up in his, he starts walking us both into the surrounding woods.

CHAPTER TWENTY-FOUR
Reunited

Alaceandra

Sorin seems to be fighting some internal battle. I glance at him from time to time as we walk. Anxiety builds within me every step we continue to stay silent. I am about to plead with him to come out with whatever is eating him up, when he finally turns to me, pausing our journey.

"Alaceandra?"

"Yes?" His tone makes my heart drop. *Please do not say you are regretting what we did already.*

"We need to talk about your betrothal."

I chew on my lip. "What about it?"

He sighs. "If we are going to continue, I need you to know that this is not some one-off thing for me. Now that I have had you, I do not intend on letting you go."

Oh. I squeeze his hand "I do not want to lose you either. There has to be a way we can make this all work."

"Well... there is one way. It is not uncommon in Ptheryeth's history for the queen to take many suitors and, at the end of their courtship, many husbands. It has fallen out of practice with the new kings, but it does not mean it was not commonplace before. The lands will accept your courting of multiple men but only if the prince decides this is acceptable. An acceptance of polyamory does not denote the acceptance of cheating by any means. Any allegations of such would diminish you in the eyes of the kingdoms. If you are unopposed to this, I will speak to the prince once we arrive back at Helomasi on the matter. You should know this is my intention."

I nod. *All of that makes sense. I just really hope the prince can see it the same way. It is not like he will not be taking many lovers himself once we are wed. He will be a king after all. Maybe I will not have to lose anyone at the end of this.*

"Good. Details can be discussed later, but until then." He knits his brows.

"Your fire has progressed in intensity and although it does not look like it is causing much damage, we do not know what all you are capable of or if it is the only power you hold. We should try to start controlling it soon."

I bite my lip. "That is fair, but who is going to train me? Our skills are vastly different. Although it looks like King Demetrius' guards share my skill. I heavily doubt they will be allowed or even want to train me. Likely no one will help me in Helomasi, save you and Sam, but Ptheryeth knows where he is." My voice breaks a little, but I clear it and continue. "No one has even offered the services of scholars to help me understand more about Helomasi's people. Frankly they have been avoiding my questions about such topics. I doubt they will want to teach me more about the powers I possess. I think the king plans to keep me weak as an attempt to control my actions further." I squeak, my foot catching on a stump. I regain my balance and continue slower than before. "Even if I had known some who might have knowledge in Tikilium, I doubt they would not welcome me back now that I have been married off, especially without the prince by my side. Ptheryeth knows the prince would not assist me, especially now we are out here in the middle of nowhere." I glance around. "He probably thinks I ran off. Who knows who or what is after us now. Or how pissed he is." I shudder. *There is still Philos. She might have some insight?* I quickly shove the thought away. I do not know if there is anyone skilled in fire in Areletos either. More than that, I do not want her more mixed up in this than she already is, *especially when she is already protecting Mandi.*

I take a moment to glance at Sorin, but he is deep in thought. I continue.

"And even if I did somehow know there was someone who could train me, it is not like I could reach out to them. I am pretty sure my letters are being intercepted, at least that is what my elvisera has hinted towards."

"You act as if all our skills do not stem from one place," Sorin says. "If we cannot find someone to teach you, I can try to show you the basics. They are usually the same amongst each skillset. I will teach you the aspects I know which should help you gain some control. When we find Sam, he will teach you too. He specializes in combat." I raise a brow at him. "What? He is our disguise master. If situations get dicey, he needs to know how to get out, and they have gotten dicey. Sam is my boss when we are out on missions. There are legions modeled after him in Tikilium, he can work with everyone no matter their skillset."

"What, really?"

"Of course! He transforms into a killer on the battlefield and is a wizard in pretty much all things strategy. He has taken down whole armies in the past. It would only make sense for him to lead the teams."

I nod. *I guess that would make sense. I just did not realize my gentle rule follower could be so brutal.*

"It would be good for him to train you." The *ifs* of the situation remained unspoken. A beat passes. "Besides, the politics of the kingdoms don't really hold sway right now because you are right. We are in the middle of nowhere and unless circumstances change, we are all we have here. We will deal with anyone coming after us when the time comes for that, but until we can either find our way away from here or to a place of safety you will learn control and how to fight and we will survive. Okay? Everything else can come second."

I nod.

He lowers his voice and stops to cup my face in his hands. "I consider the fact that you were even captured in the first place to be a personal failing of mine. It will not happen again."

"It is not your-"

"It is," he says, firmly. "We took you out on too many trips outside of the castle to be so cocky with your safety. As much as we want to be, we will not always be around to protect you. A couple of tricks with a dagger can only get you so far."

"Okay. We train. I get it. I will take it seriously."

He throws a beautiful smile my way and we continue walking.

"Good." A mischievous look passes over Sorin's features. "Plus, the sooner we can get you control the sooner we can—"

"Fuck off!" A shout reverberates through the trees. Our heads whip in the direction of the noise. The voice sounds familiar. Sorin pushes us behind a tree and some skeletal bushes, holding a finger up for me to stay quiet.

"Is that really what all this is about? I saved your life, multiple times already in spite of you idiots thinking you could outmaneuver me by taking her. A fact that would warrant your death by the way."

The voices are coming closer, and we hear one of the men sigh. "Threats now? I know you will not kill us for it, it would ruin your little plans to get back at daddy, wouldn't it?" A voice that sounds a lot like Sam's retorts.

"You are such a pain in the ass."

"That's what I thought."

My eyes widen, and I go to dart from my hiding place behind the bushes to run into Sam's arms, when Sorin's grip tightens, his eyes warning me to be still. I shoot him a quizzical look in response, but he shakes his head and motions towards his ear. *Listen.* I roll my eyes but comply.

"It has less to do with my daddy as you say and more to do with *my* Alaceandra. You being dead would complicate my dealings with her."

"Checkers or chess? Chess and checkers. Stab stab stab."

"What are you on about now?"

"Oh nothing, just imitating what talking to you sounds like."

"You insufferable..."

"Oh look! Now you're sounding like a king!"

He, whom I now recognize to be the prince, sighs. "Mocking and name calling, I see."

"You're one to talk about name calling with the stupid pet name you gave--"

"Look your obsession with my betrothed does not mean we must be enemies, if we just find her--" *Sam's obsession with me? What is he talking about?*

"It's probably plausible you got a black eye during a fight on our way here, she'd believe that right?"

"You would not be able to get close to hitting me. Are you always this violent?"

"I guess you bring out the best in me."

An involuntary snort escapes me, and I shoot panicked eyes to Sorin.

"What was that?" Sam says.

"Shut. Up." The prince replies.

I purse my lips and Sorin shoots me a look that is all at once disappointed and amused.

"Are you two done bickering or should we stay over here?" Sorin yells.

The approaching footsteps halt.

"S-Credour is that you?" Sam says in a whisper. *Oh right, the prince does not know their true identities.*

"Maybe, depends on who's asking."

Sam snorts. "Do you have Lace with you?"

I smile. "I guess it would depend on who's asking as well." I reply. We step out from our hiding place, but Sorin keeps me tucked behind him. Giving me a stern look, Sorin walks over to Sam, and they embrace.

One minute I am watching them and the next a huge gust of wind pushes me from behind, the strength of it carrying me over to the prince. My eyes widen, and I let out a surprised noise. He uses my momentary disbelief to grab my chin and starts inspecting me with narrowed eyes. His gaze pauses over a spot on my neck. Briefly I wonder if he is looking at the receding bruising from my encounter with the guard in that awful prison or some other mark courtesy of my and Sorin's recent escapades in the river. I meet his eyes in challenge, and he smirks at me. "Interesting…" He whispers. His gaze now raking over my form, probably trying to document any other evidence or new markings that might be present on my body.

A vine snakes its way around my waist and pulls me back. Sorin stands between me and the prince.

"Respectfully," Sorin starts, "please—"

"Keep your fucking hands off her," Sam says pushing his way between Sorin and the prince, getting into the prince's face. "You aren't married yet. You have no rights to her out here. We will play your little games in your palace but right now lay the fuck off."

My body is tense, but the prince only laughs, his head tilting at Sam. My jaw drops at Sam's tone and the prince's reaction, but when I look at Sorin his face is devoid of any surprise. Instead, he only smirks and lets his vine fall from my body. He walks over to Sam and claps him on the back.

"We have a lot to talk about," Sorin says and they share a meaningful look.

Sam's gaze darts to mine and the tension leaves his body. When he looks back at Sorin, he raises his eyebrows. An expression Sorin meets with a grin.

The prince has stopped his laughter and studies the two with interest. "I see…" he mutters to himself. Throwing me a smile, he turns his back on us.

"Well, now that we are all reunited. I am exhausted. Let's head back to the village."

"Village?" Sorin and I chorus. I take in both the prince's and Sam's appearances and realizing their clothes are noticeably less dirty than ours.

"Yes, the village. You both look like you can use a new change of clothes." The prince looks pointedly at my torn dress.

Sam's eyes roam over us both. "For once me and prince fuckhead are in agreeance." His eyes are sparkling when they look back at me. "Come on, they have food."

My stomach chooses that moment to growl, and I nod my agreement.

"Can we cool it with the insults?" The prince complains.

"Sure, give me your name and I will call you that instead."

The prince clenches his jaw then turns and walks into the woods.

Sam grabs my hand. "Come on, Lace, we don't want to miss dinner." He pulls me with him through the woods and I, of course, follow.

CHAPTER TWENTY-FIVE

Dinner and New Friends

Alaceandra

We arrive at a small village. A half-constructed wall surrounds the town. Clusters of cottages line cobblestone streets with roofs made of a soft straw-like material. In each set of cottages, only one holds a door, while the rest seem to be mostly underground. *How are those accessed?* The exposed walls of each cottage have ornate drawings etched into their surfaces. Some depicting people, others elvisera in mid-flight. At the town's center two larger buildings stand above the rest. Their engravings are brightly colored, unlike the other cottages. One has a bright blue sky with soft wispy clouds and the other some kind of storm. I marvel at the engravings. Their details seem to sparkle with some kind of ancient magick. *I wonder what other beauties this place holds.* No one wandered its streets nor was there any movement that could be seen in the windows of the small cottages with doors. I peer into the woods surrounding the small town and note that that too seemed uninhabited by any person or animal. *Where is everyone?* Nightfall was almost upon us, the sun almost to its resting place for the night, a slight chill entering the air. The scent of baked goods drifts through the breeze causing my stomach to rumble. *Okay so someone must be here...*

"Is it safe here?" Sorin asks Sam.

"For now. We have been here a couple days and the people have been friendly. I was transported just outside this town when I arrived. Some creature tried to attack me and one of the children who was playing outside the village." He smiled. "The adventurous nature of the little one kind of reminded me of Lace, actually. Anyway, I was able to fight the beast off mostly and get to the little girl, but ended up suffering some... minor injuries. That is when I ran into prince tag-along here and he may or may not have helped stitch up the wound."

"I saved your life," the prince chimed in. "You would have bled out if it weren't for me and you still shouldn't be walking around now. Not that you show any gratitude for it," the prince mutters.

"Anyway," Sam continues, ignoring the prince. "The little one led us to this village where we were informed those creatures have been attacking the villagers for months. We have been helping them set up defenses ever since. It has earned us boarding, food and kindness from the villagers."

"Wait, back up," I cut in. "You are wounded?"

Sam rolls his eyes. "Minorly. It is not a big deal."

"Not a big deal my ass, show me."

"I would disagree...." Sorin mutters.

"What?" I swing my gaze towards him, and he backs up his arms raised in surrender. The prince continues studying us like a puzzle and I glare at him for a second before turning my eyes back on Sam and raising an eyebrow.

Sam purses his lips and lifts his shirt. A huge gash spans his stomach, it is red and irritated, but not at the point where it looks like it might get infected. Stitches line the wound in perfect lines, but the details are lost to the darkness fast approaching. I suck in a breath and Sam pulls his shirt back down.

"It is fine, Lace I know it looks bad, but the stitches are imbued with magic for faster healing. The wound will be mostly gone in another week." I glance towards the prince again and he raises an eyebrow at me. *I will thank him later.*

"Fine. I am glad we are all back together at least. Where are the other villagers?"

"They are resting. This village is mostly nocturnal," The prince supplies.

"Yes. That is why the cottages are placed in little clusters like this." Sam points to the closest cluster of cottages. "They tend to stay inside during their waking hours, as the night around here can be dangerous, but that does not mean they are anti-social. Quite the opposite in fact. They use these clusters to stay connected with close friends and host each other. When they are able to get out, play, collect food, and forage for essentials, they etch little drawings into their buildings to stay connected to those they may not be currently hosting and to warn each other of future events."

Future events? "The person we are going to stay with is not currently hosting friends though, right?"

"Of course not," the prince mumbles.

Sam rolls his eyes. "Not for a few months, luckily. They rotate."

"Oh..." My stomach growls a little once more. I decide to shift the subject. "Did you say something about dinner?" I try to keep the hope from my voice.

A smile touches the prince's lips, but Sam replies. "The family of the little one has been awakening right at nightfall to ensure we have a hearty dinner. We have told them many times it was unnecessary, but they seem to insist, citing their love for guests and gratitude. We are not going to refuse to eat it as that would insult the family and the food is rather tasty."

"Oh... will they mind us joining? I do not want to intrude, and I have found my encounters with the people of this land thus far have been... not the most pleasant."

Sam smiles. "Yes, Lace. I had a feeling we might bump into you today. Call it lucky intuition. I asked if they could prepare some extra food just in case and they already have agreed."

"Oh."

Sam makes a noise in the back of his throat, a mix between a laugh and a snort.

"Are we going or not?" the prince asks, his form already obscured by the shadows of the surrounding skeletal trees.

"Yes, of course, let's go," Sam says, leading us through the village.

We all make our way through the half-constructed walls and through the village, until we come to a cluster of small cottages. The prince and Sam walk up to a pretty pastel blue one and knock gently on the door. Some time passes and a sleepy older woman opens the door. When her eyes land on the prince and Sam's faces her body language brightens.

"Come in, come in!" she says in a musical tone.

The men smile and walk inside, but Sorin and I hesitate.

She gives us a warm smile. "So, you did bring guests!" she calls out over her shoulder. She beckons us inside. "You are welcome in, please do not just stand out here it is going to get chilly and by the look of your red noses it does not look like you are much built for the cold."

We give her small smiles but walk into her home. It is a cozy place with a fire casting the living room in a warm glow. A little girl plays by the fire with some carved toys. She is enraptured in whatever story her imagination is conjuring up. So much so she barely notices there are new guests within her home. The girl cannot be any older than six years old. She has deep blue curly hair that is tipped with a pretty silver and thick eyelashes frame pretty teal eyes that are stark against her pale skin. Her tiny voice moves through the room jingling in much the same way as her mother's.

I inhale. The home smells absolutely amazing. Although I do not recognize the scents exactly, it smells like some kind of stew. My stomach lets out another pitiful growl and I cover it, my cheeks heating in embarrassment.

The older woman laughs, a warm sound. "Looks like someone is hungry! Good thing I made plenty. Hayford is finishing up with the food in the kitchen, feel free to make yourself at home. The boys can show you to your rooms. We have tunnels to two of the cottages outside. I have you in a room with that one over there," she points her finger towards the prince, then lowers her voice in a conspiratorial tone. "He refused to give me his name that one! But as he had helped in saving my girl Lyza, I figured I would let it slide." She raises her voice back to a level where everyone can hear her. "He said you two are getting married soon! I hope you don't mind sharing. The room only has one bed, but I figured it might be better you share it with him than anyone else." She gives me an impish smile. She goes to walk off before pausing in her steps. "Oh, how rude of me! My name is Sylvie. Make yourself at home. I will go fetch some food." Then she walks off with a flourish.

My stomach has dropped to my toes at this point, and I spare a minute to shoot my gaze towards the prince, but he is already staring at me with a smirk on his face. When he catches my gaze, he raises his brows at me. Holding back a groan, I look away and watch Sylvie as she starts passing out the bowls of stew with a man I assume to be her husband. After they finish serving us, they scoop the little girl up in their arms causing her to squeal before they leave us to our meal.

We eat. The stew is fantastic. It has many vegetables and meats with the perfect amount of seasoning, and I cannot help but make noises of contentment throughout. Although the fruit and meat Sorin procured throughout our travels had been nourishing enough we did not die, there is not much in the way of seasoning out in the middle of the woods and the flavors had been a bit lacking. Once I am finished scarfing down my food, I look up to see the men's eyes on me. I blush under their gaze.

"Sorry," I say a bit under my breath. Before they can reply, Sylvie breezes back into the room and collects our bowls.

"It is getting late for you all and you look quite exhausted," she says with motherly reproach, giving me a pointed look. "I think it is time you head off to bed."

We acquiesce and split up to head to our cottages.

CHAPTER TWENTY-SIX
Tiny Beast

Alaceandra

Dread knots my stomach as I watch the prince make his way through the tunnel. Although we had been alone before, it feels different to be alone with him behind closed doors instead of in a place Sorin and Sam could easily penetrate if they were to come looking for me. My eyes rake over the back of his form while he walks, and I feel a tendril of arousal snake its way into my lower belly. Guilt fills me with the knowledge that just earlier today I had Sorin between my legs and now... *Now you are ogling the prince like he is your next meal. Keep your eyes up Lace!*

I jerk my eyes to his back just as we make it to a rustic ladder Sylvia instructed would lead us inside our cottage. We climb up and find ourselves in a dainty building. It consists of three rooms. One with a soft blue recliner with white lace trim, a wooden table, an ice box and a large bookshelf. The other with a large bed with the same blue and white lace bed skirt and linens, a set of drawers in the corner, and a cramped bathroom. The space definitely seemed more fit for a single person than two, but I find it hard to complain too much due to my earlier accommodations. I walk back into the room with the recliner. The prince leans against the wall studying me.

"Looks like we are alone," I blurt out.

"Looks like it." He smirks at me. "Nervous without your little guard dogs?"

I narrow my eyes. "No, should I be?"

"I don't know." He pulls up from the wall and walks over to me. His energy crowding my space. "Should you?"

"Ah, I see the riddles are starting early then."

He snorts. "As is your disdain, I see."

"How did you even get here? Spyware inform you of our departure?"

"Oh, so you are aware of the spyware then?"

"I am smarter than I look, your highness," I bite out sarcastically.

"But not as stealthy it would seem." He smiles at me and then finally relents. "I followed you out, Dove. Watched you try to fly away and got sucked into the portal right along with you and your men."

I roll my eyes. His gaze caresses my face, stopping on my lips.

I turn away, feeling a little flustered, but he spins me back around holding me against his chest.

"What... what are you doing?"

"You know... I'm starting to think those guards of yours are with you for more than a little protection."

My breathing hitches. "Why do you say that?" I breathe, heart racing. *How does he already know?*

His thumb traces my lip, before lazily caressing its way to, what I now am for sure is, the hickey Sorin left on my neck. "The signs are there," he says simply.

I shudder, but do not pull away. "And if there are? It is not like you want me for anything other than these games of yours. You act like the moment we are married you are not going to just find some other women to fu—"

I am cut off with his lips crashing against mine. I freeze, my mind going haywire in disbelief before it goes blank. He pulls back lazily. "If you think my intentions with you end at marriage, little dove, you are mistaken. You will be mine. You *are* mine, in every way and although I find your dealings with those men are not exactly bothersome, it does not take away that at the end of the day," He nips at my lip. "You." He pulls me closer. "Will never." He whispers a hair away from my lips. "Escape me."

I push away from him, my mind dizzy. "I do not understand what you are implying." I clear my throat. *Did he just kiss me?*

He captures me once again, this time crowding me into the cottage wall. "Let me enlighten you, little dove. Our kings are disgusting pigs probably rampant with disease from their inability to control themselves. While, yes, I am a prince myself, you and your men seem to want to equate me to the troublesome behaviors of our fathers whilst forgetting you, yourself, are a part of a royal family. A princess no less." He gives me a pointed look. "Either way, I am not so insecure I need to try to beg for approval in the beds of the women of my kingdom. What is clear to me, though, is you and those two men are more than what you are trying to have me believe. If it pleases you to do so, you are free to pursue them. They are of interest to me, and I have started to like the impudent man you call Fadres, so I don't mind him around."

I open my mouth to… what? Refute his claim? Tell him to back off? I am plagued with confusion, my mind and body trying to sort out the motive behind this change in conversation. He stills my dizzying thoughts with a hand caressing my cheek, his eyes filled with promise and warning. I swallow hard.

"As long as you understand their being in your life does not change the fact you are mine, Alaceandra. Mine to toy with, mine to cherish, and mine to…" My mind finally catches up with his words. *There is no way the prince is staking his claim right* now! I nibble on my lower lip as I try to figure out whether to be enraged or turned on. *Staking his claim… but also… willing to share me?* Lust starts to take over my brain as an image of me between Sam, Sorin and the prince flashes through my mind causing my gaze to heat. He stops his next words, his eyes zeroing in on my lip trapped between my teeth. He growls. "It also does not change the fact that you've been eye-fucking me from the moment you stepped foot in this kingdom. As much as you seem to hate to admit it, Little Dove, you want me, and I am not going to let some asinine idea of what you think kings are and are not get in between claiming you as mine." His lips once again meet mine in a searing kiss, but this one is much more tender than the last. His lips coax me to respond, and I whimper in surprise at just how badly my body wants this. My hands tangle in his hair as he pushes me back further into one of the walls of the cottage, emboldened by my response. His lips forcefully take control of the kiss, nipping my lips to demand entry. I comply, letting him lead, but meeting his fierceness with ferocity of my own. One of his hands travels to my hip, gripping it to hold me firmly against his hardness and I let out a soft moan, my hands trailing his back, my nails slightly digging.

He lifts me up, carrying me to the tiny bedroom and crashing us both down on the mattress. Trapping my wrists above my head, he palms my breasts roughly through my dress, and I moan, straining for him. A shiver works its way through me as one of the prince's hands travels to my center. As his fingers ghost along my aching pussy. I jerk. A crash booms from the other room. We still. Letting out an annoyed noise in the back of his throat he releases me. I shudder at the loss.

"Stay here," the prince commands in a gruff tone.

Yeah right. I follow him and he shoots me an icy look. Arriving at the main room, we see little bundles of light crashing into the furniture and the walls. My eyes widen as a zing of recognition tells me these bundles of magical energy are my own. *At least I did not set the place on fire.* I think to myself. *Although I would not be surprised.* Suddenly, as if aware of my presence, the sparks all still before surging into the ground. My eyes widen in shock at the place the lights once were.

Cracks in the floor are growing by the second. I try to walk closer for a better look, but the prince places a hand on me. A furry arm shoots through the floor, and I jump back. Small gold and white flames lick the floorboards expanding the cracks. Something starts to push its way out of the ground and into the room. My jaw drops. A little albino ferret-like creature skitters out from the now small hole in the floor, before the flames extinguish and the hole closes leaving only a small scorch mark as evidence it was even there to begin with. Fast as lightening, the prince has the creature in his hands, his intent almost certainly malicious. It squeaks loudly and bites him before skittering up my body and onto my shoulder.

"*Protect me from that vile beast!*" the little creature says.

Wait says? When can animals speak. My scream gets caught in my throat.

"*I can only speak to you since you summoned me, Alaceandra, but I will not speak much longer if that beast murders me!*"

Barely audible noises squeak from the creature's mouth and are translated into words in my head. Bewildered as I am, I decide to hear the little guy out.

The prince tries to grab the creature from my shoulder, but I back away. "Do not hurt him!"

The prince looks at me with wide eyes. "Do not hurt him? He bit me! And on top of that, he is part of the demoni. He obviously came up from the realms. He must die."

"You grabbed him, it is only logical for him to bite you. Why would we need to kill him? He does not look like he will hurt us." For some reason I just know he is friendly, but I give the little creature on my shoulder a side eye as if to say *right?* Just in case.

"Looks can be deceiving, Alaceandra. That is a very dangerous creature." I ignore him.

"Yes, I have no plans on hurting you or your loved ones. I have come to only teach," he squeaks out.

"Teach?" I say aloud.

"Later, Alaceandra. The threat!" The ferret points comically at the prince, before darting under my hair. I flinch as pain pricks my scalp.

"Can you *talk* to that thing?"

"I think so," I respond.

"It is never a good thing when demoni are present, be careful what you tell it." He gives me a knowing look. "I know the creature is cute, Little Dove, but it *is* deadly. It is better if the thing is disposed of."

I consider my next words. "I think I summoned him..." I say.

"You did what? When? I did not see..."

"Yeah, well, I uh... I am apparently coming into some skillsets while... otherwise occupied. He says I summoned him, and I believe him. He says he is here to teach me."

He gives me a questioning look. "What can that thing teach you?"

"If the beast keeps referring to me as 'it' and 'thing' I will pee on his face while he sleeps."

I snort a laugh.

"What?"

I pause. "He requests you stop referring to him as an 'it' and if it was me I would, uh, probably stop referring to him as such."

The prince looks annoyed. "And why is that?"

"You would rather not know, I am sure."

The prince gives me an assessing look. "Fine. What should I call the th—" He clears his throat. "...him then?"

The little creature looks down at me from the top of my head, giving me an upside-down view of his petite face. *"You can call me Baldar."*

"Baldar?" I say aloud so both the prince and the furry guy can hear. The ferret nods his head. I look at the prince "Baldar." I giggle. The little creature is still hanging upside down in my hair. "Well, you sure have good bal-ance, Bal-dar," I laugh again at my pun. Glancing at the prince I notice he is unamused. His body is tense, and he is glowering at my hair. I clear my throat and address Baldar again. "But I am still confused. What are you here to teach me about?"

"Well, is it not obvious? About your powers, princess. Among other things. I am sure you have noticed you have been coming into some new skillsets, no?"

My heart stills in my chest.

"Um, maybe? But I... I, uh, have not run across anything like you..." The prince catches my gaze and quirks an eyebrow at me.

"Well of course not!" The little furry demoni hops from my head and skitters to the ground. I try not to flinch again at the sting of his claws. *"I have also been tasked with protecting you from the half-dead. So, you*

wouldn't have had to see anything like me as of yet." He puts tiny fists on his tiny hips, his stance meant to be one of intimidation, but seeing as he was just a small thing it looked more cute than scary. *"I have been serving from Unduli originally- hence the grand entrance- keeping them from sending anyone to activate your powers early BUT now it looks like you have gone and unlocked them yourself."* Tiny, furry, claw-tipped fingers waggle in my direction. *"So, I can finally come meet you!"* A happy squeak escapes Baldar.

"Unlocked? How did I—" I start to question, but then my cheeks flame with embarrassment.

"Looks like you got it!" A sound I know is a laugh squeaks from Baldar. *"Although I do question your choices on marking that one."*

I shoot Baldar a questioning look, choosing not to voice what he said aloud.

"Ah, a lot to learn indeed." Is the demoni ferret's only answer before he skitters back up my body.

I will need to figure out how to file his nails. I think to myself cringing again at the sharp sting of them as he races across my shoulders. Baldar huffs in what I can only assume to be a response to my thought.

"I have traveled a long way, goodnight Alaceandra." He curls up on one of my shoulders and before I can think to ask him another question, soft snoring sounds from the place he is laying.

"He, um... looks to be asleep," I say to the prince.

"What did he say to you?" The prince advances on me, his voice filled with anger and authority.

I take a step back. "Only that he was here to teach me." Baldar does not stir.

"Teach. You. What?" The prince looked on edge, his gaze tearing me apart with its scrutiny.

I hesitate. "He did not tell me anything else! He said he was here to teach me and to protect me- that is it."

"From what?"

"Something about half dead things, nothing specific, now can you back off?" I place a hand against his chest and try and gain distance. His hand captures mine and he takes a breath, before his shoulders sag.

"You are not telling the whole truth." I try to pull away, but his grip tightens. "I will excuse it for now, Alaceandra, but you will tell me. I promise it." He releases me. "We must sleep. Leave the rodent on the chair."

I huff. "He is not a rodent." I make my way over to the chair intent to sleep there as well. Shame and embarrassment have started to cover the memory of our earlier activities, and I was not sure if I would be able to be in such close proximity to him after my slip up. I close my eyes and try to adjust to the feeling of the springs of the chair digging into my hip. *This is not comfortable... but I guess better than rock.* I close my eyes.

I feel his eyes on me. "What are you doing?" He sounds a little amused.

I peek up at him. "Trying to sleep."

He sighs before he walks over to me and takes Baldar, gently this time, from my shoulder and places him on the arm of the chair. My eyes shoot open.

"What are you-" before I can finish my sentence, he hoists me from the chair and carries me to the bedroom. I flail around before being dropped unceremoniously on the bed.

"Sleep here."

"I am not going to share a bed with you."

He rolls his eyes. "What are you on about now?" He raises his brow.

My cheeks heat with embarrassment and anger.

"Alaceandra," he says firmly. "I am tired. You are tired. We need rest. I am sure there is a lot of bullshit ahead of us and I will not be responsible for your death on account of your stubbornness."

I grit my teeth. "Why does that mean we must share a bed? I would be perfectly fine sleeping in the other room or even on the floor."

"That is ridiculous."

"Why is that?"

"Why would I allow you to sleep in discomfort when there is a perfectly good bed in this room?"

"Well, why would you not—"

"What is going on here? Because before that—"

I give him a look.

"Baldar," he growls out. "Appeared you were perfectly content to—"

"That was a mistake." *Who knows what would happen if we were to continue… and what about Sorin? Sam? I know he said he would be content with sharing, but a man like him? There is no way he shares anything.*

The room stills and he stares me down. "Tell yourself that all you want, little dove." His eyes are filled with danger. "But I will tell you one thing, lying does not suit you nor does it serve you well with me. Run to your guards in the morning, but while we are in this room, you are mine to take care of and as such you will be sleeping here where I can keep an eye on you and away from whatever creation appeared to you outside this room."

I swallow back a retort, my nose wrinkling at his tone. The prince holds my gaze steadily.

"Fine," I grumble, my shoulders slumping.

"Good. Now, there is a nightdress in the bathroom. I am sure you would like to change."

I nod. Sliding off the bed off, I walk into the bathroom.

There is a simple black nightdress in the bathroom with a ruby trim. I quickly relieve myself and shower, luxuriating in the warm water. Taking a couple minutes to clean my teeth and inspect my appearance in the mirror, I pause, tracing a finger over the bags under my eyes. I do look tired. *I am tired.*

Sighing to myself, I don the new nightdress and make my way back into the bedroom. The prince has already changed into some loose pants. *No shirt though.* My eyes track over the dark lines of ink on his back, an image resembling an elvisera mid-flight adorning him along with some writing underneath. He turns towards me ending my appraisal of his body. I avert my gaze. The temperature of the room seems to have plummeted as night has fallen. Quickly slipping into bed, being sure to face away from him, I try to snuggle underneath the covers for warmth. A couple moments later he slips in behind me.

The bed is just big enough we do not quite touch when we are both laying on it, but I can still feel the heat of his body radiating to me in the small space between us. I let out a breath and try to relax. Examining the walls through bleary eyes, I try to distract myself from both the cold of the room and the heat of his body. *No plants.* I note to myself. *Maybe that means no spy ware?* I blink heavily as I feel myself being pulled toward sleep, but a shiver jerks me awake. My thoughts resume. *We are underground though, who knows what other devices these people might have down here. Or what other things might lurk in the shadows.* I shiver for a different reason, pulling the blankets closer around me, as if they could protect me from the imaginary creatures lurking around the room. My hooded eyes gaze distrustfully at the dirt floor. *Hopefully there are no spiders, though.* My shivers continue, causing sleep to elude me. I let out a soft noise of frustration and curl into myself. A warm hand touches my shoulder.

"Are you cold, Little Dove?" The prince traces his palm over my arm gently. Goosebumps race over my flesh and I jump a little at the contact. *I had not even realized he was facing me.*

"Nn-no," I say, another shiver trapped in my voice. I clench my teeth. A sigh is my only warning before I am yanked back into a warm embrace. I yelp. The prince tucks my toes between his legs in an effort to warm them... *or restrain me?* I am not quite sure which. I try to fight him albeit weakly. My weary body enjoying the warmth of him much too much for my sleepy brain to want to fight against it.

"Stop. Your body is freezing, and your wiggling is tortuous to my self-control." He angles his hips *and the erection that is currently evidence of his supposed torture* away from me. "Now, sleep," he commands, smoothing a palm over my hair. And I do.

CHAPTER TWENTY-SEVEN
Bleary Thoughts

Alaceandra

I wake up feeling off balance. My heart stills in my chest as I register it is the prince holding me close to him and not Sorin. *The prince who I kissed last night.* My brain reminds me oh so helpfully. I look up to see he is watching me. He traces a finger over my face, and I steel myself against the rush going through me at his touch. He runs a finger over my lips, and I shudder. Sleep is still pulling at my senses, my waking thoughts interconnecting with my dreams which is why I do not stop him when his fingers skate their way into my hair, and he slowly pulls me into a gentle kiss.

The feel of his lips on mine zings through me, my bleary thoughts coalescing into consciousness and I jerk away from him.

"Um, good morning." I rub my eyes.

He stays where he is. "How did you sleep?" His voice is husky.

I close my eyes for a moment. "Well, I think."

"Good."

We stare at each other. Memories flicker through my mind of last night's events and an ache starts to form between my thighs. The prince raises his hand to smooth some of the hair from my face and my eyes dart back to his lips. *What difference would it make if I kissed him one more time? Stop, Alaceandra, you cannot.* I remind myself, even as I lean into his touch. Our faces are a breath apart when a shrill voice rings throughout the room.

"I am from Unduli, beast! How dare you think doors will stop me!" Baldar squeaks indignantly from the bottom of the bed. His form appears in a puff of smoke.

I jump at the noise, pulling away from the prince.

"Stop your squeaking, demoni," the prince commands, irritated.

"Why you little—" Baldar sputters.

"Okay!" I run my hand over my face. An overwhelming urge to escape this small room overcomes me and I glance towards the bathroom door. "We, uh, better catch up with the others." I mumble, before scooting off the bed and capturing the squirming Baldar. I start to walk towards the bathroom and change but the prince's snort stops me in my tracks. I spin around.

"What now?"

A small smile graces his handsome face. "Please do not think you will get away with running from me again, Little Dove. I will catch you."

I shoot him a glare and shut the bathroom door with a bang. *If you say so, Your Majesty.* His laughter sneaks through the door and I lean against it. *This is going to be a long fucking day.*

CHAPTER TWENTY-EIGHT
Introductions

Alaceandra

I n the kitchen, Sam and Sorin jump up from the table and crowd around me.

"Did you sleep well?" Sorin asks me in low tones, casting suspicious eyes towards the prince.

I nod and he pushes me towards the table. Sylvie bustles in and sets down a plate of food filled with fruits, various meats and cheeses. My stomach growls just looking at it.

"Thank you." I smile at her.

"Of course, honey." She returns my smile before handing the prince a plate with similar contents and turning towards the doors leading to what I can only assume are the bedrooms of the house. "Please let me know if I can help with anything else." She yawns. "I have left some lunch for you all in the ice chambers." She points towards a metal box in the corner of the room. "I am off to bed, be safe and hopefully I will see you all for dinner." She places a gentle hand on Sam's shoulder before departing.

"How long has she been awake?"

"The sun has only just risen, do not worry," Sam supplies. "As much as we have tried to convince Sylvie she does not need to be awake for us nor serve us in the mornings, she refuses to go to bed until she has handed us our breakfast and given instruction for lunch."

"Even though she puts the food in the same place every day," the prince chimes in, chuckling.

"She has very strict rules on hosting." Sam smiles. "I will see to it she is repaid for all the work she has put in caring for us. Her generosity to us far exceeds the saving of her daughter. I would hate to take advantage of such a kind woman."

"You did almost die," the prince adds.

"Yes well," Sam clears his throat. "From what I understand she assisted in saving my life as well, making any debt she may have had to me paid."

The prince nods and continues eating his food.

I dive into breakfast with vigor, my stomach still not completely recovered from only eating small amounts of food from my time with Sorin. *Speaking of—* "Have you both eaten?" I ask Sam and Sorin between bites of food. Sorin stands at my back, he has bags under his eyes and his posture is tense and guarded. *He does not look like he slept well last night.*

"Yes. We have been awake for about two hours now; Sylvie was sure to hand us a plate the second we arrived in the kitchen."

I nod. "Good," I say, before stuffing another bite of creamy cheese in my mouth. Chewing thoughtfully, I observe all three men together in the kitchen and note Sam is a lot more relaxed around the prince than Sorin, who is most definitely guarding my back at the moment. *Did the prince really mean what he said about pursuing Sorin and Sam? I mean I already was kind of pursuing Sorin but Sam?* I look over at Sam. He catches my eyes and gives me a small smile.

I knit my brow and bite the inside of my lip before sliding my gaze to the prince, but he was already watching me. I frown at him, and throw my gaze back to Sam. He frowns back at me, shifting his gaze to the prince, before tilting his head at me. I shove another piece of cheese into my mouth. *Yeah, this could definitely get interesting. That is if Sam would even want me in the first place. Why am I feeling so comfortable with this idea?*

"What are we doing today?" I ask once I swallow.

"Well," Sorin starts. "I was talking with Fadres last night and we thought it might be in our best interest to start training you while we have quarters here."

Sam shifts his eyes to Sorin and then nods looking back at me. "Right. Credour told me you encountered some trouble much like I did when you first arrived here. We do not know if your kidnappers are still in search of you and while Credour did say it looks like you put up quite the brave fight against them, we both agree we have not done much in preparing you against such attacks."

I nod. "I would appreciate that. I feel as if I am gathering enemies quickly as of late." I force a smile. "No matter what kingdom I am in it seems people think they can use me to their advantage." I slide my eyes over to the prince. "It is best to be prepared in any way I can be."

The prince snorts. I feel Sorin's hands tighten on the seat behind me. "What?" Sorin all but snarls.

The prince rolls his eyes. "We probably need to work on making sure the little dove is safe from herself first. Who knows what chaos she can cause with her newfound powers."

Sorin stills. "Powers...?" Sorin comes to my side and crouches to look me in the eyes. "Did you tell him about your fire?" he whispers, his tone filled with worry.

I bite my lips and look at my plate. "I uh—no, we—"

A loud crashing interrupts whatever I was about to say as Baldar comes bolting into the room, his squeaks shrill.

"Really? You close me behind doors again?? While you are in here EATING WITHOUT ME?? Must you betray me so soon?" Baldar looks up at me, his voice filled with melodrama.

"What the fuck?" Sam and Sorin both grab one of the knives and try to crowd in front of me.

"It is okay." I try to say.

"No, it is not." Sam says sternly. "That is a demoni! They only bring chaos and death, him being here is dangerous Alaceandra. Who knows who sent him, we need to--"

"More of them, really? Nice to make your acquaintance too, Sam." Baldar huffs, cutting off Sam and causing him to bring his attention firmly back to the creature.

I squint at him. "How do you know his name."

"You can talk to him?" Sorin says, his voice filled with incredulity.

"She summoned him, as far as we know anyway, not some grand enemy, don't get your panties in a bunch," the prince says, his voice bored.

"What?" Sorin turns slightly towards me. "How did you—" He pauses and flicks his eyes between the prince and me. He raises his brows, a glint of interest in his eyes. "I see... You two did more than sleeping then." He does not seem upset, just curious and maybe slightly resigned.

The prince smirks. "I can see you have had experience with her coming into her powers as well then."

A blush steals over my cheeks. "What is that supposed to mean? If you think we—well we did not, we just—"

"We can talk about this later," Sam growls, still glaring at Baldar. He did not seem surprised by the revelation I summoned Baldar, rather just annoyed by his presence here.

"Of course he is not surprised, he's—"

Sam clatters the knife he was holding back down on the table and Baldar huffs again.

"I will be keeping an eye on you," Sam says seemingly to Baldar. "Lace, please put on some of the leathers that were left for you in your quarters. We will start training today on some more dagger work in an hour. Do not be late." He grabs a bit of cheese and scoops Baldar up before quickly leaving the room.

Sorin looks at his friend and sighs. "I-I need to go check on him," he says before racing after Sam.

Baldar's squeaks echo after them. *"See you soon!"*

Ptheryeth I am fucked, am I not?

My gaze flits over to the prince who I have once again been left alone with and I groan, looking towards the door, towards escape.

He smiles. "Looks like a nerve was struck." His tone screams arrogance, and he lets out a small laugh. "Go on now, Dove, fly along." He waves a hand in my direction. "I will not stop your retreat... this time."

With a frustrated sigh, I rise and hurry from the room.

CHAPTER TWENTY-NINE
Let the Training Commence

Alaceandra

Supple black leathers hug my body as I find myself in a position I never thought I would be in. Sam straddling me, his dagger poised at my throat. He has bested me for the thousandth time and my brow is drenched in sweat, every bit of me aching with exertion. I have not seen Baldar since Sam grabbed him at breakfast, and I really hope he is okay. For some reason I have grown attached to the small creature and his absence is unsettling.

Sam looks glorious, his toned chest glistening in the sunlight. The gentle weight of his body presses me to the ground firmly. Since the leathers are fashioned into intricately detailed pants and a long-sleeved shirt, I can feel his warmth seeping into me. Every single time we find ourselves in this position, me pinned under Sam, both chests heaving with the strain of the fight, I start to notice more and more about him. The man I always used to think was more of an intellectual than a fighter, has quite the build. His body is lean, but not wiry. His movements speak of years of training and brutal precision. *I wonder how he has kept this part of himself secret from me.* I had been crushing on him as much as I was Sorin, but now it seems like I do not even know him. Not in this form. I am battling between feeling excited by this new change in him or terrified. *Time will tell.* He shifts on top of me and I cannot help but notice the erection that has been slowly growing throughout our training session. The erection that Sam is now doing his best not to press against me. *What would this position be like without clothes between us?*

Chest heaving, I let out a frustrated groan. *Shush brain!* My body has been geared up since being in the cave *and the river* with Sorin. If that was not bad enough now there is the prince to contend with. I am a wound-up ball of need, and it is driving me insane. I should not be letting myself feel this way. I am betrothed to the prince for goodness' sake! My actions with Sorin alone would disgrace me. *But the prince seems okay with it.* I remind myself. *And so does Sorin.* Even still, I have not even hinted at my interest in Sam. It would be greedy to think I could have the three of them. *But still...* Sam twists on top of me causing goosebumps to break out along my skin. *What is wrong with me?*

"Okay, okay!" I wiggle beneath the blade. "I yield, Sam. This is impossible, you have years of experience there is no way I am going to beat you." I groan. Sexual and physical frustration ensuring my bad mood.

He sighs, then moves his wooden blade from my neck before rolling away from me. "It is not impossible. You just need more practice and to pay attention." He offers me a hand, giving me a stern look. "The creatures out here are skilled, I would know." He runs a hand over where his injury is now wrapped in bandages. "I need to prepare you to fight them if it comes to that."

The reminder dampens my arousal. "Are you sure you should even be training me? You cannot be fully healed yet. You still have six more days according to Sylvie."

He stands, readjusting his position so that we may begin again. "I am fine, Lace, I appreciate your worry, but it is unwarranted. Now please return to starting position."

"Sam, I am concerned—"

"Now, Lace. Stop stalling," I bristle.

I grit my teeth. "What is with you?"

"What do you mean?"

"You have been acting weird since we found each other."

He narrows his eyes at me, guard firmly up. "What. Do. You. Mean?"

"What do I mean? You scooped up a beast everyone seems afraid of and practically ran out of the kitchen!" He actually has the audacity to roll his eyes at me. I narrow mine at him. "A creature who knows your name, by the way." My voice is full of suspicion. "You are being more brash, commanding and short this morning and I do not know how to take it. I acknowledge this may be your disguise with the prince or how you train people, but you have never acted this way towards me. It is odd and I just want to know the cause of it."

Sam sighs and drops his blade and once again offers me his hand. I take it this time and he hauls me up. "Look, Lace. There is a lot at play here. I apologize for my behavior I'm just—" He runs a hand over his face. "Stressed." He decides. "You are not prepared for all you will have to face, and I knew I should have been training you for it sooner, but I just thought I had more time," he says the last bit under his breath.

Why does everyone have a riddle for me to solve? "More time for what?"

He hangs his head. "We really should continue training..."

"This is what I am talking about! Why will you not give me a straight answer? How am I to prepare myself for some difficult and dangerous journey when all the people I trust seem to want to keep secrets from me?"

Sam huffs. "Secrets, Lace? Really? You are the one complaining about secrets? As if we are the only ones hiding things?"

I look at him, confused.

He stalks towards me and I back away until my back bumps into the tree behind me. He puts his arms on either side of me, caging me against the tree. His mouth is just a breath from mine.

"Let's talk about secrets. Do you want to explain to me why, when we found you and Sorin, you had the scent of a female who had just freshly cum? With a hickey no less. Or this morning, you come up from your temporary quarters with your lips slightly swollen from, what I can only assume to be, the prince's lips?"

My mouth pops open. *Why does he care?*

"No? A loss for words I see." His face forms a crass smile I have never seen from Sam.

"When have my interactions with men ever been any interest to you? And for that matter how did you—" I force out.

He laughs. "How did I know? I disguise things, Lace. To disguise you must observe and know what to hide and you have been of interest to me since I first spotted you."

My eyes widen as my mind races over his comment. "Then why have you never said anything?"

He frowns. "You know the answer to that one." *My father?* The reminder of Tikilium's ruler shuts me up. He backs away from me and picks his dagger back up before finding where mine had fallen and throws it across from him. "Back to starting position, Lace, we will stop when I see an improvement."

I grit my teeth but scoop up the dagger and we begin our training once again.

CHAPTER THIRTY
Marked Ones

Alaceandra

We have been in this village for, what I think is, two weeks now, but I cannot be sure. It is hard to tell time here. Days feel like weeks and weeks feel like minutes. The plan is to stay here until I can get ahold of my powers, but to try to figure out how to leave before the solstice. Sam is afraid some of the monsters that attacked him will go after our group when we attempt to leave. Since this village has a great training ground, he wants to utilize it until he thinks I am competent enough to be able to dodge attacks should something happen on our trek to find another portal. Honestly, I am glad we are staying. This is the first place I have been where I have only had to work on myself and not worry about some broody monarch breathing down my throat. *Well, not a king at least.*

I roll over in my bed and groan. It is early morning and I have not even had a chance to eat breakfast. *I already feel like I am ready for bed.* Staring in the mirror after a brutal training session with Sam, I take note of the bruises which have started to form from falling on my ass time and time again. I am sore, tired and debating if sleep might be a better idea than food at the moment. *I could really use a nap,* I think to myself, glancing at the bed longingly.

As hard as Sam is being on me, the results of his training speak volumes for its effectiveness. My strength and agility are improving and there is the barest hint of muscle growth in my body. I have also ended up beneath him a lot less. *A fact which I am not sure if I am happy about or disappointed in.* Time has caused the bruises around my neck to vanish along with Sam's injuries and I am glad to be rid of the evidence of my encounter with that guard.

I wish I could say training with Sam is fun, but he has still been acting off and colder towards me lately. I am trying not to badger him about it, but I miss him. Even at his worst he has never been such a grouch with me. His distance is concerning. I thought as I trained with him more, he would loosen up, but it has not proved the case. *I even got my dagger near his throat today,* but nothing. He disarmed me easily after the small success, so maybe I should not expect much in congratulations, but still, the old Sam would have beamed with pride at the achievement. I sigh.

I wish I could write to Philos. I think I might actually shock her with all I have been up to as of late. I try to imagine what she would say. I smile. *She would probably encourage me to explore the men as much as I can but caution me to be safe. She would remind me if my father caught wind and/or if I needed a safe place to land, she would always be there for me. She would then probably make a joke that would be just funny enough to make me forget about the seriousness of the situation.*

Tears sting at my eyes and I press them with my palms to stem them from falling. I really miss her.

A warm feeling fills my body, peace and contentment overwhelming my previous despair, when suddenly, Baldar is twining around my feet. He climbs me and nestles himself in my hair.

"You will not believe the portals I had to go through to get here!"

I jump, pulling him from my head and holding him close to my body. "Where have you been?" I whisper. Baldar has been gone since Sam walked off with him the second day we were here. I was starting to think I would never see him again.

"Everywhere!" he squeaks.

"What?" I look at Baldar dubiously, tears momentarily halted.

"You heard me! Like I said it has been crazy trying to get back here, but I did it," he preens. *"Now, unfortunately this slight delay has cost us valuable training time and we are dreadfully behind. We must get started post haste!"*

"More training?" I groan, my muscles giving another ache of protest.

"Yes, but do not worry, there will be no sword swinging involved... well at least not the normal kind." The ferret makes a sound disturbingly close to a snicker. *"Now move your ass and grab your men. Meet me in the back forest this afternoon, twice past the sun's highest point. Oh and..."* His squeaky voice turns serious. *"Try not to alert Sam."*

I furrow a brow. "Why is that?"

"Why do you question me?!" Comes an exasperated squeak. *"He is not a marked one!"* he says, as if it is obvious. *"...and, well, I am not particularly pleased with him at the moment."* His tone turns sheepish.

"You and me both," I sigh.

"Great! Now please follow the instructions! I will be napping on the recliner." With that, he jumps from my arms and skitters out of the room. I hear a crash on the other side of the door then silence. I stare at the door for a moment, but honestly, I really do have no desire to argue with the

little creature, especially after he has been gone for so long. It is not like he will bother anyone with his shenanigans here.

The prince has already left the room, likely sometime after I went out to train with Sam this morning. He too has been more hands-off these last two weeks. His gaze more observant. I would find this worrisome, but this nature seems to end once we reach the threshold of the cottage. Once we arrive back to the room in the evenings a switch seems to flip in him. He becomes more relaxed and mischievous, using that silver tongue of his to coax a reaction, any reaction, he can out of me. Once we both decide it is time for sleep, he pulls me into his arms and commands me to close my eyes. If I question his motives, he makes some comment about the ridiculousness of him allowing me to be uncomfortable if comfort is easily provided. *It is downright confusing.*

I have awoken in the prince's arms every single morning, my back pressed firmly against his front. It has taken a lot of willpower to pry myself away from him and go out for training with Sam, but it must be done. By the time I get back he is always gone, and I do not see him again until the end of the day when we once again get ready for bed. My attraction to him has not waned in the slightest. Not that I am surprised. Sleeping snuggled in a man's arms does not exactly cause feelings to wane, but it does not feel right to act on anything, even if he is my betrothed, with things so tense between the four of us.

Sorin has not really been around either and I cannot help but be upset by that fact. Our time in the dark lands alone meant the world to me. I feel like some piece of me is missing without him around and yet it seems he has no trouble being apart from me. He is usually at breakfast in the mornings and dinner in the evenings, but otherwise I do not see him for the entirety of the day. When we are at meals, he stands behind me and guards my chair, his fingers brushing my shoulders while I eat. He always appears deep in thought but has not elected to speak to me in order to share any of those questions I can see racing across his features. He does not seem upset per se, just preoccupied with something.

The change is causing me to go slightly insane. I do not understand the men's sudden distance. Something has awakened in me and with every day that goes by without my continued interaction with them, I grow more and more on edge.

This longing is not helped by Sam's continued contact with me either. His coldness does not negate the closeness training has encouraged. I never thought Sam was interested in me, but his anger with me as well as his body's signals from training have been telling me a different story. It takes everything in me to force myself to grab my blade and try to defeat him instead of begging him to explain to me exactly what he has run out of time for and what all these riddles mean, but I know that it is smart to prioritize my training, and I do not want to push him farther away.

I splash cold water on my face and make my way towards the main cottage for breakfast. Hauling myself up the ladder to Sylvie's cottage, the voices of all three men filter through from the kitchen. I creep towards the door to catch Sorin speaking.

"Are we understood?" Sorin's tone is unyielding.

Something creaks and they all turn in my direction.

The prince smiles. "Ah, perfect timing."

CHAPTER THIRTY-ONE
Negotions

Sorin

Sam has been fucking annoying to deal with over the past two weeks. He had not taken the news of Lace and I well.

"You interfered," he growled at me.

"We were already interfering by following her to Helomasi! And then I had to save her from that guard and things just... happened. I didn't fuck her."

"You unlocked her powers! Before the prince could! Do not bullshit me. Whether it was your fingers or cock does not matter. It is basically the same thing. Now everything is out of order."

"What are you talking about?"

Sam glares at me. "I guess we will find out, won't we?" Then he stormed away.

He normally gets out of these growly moods more quickly, but I think his training sessions with Lace in the mornings are only making him more of a grouch. He has been stomping in going right in to the shower to 'work off some tension' and ignoring me. You would think his release would help but he exits in just as much of a sour mood as he went in. The sexual frustration must be killing him. *I know it is killing me.*

Despite his frustrations with how I handled things, I do not regret it. I miss having Lace in my arms at night and watching over her into the late hours of the morning. Not having her body against me is worse than torture. Without her a piece of me feels like it is missing and the longer I go without feeling her against me the more and more lost I feel. I don't like pissing off Sam though nor do I want to ruin Lace's future by testing the prince further. I only allow myself the most innocent of touches during mealtimes, but I am at a point where that is not enough. It is taking all of my willpower to not give into my desires. Especially when I see Lace's crestfallen gaze as I leave the kitchen each morning. I have tried to supplement my craving for her by allowing myself to watch her as she trains with Sam, but even that does little to make this empty feeling go away. *The way she looks at him though...I need to do something.* When Sam walks into the room after his morning training session with Alaceandra I stop him before he can make his way to the shower.

"What, Sorin? I'm busy."

"Look. We need to talk."

"We have."

"No all of us. Including the prince."

Sam arches a brow. "About what?"

"Lace."

Sam snorts.

"Look we all want her. There can still be a chance—"

"Maybe for the prince and you," Sam mutters.

"What? No, Sam. You too. You should see the way she has been looking at you lately. Her eyes are basically devouring you during those training sessions."

"The one's you've been watching from the forest?"

Yeah, he knew. "Yeah those." I say, scratching the back of my head.

He lets out a breath. "Look, I get it. You miss her. I miss her, but there is no way it is going to work. Not now that things are out of order."

"Where is Sam and what have you done with him?"

He rolls his eyes, and I place a hand on his shoulder.

"You have been scheming and planning to be with Alaceandra since you revealed to me what she means to you. There is no way you just throw in the towel right now."

"That was before all... this." He motions around. "What happens when she finds out who I really am? There is no way she can accept it under the current circumstances. What will we do then?"

I sigh. "We will figure that out when the time comes to it. For now, can we just talk to the prince? Maybe he might be more open than we think. He has been watching all three of us and he seems more curious than anything."

Sam rolls his eyes. "That jackass? Maybe. It is Lace's willingness I am more concerned about."

"There is no harm in trying."

"Oh, there is plenty of harm."

It is my turn to roll my eyes. "Just say you will do it."

"Fine, let's go talk to him." Sam says before leaving the room. I, of course, follow.

CHAPTER THIRTY-TWO
Perfect Timing

Sorin

We make it to the kitchen and find the prince sitting there smiling at Sylvie, his plate empty.

"That was amazing, Sylvie. Thank you again."

"Oh! It is no problem at all!" Sylvie glances over at us. "Come in, come in! I will grab your meals right away." She waves us forward.

"Actually Sylvie. Can we wait until Alaceandra comes down for our meals? Would you mind giving us a bit of privacy?" Sam smiles at the older lady.

She tilts her head. "Well, sure I will be in my quarters. Please come get me when the young lady arrives." She pets the prince's back and departs towards her room.

Once the door closes, we turn to the prince. He is already looking at us expectantly. "What do you want?" he asks in his usual bored tone.

"We don't trust you," Sam starts.

Not the way I would have begun this conversation but the truth, nonetheless.

The prince smiles. "Seems we are on the same page."

Sam smirks.

"Nevertheless, I think we all know why we are here," Sam continues.

"And whatever is the reason for that?" the prince asks, leaning closer to us, his arms on the table.

"Alaceandra," I butt in. Tiring of their hedging.

"Oh?" A glint of interest passes through the prince's vision.

"Don't act like you aren't aware, asshat," Sam says.

The prince's eyebrows furrow. "I don't think insults are the way to go here, Fadres," the prince chides, amusement in his tone.

Sam gives him a dry look.

The prince leans back. "So, I might have had a suspicion," the prince provides. "But I already told my Little Dove she was free to pursue you two if she so wished. The connection between the three of you is apparent and I have no intention of stunting Alaceandra's growth by stopping it. So, pray tell, why are you coming to me?"

Sam and I share a glance, taken aback by the prince's news. *He knows.* I curse to myself. A smile filled with pride takes over his features.

Sam glares. "What are you after here?"

An odd look flits over the prince's features before his arrogant mask is back in place. "We all have our motives, including you both, or would you have me believe your wanting of her is rooted in childhood love?"

The room darkens slightly. "You are such a—" I jab Sam and the room goes back to normal. Sam takes a deep breath smoothing a mask of cool indifference on his face.

"Lace has never had a choice in her life," I supply. "She needs all of us. We need to all be in agreeance here on what the terms are, seeing as it is apparent now we all know there is more to her than meets the eye." I give both men a hard look, which they return with a nod. "She has a hard path ahead of her and she is going to need all the help she can get." I pace the small kitchen and sigh, looking up at the ceiling. "The more allies she has the better and seeing as she has already marked the two of us," I shoot the prince a sidelong glance. "It is only a matter of time before she inadvertently does the same to you." I point a finger towards Sam "especially with the heat coming off of the two of you during those training sessions." Sam cuts his eyes away from me. "Alaceandra had not mentioned to the both of us what you had consented to. I think it might be a good idea for us all to talk to her about this together so there is no room for questions when it comes to our intentions. There needs to be no barriers."

"As I said we are on the same page." The prince smirks. "I was right in my assessment of the two of you. What an interesting pair the little dove has aligned herself with."

Sam rolls his eyes. "Sure," he says blandly.

"We need to be careful though," I ignore them, continuing. "Alaceandra is still a virgin, and her newfound powers and marks are going to being pushing on her to... fully unlock them with all of us." I say delicately. "We have to do our best not to overwhelm her, are we understood?"

The prince nods, but Sam stays noticeably silent, his face concentrated. I arch a brow at him.

"Are we understood?" I repeat.

A creak sounds behind me and I spin around quickly. Lace stands there; eyes wide.

"Ah, perfect timing." The prince says with a smile.

CHAPTER THIRTY-THREE
Rendezvous

Alaceandra

"Um, hi," I say awkwardly. "Where's Sylvie?"

Sam focuses briefly and then calls out. "Alaceandra is here."

Some rustling sounds from the direction of Sylvie's room and then she appears with a smile. "How are you today, Alaceandra! I hope you're hungry!" She pats my cheek and walks around the kitchen before setting a bowl of fruit and a plate of meats down for myself, Sorin and Sam.

I smile at her and sit down across from the prince, looking at Sorin and Sam's plates curiously. "Have you both not eaten yet?"

They do not answer me, instead they take their seats on either side of me. My heart races as the tension in the room grows and I scrunch my brows up in confusion at their odd behavior. *Something must be going on.* "I am off to bed!" Sylvie throws over her shoulder before she bustles back down the hall and into her room. The soft lock clicking behind her. The cloying anticipation of the room only grows at her departure. Sam closes his eyes briefly and I realize he is putting up a sound barrier. *But for what?*

"No not yet." Sorin finally answers, his disposition unusually sunny.

"Why is that?" Pretending to keep calm I start to eat, purposefully avoiding the heat of each of their stares. They allow me to eat a couple bites before the prince breaks the silence.

"We have all decided we will pursue you and will let you decide if you would like all, one, or none of us," the prince says calmly.

I choke on a piece of salted meat. Sorin rubs my back as I cough.

"Um what?" My voice is raspy.

The prince chuckles. "Is that not what you wanted, Little Dove? A chance to have all your men?"

I shoot him a wild look. "Wha-what?" *I guess Sorin was serious about talking to them.*

"Let her process, asshole," Sam mutters.

I must be going insane right now. I honestly was not sure if they would agree. Am I seeing things? Hearing things?

Sorin takes in my frazzled state and gets up from his chair. Spinning mine to face him. He tucks a strand of my hair behind my ear. Lowering his voice he whispers, "We do not have to do this if you do not want to. But we have all agreed we would be open to this if you were. Are you?" A brief look of vulnerability washes over his features.

A million thoughts race through my head at once. *This is absolute insanity. I know Sorin said kingdoms have had many rulers in the past, but the current people would never allow this! Further, do they even all want to be with me so much they would face those people who would stand against us? Whose idea was this anyway?* I stare into Sorin's eyes. They sparkle with hope, a dash of fear, and more than a little bit of heat plays through them and my stomach flips with trepidation. *Am I open to this?* I look at the prince, Sam and Sorin, their gazes meeting mine expectantly. *If they are then...* Something inside me gives a lurch, screaming at me. *Yep. Yes. Yeah. I am.* I look through my eyelashes and give Sorin a nod.

"We need to hear you say it," Sam growls. *He growls at me!* His voice causes a shiver to rush through my body and I dart my eyes away only to meet the prince's smirk. *What am I agreeing to? Three is so many men, so many—*

A blush creeps over my face. "Yes, but—"

"But what, my sweet Firefly?" Sorin cradles my cheek with his palm.

Cocks. So many cocks. I am still a virgin for Ptheryeth's sake. What am I to do with so many? I bite the inside of my cheek. "I need to know what this means. What does this pursual entail?"

"What do you want it to entail?" Sorin's voice is husky with desire. I do not know whether I am about to panic, crawl into the ground and die, or ask each man to take his clothing off one by one right in this kitchen.

"Whatever you are comfortable with, Alaceandra," the prince cuts in. "I will not withhold you from these men as there is a certain... power in your association with them, but be warned once certain steps are taken, they cannot be withdrawn." I glance over to the prince who is gazing at me steadily, his face a blank mask. *Really? I thought we were done with the stupid riddles!*

"Okaaaay." *What a mood killer.* I draw out the word, then look down at my hands, insecurities creeping in. "And you all truly want this?" I peek over at Sam who has been decidedly silent.

"It is what we have agreed," he says, meeting my gaze.

That is not exactly a yes... but I nod anyway. "Okay then, I would... um... like to try this," I wave my hand across the room shyly, "then."

Sam nods, striding across the room he picks up his plate. Brushing a lock of hair behind my shoulder he whispers in my ear. "See you soon, Alaceandra." Then he walks out. *Umm... okay.*

Sorin recaptures my attention with a hand on my chin. "Good." He presses a gentle kiss on my forehead and stands. "Eat your breakfast, Firefly." Making his way back to his chair he sits, picks up his fork and starts eating.

My eyes dart back over to the prince whose eyes are on me, assessing. My brows knit. *What a weird morning...* Clearing my throat I continue to pick at my breakfast, trying to ignore the prince's gaze on me, when I remember Baldar's instructions from this morning. *But how to bring it up...*

Sorin starts to get up to put his dishes away when I finally speak. "Um, hey guys?"

"Hmm?" Comes the prince's reply. He has been watching me this whole meal. *It is unnerving.*

"Can you meet me out in the back forest two hours past the sun's highest point?" I ask.

Sorin glances outside. "Um sure, that's in..." He squints his eyes. "Three hours?"

"I think so," I say, hesitantly. It has been hard keeping track of time here.

"Why do you ask?" The prince says quietly. I side eye him.

"I will tell you once you meet me out there, I do not want to share any more details here."

Sorin gives me a distracted nod. "Alright, I will let Sam know." He runs a hand through his hair.

"Fa-" I start to correct but decide against it. *Maybe the prince did not notice the slip up?* I glance towards him; his eyes are sparkling with interest. *Fuck, he definitely caught that.* "No, no need. It just needs to be you two for now." I try not to panic, keeping my voice neutral.

"Is this about him walking out earlier? I was going to talk to him about it, but I do not think we should leave him out, especially not so soo—"

"It is not that. What I need you two for has nothing to do with our conversation earlier."

"Then what?" Sorin crosses his arms over his chest.

I narrow my gaze at him. *Stop with the questions.* "Look you have kept much from me and have still expected me to trust you. Please give me the same respect."

Sorin grits his teeth. "Fine. I will be there. Alone."

I look to the prince, my face steely. "The little dove has her own secrets?" he whispers, then smiles. "Of course you needn't worry, Dove. I have no plans to inform anyone of your whereabouts, I am much too interested in the games you are playing."

"Thank you." Grabbing my dishes, I deposit them where Sylvie had instructed and then head back to my and the prince's quarters.

CHAPTER THIRTY-FOUR
Secrets

Alaceandra

Sometime later I find myself leaning against the thick trunk of some kind of oapik tree. Baldar skittered up its branches when we arrived and is now currently nestled in the blackened leaves taking yet another nap. From the edge of the woods, the prince approaches.

"Hello, little dove."

"Hello, prince."

"Still have yet to find another name for me I see." His gaze sparkles with mirth.

"Could be easier if you gave me your own."

"Perhaps, but has the dove learned how to join the fray, or only how to fly away?"

I wrinkle my nose at him. "You are an aggravating one, are you not?"

He approaches me. "I guess that might depend on the circumstance, no?" A flash of desire and something else crosses his features as he moves a strand of my hair behind my ear, his touch gentle. A small sound drags his gaze up and away from me and he chuckles, noticing the sleeping demoni above me. "Looks like your demoni has come back to haunt you." His voice is slightly husky.

"I would not call it that." My voice comes out a little breathier than I intended.

"Oh? What would you call it then?" His lips are mere centimeters from mine. His large body caging me against the tree.

I stare at him. "He is napping. All he has done since he arrived is sleep, not much haunting can be done when one is unconscious."

"Perhaps." He repeats his earlier sentiment.

Clearing my throat, I decide a subject change is in order. "Where is Credour?"

This causes him to pause. He leans away from me slightly. "Last I saw, he was in his cottage, likely talking to Fadres about his earlier departure," A pause. "Or shall I say taking to Sam? That is what your other man has referred to him as, no?"

"I do not know what you are speaking of," I evade, breaking eye contact.

"Oh, I think you do." A hand to my chin has me meeting his eyes again. "Does your dear Credour also go by a name unknown to me?"

"Names have power," I echo, unflinching to his searching gaze.

"Hmm." He drops my chin and takes a step away from me, his face shuttering before transforming back into his usual arrogant facade. I glare at him. He returns my look with a rehearsed cocky smirk. "Sneaky little princess. You should be careful who you lie to. If it is found out by my father you have snuck two men under his nose, he would not be pleased." His tone holds a bored note.

"And how would he find that out? Are you going to tell him?"

He shakes his head slowly. "No. I will not." He wipes his hands along the front of his clothes, smoothing out imaginary wrinkles. "If you are to keep secrets you mustn't be so easily read. We will need to work on that."

I pause. "Are you not upset?"

He tilts his head at me. "Upset?"

"Yes!"

"No. If I were in your situation, I would have done something similar. Allies are important. You should be glad you have them."

"Oh." I nibble my cheek.

He looks towards the tree line. "Credour is walking up now. I would recommend waking Baldar."

"*I am awake, hard to sleep with all your yapping,*" Baldar squeaks from his perch, I jump at the sound and swing my gaze up to him. He gives me a disapproving look. "*So much to learn...*" He mutters and then scurries off the tree.

"Sorry I'm late!" Sorin comes running from the trees. "It is hard to gauge time here."

"*Easy to do,*" comes Baldar's voice. "*Time moves differently in these lands, much to our advantage. Now get moving.*" He scampers to the middle of the field.

"Um... okay." I decide not to question that too much. "Will you two follow me?" I start to walk towards Baldar, but Sorin catches my arm.

"Why did you bring us out here?"

The prince glances at the two of us and then looks towards Baldar. "See you over there in a minute then?" He nods to the place where Baldar now stands expectantly.

"Okay," I say, slumping my shoulders.

Looking at Sorin, I sigh. "Look I need to learn more about my powers and Baldar seems to think he can teach me. For some reason, I trust Baldar. This training though apparently needs you both present for it to work. We talked about me learning more control, so I am doing that. Are you going to help me?"

He pulls me closer. "Why can't Sam join?" Sorin whispers, glancing at the prince.

I hold back an eyeroll. "Baldar?" I pitch my voice up so Baldar can hear me. *A little help please?* A small scuff is my only reply. I pinch the bridge of my nose. "They, um... got off on the wrong foot and I have not... grown as close to him as I have you both over the last couple of weeks. Since he has not triggered one of my powers, it would make no sense for him to be here," I guess.

Sorin nods. "Okay... so I take it he does not know Baldar is here then."

I shake my head.

"Great..." He looks skywards. "Okay." His eyes once again find mine. "Let's get you trained, but I cannot keep this from Sam. Honestly, I cannot imagine he is not already suspicious as it is," he warns.

I figured as much. I sigh.

Sorin grimaces. "I am not sure how much time we have." He glances to the woods. "We should start training now." He holds at his hand.

I take it and we make our way over to our new training grounds.

CHAPTER THIRTY-FIVE
I Have To Do What Now?

Alaceandra

"*A gain, Alaceandra.*" Baldar directs me as I try once more to make something appear or catch anything on fire. *No dice.* I groan in frustration. This training exercise has proved to be downright embarrassing. For one, I lack the ability to make anything appear. Two, there is the fact that the men are just staring at me as I fail time and time again. *Why do they need to be here anyway? I cannot believe they have to watch this after our conversation in the kitchen this morning. I must look mighty attractive covered in sweat trying to make floaty lights appear. Not.* I huff.

"*Just how much have you done with your marked men?*" Baldar's squeak startles me from my thoughts.

I mutter a reply. "Why does that matter?"

"Because it does." Baldar answers unhelpfully. *"Now answer the question."*

"We've just kissed," I whisper, biting at my bottom lip.

"Oh," Baldar gives me a bland look. *"That makes sense then."*

"What makes sense then?"

"I thought you all would have progressed further in my absence. You will need to kiss one of them, Alaceandra. Looks like the bond needs an extra kick in the ass to get things running for now." He gestures towards the two men and I stare at him. *"We do not have all day."* He taps his foot, impatiently.

"Kiss one of them?" I stare at him incredulously.

"Correct."

"And you think this will trigger my powers?" I ask.

"Correct."

"Can we not do something else to trigger them?"

"Eventually, yes, but right now this is the fastest option."

"Fastest? Meaning that a slower option *is* available?"

"What are you guys talking about?" Sorin asks.

"We are just going over how to trigger my powers for training."

"And that is making you blush?" The prince is smirking at me.

I breathe out harshly. "He wants me to kiss one of you." I try not to melt into the grass from embarrassment.

"Does he?" Sorin gives Baldar a curious look. "I guess that makes sense."

"Yeah, but-"

"Feeling shy?" I can hear the prince's smile in his voice and it grates at me.

I rub at my eyes. "Look we all have just decided this thing between all of us is something we are going to try. I do not want to fuck up something that is tenuous at best due to its newness. It is one thing to practice my powers through channeling with you both here and quite another to outright make out with one of you in front of the other without some sort of discussion first, especially because Sam does not even know of this rendezvous. Maybe we should wait on training until we can talk about all this a little more."

A branch breaks somewhere in the trees. I whip my gaze in that direction as a voice echoes throughout the clearing. "You need to train, Parum Bellator." Sam steps out from the darkness. "Stop worrying about the implications."

I narrow my eyes. "Sam? How did you—" I process what he said. "Wait, do not tell me you are joining this whole nickname train too! What does that even mean? Also, how long have you been there?" *Well, there goes that excuse, this is just my luck...*

He smiles at me. "Not long."

"Ugh now you've done it." Baldar's tone is filled with annoyance.

"What do you mean I have done it? What did I do?"

Baldar ignores me. *"Are you going to kiss one of those two now or are we just wasting time."* He snaps.

"Fine." I grumble. *Who though?* I stare at both the men then look at Baldar. If I am going to do this the only real choice is Sorin. Not only because I trust him the most of the two, but also because fire is much more predictable than little furry creatures roaming about. I can barely keep track of Baldar as it is. "Do we have water? Or something to put out flames?"

"Ah, so Sorin then. Good choice, although I am quite adept at fighting off demoni it might have been quite the challenge with everyone around." He runs over to Sorin and grabs his pant leg dragging him into the middle of

the field. Sorin allows this warily. Once he releases him, Baldar mutters *"I so did not feel like cleaning up guts today, fire is much easier."*

"Cleaning up guts?" I ask. *Why would he have to clean up guts if I chose the prince? Was he planning on killing the other demoni?*

He jumps, startled. *"Of course not what a silly question."* He replies before laying at Sorin's feet. *"Come here."* I look at the prince and Sam to notice that they are both now sitting on opposite sides of the field, leaning against one of the large trees.

The prince notices my stare and makes a shooing motion towards me, his face filled with interest. One more look at Sam shows he too seems interested about what is going to happen next.

I swallow and then make my way to Sorin and Baldar. Standing across from Sorin, I lower my voice. "Did you tell him that we would be here?" It does not truly matter, but seeing as I specifically asked him not to, I need to know.

He shakes his head. "I did not, but I knew he would figure it out. Sam has a weird way of just knowing things, especially when they are meant to be secret."

"Shush!" A loud squeak ends our conversation. We look down at the demoni. *"We must begin,"* he says and his white fur starts to glow.

"I- I heard him," Sorin says his eyes rounded.

"Yes, now kiss the girl." He waggles his fingers at us.

A mask of determination seems to slip over Sorin's features and I have only time to notice Baldar running behind me before Sorin is pulling me to him. His fingers slipping into the strands of hair at the nape of my neck. My skin tingles. His fingers tighten as he wraps his arm around my waist, fitting my body against his.

"I have missed these lips so fucking much," he whispers before kissing me with such passion, I lose track of everything else. My eyes flutter shut as warmth spreads throughout my body. I return Sorin's kiss, my body relaxing completely in his hold, and whimper when I feel his vines start to twine themselves around my ankles. They continue to work their way up my body, weaving themselves between us until we are bound together. "So. Fucking. Perfect." Sorin breathes between kisses. His lips leave mine and start to make their way over my chin and down to my neck.

The warmth quickly transforms into an inferno heating my entire body and I moan, letting my head fall back, dizzy with lust. I grasp at Sorin and he chuckles before I feel vines twine around my wrists and gently urge me to release him, as I do the vines around my legs tighten, pulling me until I am forced to turn completely. My ass is now firmly pressed against Sorin's cock. I yelp and open my eyes at the change only to gasp at the sight before me. Flames of blue, green and gold dance across the clearing, stopping short a foot from the edge of the tree line. I feel Sorin's lips at the shell of my ear. "Look what beauty you have created, the power you hold is magnificent, Lace." The flames glow brighter at the compliment and I chance a glance towards each end of the clearing. Sam and the prince both watch with intent expressions. The flames give them a wide berth and I wonder if that is something I am doing subconsciously or if it has something to do with Baldar.

"It is you Alaceandra," comes his little voice. *"Your soul recognizes them. It will not burn them."*

"Recognizes them?" My brain is coming out of its lustful haze at hearing Baldar's voice and the flames start to dim.

"That is something to explain later," Baldar says quickly. *"You are losing your flames. Focus Alaceandra."*

Panic fills me. "Focus on what?" I ask. The flames shrink further, their light now more of a sparkle against the grass.

"The warmth, Alaceandra. Focus on the warmth."

The warmth? I question internally. Sorin, along with his vines, remain twined around my body but they have gone still. I think back to a couple minutes ago. I did feel a warmth but I have always chalked that up to arousal. I try to focus on the sensation anyway. As I focus, the warmth once again grows in my body, racing down my arms and into my fingertips. My eyes widen as the sparkling flames grow into small fires.

"Good," Baldar praises. *"Now we are going to try to move them closer together. Do you see how they are all spread out? We are trying to concentrate those flames into one."*

I focus on one of the smaller flames, my brow wrinkling in concentration, but nothing happens. I keep trying, a small headache forming.

Hours pass of me focusing on the sensation and trying to get the flames to move with no luck. Finally, I throw my hands up in surrender.

"This is impossible." My headache is now firmly a migraine. An agonizing pulse forming behind my left eye.

"You are giving up far too easily," Baldar chides.

"I have been trying for two hours! They will not move."

"Then keep trying," Baldar states flatly.

I am about to scream when a gentle touch along my back catches my attention.

"Instead of imagining pushing them together," Sorin's soft voice is back in my ear. "Imagine a flame in nature, what might move a steady flame?"

I sigh. *A flame in nature?* Wind caresses my skin and I shiver. *Wind would move a flame, would it not?* "A breeze?"

"Exactly," Sorin whispers, his tone filled with pride. "Now, try imagining a breeze pushing that flame into one of the ones around it." He points out a group of flames near each other. "Test the air, where is the wind blowing? We want to work with nature not against it."

I nod and do the only thing I can think of to test the winds direction I lick my finger and hold it up. Noting the direction of the breeze I re-concentrate on the middle flame, this time imagining a gust of wind pushing the fire towards its mate. The top of the flame flickers before leaning in the correct direction. That is all I am able to manage before exhaustion crashes into me making my legs go weak and my body sways. As I start to drop the flames extinguish themselves. Still, I smile at the little victory.

"It moved!" I say, my voice faint, I can feel my eyes rolling back.

"It did. Good job Alaceandra."

"Good job, Firefly."

Those are the last things I hear before my vision blurs and pain overwhelms me as I lose control of my body and crash to the ground.

CHAPTER THIRTY-SIX
What Happened?

Alaceandra

A red light flashes and I find myself in the middle of a field, the sun sinking into the horizon. I look around and realize I am alone. To my left, I notice a dark puddle in the grass and a wave of nausea washes over me. A force urges me to walk and I feel my legs start to move in the direction of the puddle. The land is wet, making my legs and ankles drenched with each step. The foreign force urges me to pay no mind to the sensation, instead it encourages me to only continue walking. Squatting down, I press my fingers into the puddle and pull them up to look at the substance. My hands shake. Blood. Why is there so much blood? *I look around and notice that the field is covered in the scarlet streaks. Not only that but bodies also lay strewn about, daggers and arrows protruding from their forms. My heart starts to race, and I jump as something moves at my feet. I whip my head back to look at a form now laying where the puddle had been only moments before. Recognition sweeps over me but* no, it cannot be. *I shake my head and fall back, crawling away from the form.* "It is fated, Alaceandra." A voice whispers in the wind as unseeing eyes stare back at me. "It will not be stopped." *A dark laugh echoes, and I scream.*

I wake to a cold cloth pressed to my forehead and the worst headache of my life. Groaning, I roll to my side, causing the rag to fall off my head and to the floor. I peek my eyes open, but darkness greets me. *Thank Ptheryeth, I think light might have killed me.*

"You're awake," Sorin whispers to my left, an uneasy feeling rolls through me.

"It seems so." A small light flickers on in the corner, bathing the room in a warm glow. I shield my eyes against the light.

"Sorry, should have warned you," Sorin says sheepishly before grabbing the cloth from where it had fallen beside me and placing it on a plate next to the bed.

Blinking rapidly, I take in my surroundings. I am in a room of carved dark wood with ornate red rugs lining the floor. The bed I am laying on is made of the same material and has iron accents running through it. The same goes for a small desk in the corner. Tiny iron figurines decorate the walls and there is a room off to the right that looks like it might lead to a sitting area. *So definitely not in my cottage, then. This one seems much more masculine... and red. Where am I?*

Sorin sees the confusion on my face. "This is where they have Sam and I staying. Here, take these." He shows me silver capsules in the palm of his hand.

"What are they?" I ask.

He chuckles. "They are for the headache I can tell you are harboring at the moment."

I eye them warily but decide to take them from him. He hands me something to drink and I pop the capsules in my mouth and gulp down the liquid. I cannot help but be glad that he is the one here to take care of me. Although sleeping in the prince's arms is nice, it is not the same as being with Sorin. The amount of comfort and peace I feel in Sorin's presence is something I share with no one else. My heart squeezes as I remember how distant he has been lately, and I reach out for him.

He walks over to me, and takes my hand in his, brushing his lips over my knuckles.

"I have missed you," I whisper.

"I've missed you too, Firefly." He sits at the edge of my bed and softly runs his fingers over the strands of hair sticking to my forehead.

"Why have you been avoiding me then?" I ask, glancing away from him, cursing at the vulnerability in my tone.

"Lace..." His voice is pained. He pulls my face so that I have to look at him. "I told you in the woods that we had to do this correctly. You are my number one priority. I cannot have you unless I know for sure that it will not harm your future. I know you also share feelings for Sam and the prince. I will not strip you of your choices nor will I take advantage of your inexperience. I have to make sure you are certain of what you want here."

Anger flares, but I do not dispute his claim. *I do have feelings for the other men, but...* "That does not mean that you have to avoid me. Watching you leave me every morning after meals has felt like you leaving me to my father's wrath in the woods. Although I know you have reasons for your actions, I cannot stand the uncertainty that comes with them. I know that our circumstances here are unconventional, but I cannot do this without you." Tears brim in my eyes, and I look at my hands. Truthfully, I know I am falling for Sorin. Hard. It was only a matter of time. *Sorin is the only one I could ever truly depend on. If him staying away from me is the only reason I have a bright future, I would rather be damned.*

Sorin pulls me into his lap. "I am sorry, Lace. I promise that I will do everything in my power to never make you feel that way again," he whispers this pledge to me before pressing a kiss to my forehead. A humming fills my body, my bracelet warming against my skin. After a couple of moments, the sensation vanishes, and I glance up at him.

"I will take you at your word, but do not make me regret it," I whisper. "What are we to do now?"

"The prince and Sam are in the sitting room out there. When you start feeling a little better, we should see them but take your time."

"Okay" I whisper. Sorin leans against the headboard with me in his arms and I stare at the ceiling for a bit until my headache starts to subside. "What happened after I passed out?"

"Nothing much, Baldar disappeared. I grabbed you and carried you inside while the prince and Sam stalked after me. The noise woke up Sylvie and she popped her head out of her room, took one look at you and grabbed us some medicine to give you when you awoke. Since the tunnels to our quarters are a bit shorter than yours, we all decided to bring you here. It has only been about three hours. We have been waiting for you to wake up. You really scared us."

"Okay." I pull myself from Sorin and coax my legs to stand, holding on to the headboard when the room starts to spin a little.

Sorin rises next to me and scoops me up in his arms. "Maybe you shouldn't be walking right now."

I nod and lay my head on his chest, trying not to lose my lunch. "Let me see everyone."

"Are you sure?" Sorin's eyes fill with concern, and he smooths one hand over my forehead.

"Yes, please. I am sure this will wear off eventually. I am just tired. Who knew coming into your powers would be so exhausting?" I laugh weakly.

Sorin throws me a sympathetic smile but complies with my request and walks me into the other room.

CHAPTER THIRTY-SEVEN
From A Distance

Sam

Some hours earlier...

I am sitting against one of the large trees lining the clearing watching the little warrior's fire flit across the grass when I see it. A boot, then a figure darting away to my left. I stand ready to go after whoever dare lurk in the woods while the little warrior trains, when I see her fall. I flash over to her, but Sorin has caught her before I can make it. *Good man.*

We run back to Sylvie's cottage where I collect a bit of meat for Alaceandra. The pest who calls himself a prince follows behind us until we reach mine and Sorin's cottage. There, we wait. I do not mind the pest's company nearly as much as I did when I encountered him. In fact, he has grown on me quite a bit, not that I would let him know that. His ego is much too large as it is and I will not help in inflating it. Still, he did help me get to safety when he thought my life was on the line, and for that he has earned a modicum of my respect. Although the injury would not have proved fatal- seldom do for those of my kind- the true fear the man showed on my behalf was one I will remember. I sit with him now on this tiny sectional, waiting for my little warrior to awaken. I know she will and yet I find I am stressed at the reasoning behind her fall. It is unnatural that such a small task would exhaust her so much. Moving a bit of her magick around should have been child's play once she figured out how to do it, and yet... and yet it was not. My mind flashes back to that figure in the woods. I must find them and figure out why they were watching Alaceandra. Maybe they can provide me some information.

Wood creaks and I stand with the pest. My little warrior looks exhausted as she is carried into the room and placed on the sectional. My brow knits in concern.

"How are you doing?" I ask.

"I am okay, just tired."

"She almost passed out when she stood from the bed."

That is definitely worrisome. She should be recovered it has been three hours. I must catch the lurker. "Seems like more than a little, Lace. Here eat this." I hand her the bit of meat that I procured and watch her take a bite. "You should rest today and we will continue your training tomorrow. There has to be a better way to train you without exhausting you." I start to pace. *She must be recovered by tomorrow. We will need to ramp up her training especially if she is being watched. She is improving in her dagger skills but not fast enough. We are far too close to the solstice; we cannot be delayed.*

"Is it not normal to be tired after training a new skill?" she asks through a mouthful of food. My racing thoughts pause at how adorable she looks when she eats.

The pest's snort jars me from those thoughts. "Nope," he says dryly and I glare at him until he meets my eyes. He raises his brows at me, his gaze challenging and I hold back a snarl.

Taking a breath, I answer Alaceandra's question "Tired, yes, but not like this. Think about how you feel after our trainings in the morning. Your muscles are sore and your body weary but you are still able to function. It should be much the same when training your abilities. You should be mentally maybe a little drained, but not so much so that you lose consciousness for three hours. Unless, of course, something interf-" A thought hits me and I stop pacing. *What if they are the reason she cannot control her powers yet. It would only mean war if they did, but I have to ask.* "Did you... dream at all?"

"Dream?" She is understandably confused, *but I need her to answer.*

"Yes, dream. Try to remember. Was it all darkness or did you see anything?" I press.

She concentrates on something. "I- I do not remember. Maybe... there was a voice, I think?" I suck in a quiet breath, ice filling my veins. "No, I am sorry. Nothing is coming to mind." She lays down, but I have enough to go on. *I must find that lurker. Now.*

Looking back to my old friend I say, "I need to go. Sorin, can you watch, Lace?"

The pest rolls his eyes. "I can watch the princess." I have no time for his childish antics. I need to go.

"I will need you at the north wall today, I have something I must attend to." Luckily he too knows the dangers that this place holds, so he takes his watch seriously whenever I ask him to take a shift.

"And that is?" He narrows his eyes at me, and I have to take a deep breath as to not deck the man.

The room darkens marginally as I say, "Something we will speak of later." I glance at Alaceandra to see if she noticed my loss of temper but she appears to be none the wiser.

"Fine," the prince says through gritted teeth before storming over to the floorboard that holds the exit. He whispers something to Alaceandra before jumping down the hatch.

The fear that flashes across Alaceandra's face at his dramatic departure has me balling my hands into fists. "How far down is that drop? Is he okay?" She strains to look but Sorin quickly shifts her back into him as she sways. I give him a nod and make my way over to the hatch to follow after the fool.

"He is fine," I growl. "The asshole is just being dramatic. We will be back soon." I then quickly climb down the ladder and flash to catch up to the prince.

"What was that?" I ask pulling the prince to a stop.

He turns on me, eyes flashing with anger. "What do you mean 'what was that?' Alaceandra is injured and you have me on border patrol for the evening? What is that about?"

I walk ahead of him and he reluctantly follows. "I need to check the woods, I saw something or someone right before Alaceandra passed out, which will leave the north wall empty for the evening. I need you to make sure it is secure while I investigate the threat."

"Why me? Although it seems you have some sway with that Credour man, I am not under any charge of yours. I do not take kindly to being ordered around."

It is my turn to roll my eyes. "Yeah, yeah. You are a big tough prince, but when it comes to the matters of Alaceandra's safety I need someone I can trust watching out for her while this is taken care of."

"And you don't trust me, so you have Credour watching the dove?"

"We have been over this, of course I don't trust you I can see your agenda written all over your face. You care more about getting back at daddy then you do anything else. Alaceandra is just your tool to getting there, why she wants to go after you is a mystery to me."

"And yet you would allow it."

"I cannot nor will not control Alaceandra's actions. She alone decides her future." *Whether I like it or not.*

"Ah now it is you that speaks in riddles." We share a look of mutual understanding as we reach the ladder to Sylvie's cottage. "Fine, I will check out the border, but I will only be out there for two hours. Only two hours. After I will switch out with someone else. I do not want to leave the Dove for too long." Worry flashes over the pest's face, and I nod at him.

"Fine. I will finish my business swiftly and meet you back at Sylvie's in two hours." He nods at me.

The pest climbs the ladder, and I follow after him. We round the corner finding Sylvie in the kitchen finishing up dinner. I grimace. "Sylvie, I think with Lace's incident earlier, it might be best if she gets some rest. I am not sure if we will be able to eat in your kitchen tonight." Lyza sits at the table playing with a small wooden doll, and I smile at her warmly.

Sylvie spins around beaming at me. "Oh, I figured as much!" She says, amicably. "I am making your dishes in little portable containers, feel free to carry them to her room when you are both done with business tonight." She bustles over and gives us both a kiss on the cheek before resuming her cooking. "Be safe out there!"

"Thank you, Sylvie. You are far too kind," the prince drawls.

"Oh hush." She turns a little pink.

I push the prince out the door.

"Two hours?" I ask

"Two hours," he repeats.

CHAPTER THIRTY-EIGHT
Drained

Alaceandra

I watch Sam leave and cannot help but be annoyed that he avoided my question. I look at Sorin. "Where are they going?" I repeat.

He looks away. "Um... I am not sure."

I do not believe that one bit. I huff. "Really? Again with this?"

He sighs, his foot tapping, before he finally relents. "The prince and Sam have been keeping watch of Olvaria during the day from any potential threats. Just because Sam has defeated one of the creatures before doesn't mean they will not be back. He has been on guard whenever he is not training you, I assume they have gone to check on that."

"Olvaria?" I ask.

"The village. I learned that is what they call the place while I have been out helping the villagers build the wall around the perimeter."

"Oh." *Well, I guess that explains Sam's absence then. I had not even thought that the village had a name, but of course it does, why would it not?*

I feel my cheeks heat with embarrassment. *With all the training I have been going through, I have not done much exploring of the place outside of the training grounds and Sylvie's cottages, no wonder I had not seen Sam and the prince around much.* "Why is he being so cagey about that? And what is important about the north wall?"

"That I do not know," Sorin says. "But that is near where we were training you earlier. Maybe something happened he needed to look into?"

I hope not. "Maybe, but I did not notice anything when we were out there."

"You wouldn't have. Like I said Sam is good at detecting things people don't want found. He probably saw something that we did not catch."

"Is it safe out there?" I ask, because honestly it does not seem like whatever thing Sam is looking for is easy to conquer, seeing as it had almost killed him in the past. I know he has the prince as a backup, but I am still unsure how reliable the prince is. He has admitted to me that he is only really playing for himself. What if he views Sam and Sorin as his pawns as well in his grander scheme? Is that why he is willing to play along and let me have them for now? Will that all change the moment he gets what he wants?

I hate that my newfound powers are more of a hindrance to us here than a help. It seems like Sorin and Sam have been close comrades in my father's battles, and I know that Sam would likely much prefer Sorin's help over the prince's, but my lack of training makes me a liability, leaving Sam without a valuable ally.

"Nowhere is truly safe, Firefly," Sorin says softly, placing a gentle kiss on the top of my head. "Wherever you go there will be a battle that needs to be fought. A piece that needs to fall before you can get to your final destination. It is something that Sam and I know well, and you too will learn. Sam can handle himself. I have no doubt he will be fine."

"Okay, but if he is not back soon, we must go find him."

"If he is not back by dawn, I will go find him, you should remain here with Sylvie if that is the case." I give him a look. "I will come back, but we both do not want you in any danger if we can help it."

I do my best to remain calm. "Fine." I acquiesce, slumping back against Sorin. *I guess he is just as aware of my helplessness as I am.* My thoughts sour further.

Sorin notices and pulls me to face him. "It is not that I think you incapable, Firefly," Sorin whispers, running his fingers through my hair. "I believe with my whole being that one day you will far surpass even Ptheryeth's most skillful, but I hold true to what I said before. If there is ever a possibility for you to get away from an encounter before it is life threatening, I need you to run. I refuse to take you into a situation where that could be the case unnecessarily. If Sam was to somehow go missing and I were to take you with me to find him, the possibility that you would not survive that encounter is far too great. I will not endanger you, Lace. I refuse to put you at risk and most of all I will not lose you." He kisses me and I return his kiss with fevered passion.

His fingers tangle in my hair as he pulls me onto his lap. I feel his thick erection straining for my entrance through the coarse fabric of his pants and I moan rubbing myself gently against it. "I love the way you taste." He whispers against my lips as a thick vine wraps itself around my waist. His hands trace themselves up my waist making their way to my breasts before he squeezes them gently. I cry out as he pinches one of my nipples and he chuckles against my lips. I pull away from him, my heart racing as I remember that this activity has consequences, but when I look around, the room is not bathed in fire.

"H-how?" I whimper out as he presses gentle kisses along my collarbone.

He pauses his kisses to glance around the room. "How are you feeling?" he asks. His hands still caressing me softly.

Horny as fuck, but... "I do not feel the same warmth I usually do," I whisper.

He nods. "You likely drained yourself during training," he says a small smile at the edge of his lips.

"You can do that?"

"Definitely," he says. "If you do too much at once you need to recover, during that period it is harder to access your powers. Not impossible to do but it is dangerous."

"So does that mean..."

He smiles. "You aren't going to burn down the cottage... if you would like to continue?" He pauses.

I answer him with another kiss. Lifting me, his vine tightens around my waist as he walks us both back over to the bed in the other room and places me delicately on the mattress. Pulling off my clothing, he sucks in a breath at the sight of my dripping pussy. Ripping off his shirt, he pulls my legs until my ass sits at the edge of the bed before he kneels before me, throwing my legs over his shoulders, and starts devouring my pussy. I clutch at the blankets and my body starts to hum. I squirm against his masterful tongue. His vine holds me firmly, ensuring I cannot wiggle out of his reach as he sucks my clit into his mouth. Firelight flickers at the edge of my skin but quickly dims and extinguishes. I pant, desperately trying to hold onto anything to keep me grounded.

"You are so fucking responsive." One of his fingers slips inside of me, curling to rub just the right spot. "Such a beautiful pussy, Firefly. I can't wait to bury myself so deep inside of you that my cock is all you can think about for the next week." His thumb is rubbing circles along my clit as his finger rocks itself in and out of me. "Do you think you can take that, Firefly? Can you take my cock like a good girl?" I explode into a million pieces around his finger. "Such a good girl," he growls. "Again." He sucks my clit back in his mouth, continuing to pump in and out of me as his vines encircling my breasts flick at my nipples. I let my eyes drift shut, overwhelmed. My body feels hot as tiny currents are zinging their way along my skin, heightening my euphoria. I try to focus on them, but find that my thoughts are fractured. My body too focused on reaching for its next orgasm to allow my brain room to think. I open my eyes and reach for Sorin's hair as I feel my orgasm attempt to take over, but before it can crest, the room darkens causing Sorin to lift his head. I whimper in frustration, pulling at the strands.

A chuckle sounds in the doorway and Sorin grabs some blankets to shield me from our intruder. *Another fucking cock block, you cannot be serious.*

CHAPTER THIRTY-NINE
Taking Care of Business

Sam

Finding my way back to the field, I notice dirt that looks out of place around the same spot I saw that boot earlier. Touching the ground, I rub the soil between my fingers causing sparks of magick to zing up my arm. *Hmmmm...* Sensing that the magick travels deeper into the woods I follow its path trying to find where it leads. The way it weaves about the trees makes me certain that this path is not made by some sort of animal. It curves and doubles back meticulously, making its origin and ending hard to find. *No, whoever was here attempted to disguise their tracks, making them difficult to follow for the average person.* Unluckily for the interloper, I am a master in all things having to do with concealment. I make easy work of discerning which path will take me to where they ultimately ended up. Passing a few caves along the way, I take note of them in case they may prove useful later. As the path of magick grows stronger, I mull over what disguise I will use when I eventually come upon the intruder.

I find a clearing that has a thick cloaking spell around it. *Ah there you are.* Testing the spell, I try to see what kind of magick I am dealing with. *Looks like a redirection spell.* I trace the little streams of air whipping around the area. *The air currents are supposed to direct whoever may come upon it to travel in a different direction, but these are not foolproof. If someone is already lost, they can easily wander past the spell. Its biggest weakness is that it is only useful at cloaking against those who are looking to find it. I wonder what his back-up plan is if anyone were to find this place accidentally as it is not terribly far from the main cottages.* Deciding on the perfect disguise, I puncture the magick with a finger and it crumbles deliciously, revealing a large tent framed in wood, rope and white sheets. I absorb the residual magick into my skin, prohibiting it from alerting its owner of my arrival. Walking deeper into the clearing, I change my appearance as I go so that I look to be an older, weaker man. My hair greys, my limbs turn frail and I change my gait to more of a hobble. Arriving at to the tent I rap on the wood, a commotion sounds from within. A glass breaks followed by a barely audible "shit," then silence.

I wait a minute before letting out a feeble "Hello?"

The white sheet peeks open. "Who are you and how did you find this place?" A large man stands on the other side of the tent door, a large axe in his hand. I roll my eyes internally.

"Oh... I am sorry." I feign fear. "I-I got lost in the woods on my way back to my cottage and came upon this place. I was wondering if you knew where I was and maybe how to get back?" I force my body to quiver with my words.

The big man's grip on his axe tightens. "Sure, old man, why don't you come inside." His voice is filled with anticipation.

I walk past the man, noting that he does not drop his axe. His smell hits me on the way inside. He reeks of death and decay and is doing very little to hide it. Holding back a grimace, I sit at one of the stools surrounding a small table in the center of the room. The table has a bit of rope, a broken glass, some parchment, and a little quill on it. The man smirks at me, throwing his axe over one of his shoulders.

"Quite the place you have here," I say conversationally. "I have never seen a tent here before, are you visiting someone in-town? We don't get a lot of visitors! They must be glad to see you." Sylvie mentioned a lack of guests in the past, not that I am surprised. The only way to access this place is through the portal Sorin and Alaceandra fell through, and it has been quite selective over the years of who it allows entry.

The man approaches me, his steps slow and measured. He is pulling up to his full height which I know is his attempt at intimidation. *Tsk tsk tsk...* I purposefully ignore the menacing aura. He studies me. *He is likely looking for any weapons. I am sure I seem like quite the easy prey right now. Someone stupid enough to not be fearful of a big oaf wielding a deadly weapon, is someone easy enough to kill afterall.* He fiddles with his axe, tossing it up so he can rest the poll of the weapon on his other hand and caress the metal, his eyes never leaving me.

"I am in town doing some research," he replies. "I think I have found all that I needed to though so I will be leaving soon." Anticipation is growing in his tone, making his voice raspier.

"Research? What kind of research? I did not realize anyone would be interested in our little town."

"Yea, well... it seems that your town has been getting a lot of interesting new faces," the man grunts, more to himself than to me.

"Oh! I did not realize!"

He grunts. "Come on, old man." He grabs a bucket in his other hand and tries to smile. His crooked, rotting teeth are unsightly and I do my best to remain unfazed. He motions for me to lead the way. "I'm hungry, let's get going."

I jump up and push the stool under the table. Using my back as a shield, I grab up the bit of rope and stow it in my sleeve for safe keeping before casually walking out of the tent.

"This way." He takes me to a narrow path on the other side of the clearing. One that is definitely in the opposite direction of the cottages.

"Thank you!" I say enthusiastically. The path is short and the man stalks behind me, his breathing ragged. We reach another small clearing. This one also has a heavy cloaking spell surrounding it. I try to get a feel of what is hiding beneath it without breaking the spell. The clearing reveals itself to me for only a second, but it is enough. *Bodies.* Corpses litter the clearing in various states of dismemberment and decay. *This must be why he smells so awful.*

The changing of the wind is all the warning I get before the man's axe comes whizzing past my face. I jump to the side, spinning around.

"Shit," the man says, before winding up to swing the axe again. I evade him and he growls. "Why are you so fucking fast," he mutters more to himself as he chases me. On his third swing, I step into him catching his arm pulling it straight and twisting. I hear his bones give way and snap. The axe clatters to the ground. He yells, swinging his other arm to punch at me, I block and use his outstretched arm to vault onto his back before wrapping my legs around his back and my arm around his throat. Placing my hand on my bicep I put my other arm around my hand to help me squeeze the man's thick neck. He pulls, punches and scratches at my arm to no avail. Running, he tries to ram me into the nearest tree, but before he can make it, his legs give out under him and he passes out. We hit the ground hard and I do my best not to lose my grip. Holding on for another minute to make sure he is actually out, I release him and make quick work of tying both his arms together. As I am finishing up the last knot he starts to rouse. A quick uppercut is all it takes to fix that issue. I sigh as I cinch the last knot on the man's restraints. *What a waste. I hope I didn't cause too much brain damage. I need to know what all he was sent to do.*

I absorb the cloaking magick to reveal the clearing once again. Stray limbs are strewn about and blood soaks the grass, I look down, *and now my clothing.* I sigh. Well, I guess I now know where he was taking the people that wandered to his tent then, but I will have to find a change of clothes before returning back to Alaceandra and clean up this mess. People will likely think the monsters lurking the lands caused this massacre. I should move them closer to the border to corroborate this, but that will have to be done later. The less people that know about this intruder the better. Recloaking the field, I release the old man's form so that I am once again Fadres and get to dragging the man back to one of the caves I saw earlier. *I knew those would be useful.*

A couple of minutes later, I have him strung up in one of the caves closer to the cottages. I weave my magick intricately around the area so that no sound can escape. I also cast my own redirection spell, this one more complex than this man is capable of. It should lead anyone who comes close to here away from this spot whether they are looking for it or not. Checking the sun's placement in the sky I realize it has been close to two hours already. *I will have to question this man later.* Checking my knots again, I leave him and make my way back to the tent. Finding a spare change of clothes, I sniff them. Luckily, they do not smell like death, so I change into them. The shirt is far too long and looks more like a dress than a shirt on me but it will work. Leaving my clothes, I grab a fire starter, flick it open and toss it into the tent. The fire catches quickly, eating the wood and white linen until all that is left of the man's residence is ash.

Turning away from the mess, I make my way back to meet with the prince.

CHAPTER FORTY
Cuts and Bruises

The Prince

"**Y**ou're late." I look at Fadres *or I guess Sam* now. He has changed into ill-fitting clothes that look more like a night-gown with pants than an actual outfit and has scratches along his arms. "What happened to you, and why are you dressed like that? Did you fall in the shower?"

"I was taking care of something," he says flatly.

I roll my eyes. "You said that. I was more so asking about what that was."

He glares at me. "None of your concern, asshole."

The names again. I sigh. "I see. Well, you cannot go to see the little dove looking like that. It will startle her. I will get something to patch up those cuts of yours and grab you some of my clothing. It will fit better."

He crosses his arms. "Thanks," he says curtly.

Making the trek to my and Alaceandra's cottage, I grab the required items. There was not much of anything on the northern border. Sylvie mentioned there have still been attacks from the creatures since we have been here, but it seems to have calmed down with us keeping watch in the evenings. I am grateful that we are able to provide some help to Sylvie's people. It would have been quite miserable to have to find food and shelter out here had it not been for her. The north wall had been anti-climactic; after walking the border a couple times, I checked the potion bottles to make sure that whatever Sorin had kept in them was still full before finding one of the other guards to relieve me. The construction is almost done out there, so we have been seeing fewer monsters at the borders. Although this is a great thing for the people, it does mean that now my watch consists mostly of walking around and looking at nothing rather than having to fight off intruders. Which, honestly, is a bit on the boring side. *Maybe we can think about having less people sitting around out there. I am sure they would love to go home to their families early.* After I had made my way back to Sylvie's, I had to wait another hour before Sam made his own appearance. I would have left him and returned on my own, but I was far too curious about what he had gotten up to. Although usually tardiness irks me, his ragged state upon arriving tells me he was not just dragging his feet out there.

Sam is sitting at the kitchen table when I return. I hand him the bandages and he quickly dresses his wounds. Once he finishes, I give him the set of clothing, which he quickly changes into. Dressed, he gathers his old clothing and starts a fire on the stove before throwing the ill-fitting set on top of it.

"Why are you burning those?" I ask, watching him.

He shakes his head and watches as the clothing becomes ash, then he shuts off the stove and uses a broom to sweep up the ashes. Opening the door, he throws the ash outside.

What are you hiding? "We need to get back." I say.

"Then let's go," he says before walking towards the pathway to his cottage.

When we find our way back to Sam's cottage, no one is in the sitting room. My ears perk as I hear breathy moans coming from the bedroom. I smirk. I can tell Sam hears it too because he walks over to the bedroom, and I follow closely behind. He stills in the doorway before letting out a deep chuckle. Moving him aside I make eye contact with a very naked Alaceandra. Sorin lays near her clutching a blanket over her form. *Naughty girl.* I raise an eyebrow at my Little Dove. "Are we interrupting?"

CHAPTER FORTY-ONE
Welcome(?) Interruptions

Alaceandra

"That depends," Sorin says looking at me. "Would you like them to leave, Firefly?"

I must resemble an elvisera with how red my body is right now. *Do I want them to leave?* I stare at Sorin. *I definitely do not feel like stopping right now and the idea of them here with us... or even them joining in with us is definitely not a turn off.* I squeeze my thighs together. *Nope more like the opposite in fact.*

"Doesn't really look like the little dove wants us to leave," the prince drawls.

"That is for her to decide," Sam growls. My gaze flits over to him. *I do not remember him wearing those clothes when he left...*

I shiver as Sorin's hand traces up my thigh. "Lace?"

"Um... no. If-if you want to stay then... you can." My body is still on edge from being denied my last orgasm. I shake my head a little to try to come back to focus.

"I think they want to do more than stay," Sorin whispers to me, conspiratorially. I cannot help but flick my gaze down to the hard cocks that are tenting Sam and the prince's pants. "I can kick them out if you need me to."

"No. I- uh would like them to stay and um... participate if they wish."

"Oh yeah?" Sorin's eyes are glittering.

"Yes," I say feigning confidence. "If we are going to um, all pursue each other then I think this might be a good test to make sure that we are all okay with what that might mean."

"What might that mean, Parum Bellator?" Sam's voice has an edge of something dark, and I hold back a shiver at the tone.

I clear my throat and stare at my hands. "That we all might be-"

"Look at us," Sorin says gently.

I move my gaze to each of their eyes before stopping at Sorin's. "That we all might be... intimate with each other. I think that should be something we are comfortable with." I motion to the three of us.

"Ah, the little dove would like to fuck all her men?" the prince questions as he and Sam approach the bed.

The look he is giving me.... It is filled with lust, longing and so many dark promises that I feel myself clench around nothing, heat coiling tight in my body. "Yes." I lick my lips. Sorin traces his fingers along my thighs and a slight tremble invades me.

"We didn't hear you," Sam says his voice deep with arousal.

"Yes," I say louder.

"Good girl," Sorin coos before uncovering me once again. The other two men suck in a breath. "That is all I needed to hear," and then he is on me again, sucking my clit into his mouth and throwing me sharply into yet another orgasm. I scream and clutch onto him, squeezing my eyes shut as my world once again loses focus.

A hand on my chin has me opening unfocused eyes. Sam kneels by the bedside, his thumb softly caressing my cheek. "Eyes on us, Parum Bellator, we want to see all of you."

I bite my lip and nod. He smiles at me before releasing me. Another set of hands lazily move across my torso and I look down to see the prince tracing his fingers up my form. "Such a pretty Little Dove. Do you like being all tied up in vine?" He drifts a finger over one of Sorin's vines and Sorin's eyes whip up, flashing at the prince. The prince chuckles, removing his hand from the vine as Sorin continues to torture my pussy with his tongue and fingers. My body feels as if I am filled with a current, Sorin's tongue masterfully bringing me back to the edge of yet another climax, and I want to cry. I do not know how I can possibly cum again. I am a quivering, aching mess and yet my body is waiting for *something*. I watch as the prince continues to trace his way up my body, letting his fingers drag over every dip and curve until they reach my breast. He pinches a nipple between his fingers as Sorin adds a third finger inside me, deliciously stretching me, and I explode. The noise escaping me can only be described as a wail as I feel power erupt from my core, exploding throughout the room. Suddenly, the small space is bathed in darkness, my heart quickens in my chest.

"Don't worry, Parum Bellator." Sam's voice is at my ear. "Just focus on us." I feel my body flipped around until I am on my hands and knees, the soft bedding beneath me. As I focus on Sorin, Sam and the prince, slowly their forms along with the bed appear before me. The prince stands in front of me his cock on full display, his hand lazily stroking his length. His cock is large, almost as long as Sorin's and a bit thicker. I swallow as

I eye it. Sorin is behind me just out of view, but his presence is a heat at my back. Sam is.... I swing my gaze away from the prince's cock to find him. I spot him at what I can only assume to be the edge of the room, his eyes boring into me. When he speaks though, it almost feels like his lips are caressing my ear.

"Have you ever sucked cock before, Parum Bellator?" I shiver.

"No," I breath out.

"Would you like to?"

I lick my lips and nod before remembering that they prefer me verbal. "Yes."

Sam smiles and makes eye contact with the prince before returning his gaze to mine.

The prince runs his finger over my hair before coaxing me forward. "Open your mouth, little dove." I do as he says and he guides his cock into my mouth. I lick it lightly with my tongue testing the feeling of him and his grip tightens on my hair. "Good. That's good, now try to suck but not too hard." I suck him gently, gazing up at him and he groans. "Perfect, little dove. I am going to move you back and forth, just keep doing that. If it's too much tap on my hand and I will stop, okay?" He pulls me off of him.

"Okay," I whisper.

"Good, now open." I do and he guides me back over him, his length stretching my mouth until it's full of him before withdrawing and repeating the movement. He tastes just a tad salty, but not in a bad way. Flutters of excitement race through me as he rocks into my mouth a little harder, nearly causing me to choke on him. I brace one hand against his thigh to try and keep my balance. His cock is a perfect contrast of hard and soft and I cannot help but let out a little moan as his hands continue tightening in my hair as his pleasure increases. The sting of pain at my scalp causing a zing of pleasure to shoot right to my core. My teeth scrape him on his next thrust and he lets out a small hiss. I try not to giggle at the dark look he gives me. I continue working the prince with my mouth and tongue and Sorin strokes my back as I do. My body strums higher and higher at the sensation until suddenly the prince pulls me away. I whimper.

"I'm about to cum," the prince says with a strained voice, trying to explain.

"I do not care," my voice is breathy and high pitched. My mind is dizzy with the need to finish this. "Please, I want you to cum in my mouth."

"I will not be gentle," he warns.

"I. Do. Not. Care," I say firmly, challenging him with my gaze.

His eyes darken and he lets out a primal sound, pulling me forward once again, but this time he does not let me lead. He uses my mouth, his hips pumping hard, and I grip onto his thigh for dear life, trying desperately to keep up with his quick movements and not choke on his cock as it invades me. After a minute, he loses his rhythm, his hips jerking erratically before his cum floods my mouth. I swallow and he pulls away before kneeling before me, his eyes wild. Grabbing my throat, he lifts me, so I am at eye level and captures my lips with his. Moaning, I kiss him back, holding his arms as my body sways slightly. He releases me and vines pull my body until I am once again on my back, my ass at the edge of the bed, while Sorin's hot gaze studies me. My body is swimming in sensation, and I am almost certain I see sparks leaping from my skin. Sorin's lips capture mine in a heated kiss.

"Are you still having fun?" he checks in, his face near mine.

"Yes," I say, my voice raspy.

"Good." I feel Sorin's finger circling my entrance before he pushes it inside me and I clench around him, my body craving more. He chuckles.

"I think you are ready," Sorin says, dragging his finger in and out, rubbing at the building ache deep inside of me. I moan, my head falling back against the mattress. "Is that what you want, Firefly? To feel my cock inside this wet, tight little pussy?" He rubs the head of his cock along my slit, and I jump.

Please. I beg internally. Sorin's cock is smearing the evidence of my need all over my thighs and it feels as if my very soul is yearning and demanding for him to take me *now*.

"Yes, Sorin. Please..." I gasp, my heart hammering in my chest. At my words more vines shoot from the ground weaving themselves around my legs and torso so that my hips are pressed upward, and my legs are pulled fully open, my pussy now even more exposed to Sorin's devouring gaze.

Sorin growls, pulling his hand away and notching his cock at my entrance. His grip is tight on my hips, and I can tell he is doing his best to maintain control of himself. "I will try to be gentle." His voice is strained, his words more to himself than to me. Slowly he starts to push into me.

My fingers tighten on the blanket as I let out a breath of air. I knew he was big but *holy shit.* "You are too big," I whimper, squirming beneath him.

He chuckles but pauses his motion. "You can take it, Firefly, I promise." He reassures me and I nod, trusting his words. Instead of continuing his movement, he drops a hand between us and starts to trace circles over my aching clit. I scream as another orgasm crashes over me. As it does, Sorin pushes deeper inside of me causing a jolt of pain to rip through me before a throbbing pressure invades. Fully seated, he pauses, one of his hands brushing my hair away from my face. "You are so fucking perfect, Lace," he growls. More sparks shoot out of me, and I startle as I see one fly up before being overtaken by darkness.

"Do not fear it, Parum Bellator. You will cause no harm." Sam's voice is once again caressing my ear. My heart rate slows and I allow myself to fall into the sensations buzzing through me. "Good girl," Sam praises.

"You look so beautiful, Firefly," Sorin breaths. "I wish you could see yourself right now." He rubs a strand of my hair between his fingers and leans down to kiss me softly. I whimper as I feel him move, my pussy trying its best to hold onto him. He straightens, his eyes softening. "Tell me when you are ready, we will stay just like this until you tell me you want me to move." Tension holds him rigid, but he only grips the bed, ensuring he stays completely still so that I can adjust. We sit like this for a few minutes, until the painful ache starts to subside and an urgency to move overtakes the desire to be still.

"I am okay," I whisper.

"Are you sure?" Sorin asks.

"Yes. I need you to-"

My sentence is cut off by the drag of Sorin's cock sliding out of me. A moan tears from my throat as the world dims and only sensation remains. Only the single connection of our bodies registers as I become hyper sensitive to his movements. The darkness moves in closer as my skin sparkles and light dances away from my body. My clit is sore and aching from all the orgasms he has given me over the past couple of hours and I pant as I feel another curling itself inside me. I reach for it but it evades and I whimper in frustration. He continues to move in and out of me. *His movements are too controlled.* He keeps his eyes firmly shut a battle raging over his features as he fucks me. I do my best to meet his thrusts, fighting against his vines. "Let go, Sorin, you do not have to be gentle with me." His eyes shoot open, and he stalls his movement, his grip and vines tightening around me, the pressure almost enough to bruise. His eyes burn gold.

"You feel too fucking good, Lace. If you move...." His eyes start flashing between the pretty gold shade and his normal green. "I do not know how much I will be able to control myself and I don't want to hurt you."

"You know you will not hurt me, Sorin," I plead. "I need you fully and completely, please do not hold back."

The gold in his vision wins out and I am hauled into his arms, his vines supporting my weight as he pulls almost completely out of me before slamming me back onto his cock. I cry out, gripping and scratching at his back as he continues to slam in and out of me. He dips his head down to suck my nipple into his mouth, before biting the flesh and I yelp. His movements are animalistic and his pace punishing. The pain only heightens my pleasure, and I once again struggle against Sorin's grip not knowing whether I want to push him away or pull him to me. He snarls at me, his hand gripping the back of my neck as he shoves himself in and out of me. His other hand makes its way to my clit to circle it softly. My eyes roll back and my toes curl as my orgasm slams into me hard. I scream his name.

Throwing me back on the bed he traps me underneath his body as he continues to punish my pussy. My orgasm continues to roll through me, and I start to make unintelligible noises as wave after wave of pleasure rips through me. His hip movements start to become jerkier and with a shout of his own he releases inside of me.

Something clicks and I gasp as a searing sensation rips through my skin. All at once the room comes back in screaming color and I do my best not to shield my eyes from the sudden onslaught of stimuli. Sam and the prince approach us in a rush.

Sorin pulls out, his face filled with panic. "Fuck, Lace. I am so sorry. I knew I would be too rough. Are you okay?" I whimper at the loss, the sensation quickly retreating and clutch at the thigh that was the source of the pain. Sorin studies my face before his gaze travels down to where I am clutching my thigh.

"What is it, Little Dove?" The prince and Sam are now standing next to me.

I uncover my thigh to reveal a delicate gold vine tattoo that is now encircling the flesh. Tracing my fingers over it, it tingles under my touch. "What is this?" I direct the question to Sam who looks the least surprised about the new tattoo, but his face is a mask.

"I will look into it," the prince replies for him tracing a finger over the tattoo. I shiver at the contact. Looking at Sorin, I notice he has already donned a pair of shorts.

"Are you hurt?" Sorin's leg is twitching, his expression filled with worry.

"I am okay. It hurt for a second, but the pain melted away quickly."

"Are you sure?" Sorin presses.

I take stock of my body. I will definitely be sore tomorrow, but it feels like otherwise I am doing okay. "Yes, I am sure." I smile at him and some tension seems to release from his body.

He smiles back at me and scoops me from the bed. "Good. Let's get you cleaned up."

CHAPTER FORTY-TWO
Aftercare

Alaceandra

Sorin leads me to his bathroom where he gives me a towel and wash-cloth before showing me where the soap is and how to turn on the water.

"Normally, I would prefer to wash you myself, but you have a lot to process at the moment, so I thought it might be nice to have a bit of alone time? I will be right outside. Call for me if you need anything, okay?"

I would question how he would know I would prefer to be alone right now, but it is Sorin. Of course he can see that my brain is running in circles. "That would be nice," I admit. "Thank you." I take the supplies from him and he leans down to kiss me.

"See you in a bit," he says. "I will see if I can find us some food." Then he leaves me alone in the bathroom. I touch my lips.

Turning on the water I wait a minute before stepping in the spray, then it all hits me. *Holy shit, holy shit, holy fucking shit.* I mentally chant.

I just lost my virginity. I lean against the cold rock of the shower wall and stare at the water as it cascades down. *While Sam and my fucking betrothed watched.* My cheeks heat. *After sucking said betrothed's cock until he came in my mouth.* A tiny noise escapes me and I sink down to the shower floor and sit there for a moment. Examining my body, I pay closer attention to the little vine wrapping around my thigh. *Apparently, I have you to show for it, huh?* I do not know whether I feel like laughing or crying at the moment. Likely both, but I definitely do not have the time for all of that. *Sorin took my virginity.* I repeat to myself. *Philos would be so proud, but if my father ever finds out? He is going to kill me. I might have completely screwed myself over in the eyes of Tikilium but I refuse to regret it. Sorin was... perfect. He made the moment all about my wants and desires, something I have never been afforded before. No matter how everything turns out once all this political bullshit comes to a head, I will cherish the memory of being with him. Til the day I die.* Running my fingers over the mark, I feel it once again tingle at my touch. *What do you mean?* I ask the little vine. *Are you a physical impression for whatever mark Baldar says I placed on them or something else?*

My mind continues to whirl, refocusing on those weird lights that seemed to lift from my skin when I was with Sorin. They looked like the lights that summoned Baldar. So, they are likely a manifestation of my powers but I was supposed to be drained from training. *None of this makes sense.* And the darkness. Where did it come from and what was its purpose? It did not feel like a malicious presence but still, it definitely seemed like it did not originate from me, instead it seemed to absorb those little lights as they sparked. *So many questions and yet... I have no one who I can ask who might actually be able to provide me with answers.* I sigh, standing and grabbing the washcloth before running it under the spray and lathering it with soap. I wash myself and realize that I am a bit more sore than I had originally thought. *Guess I will not be doing that again anytime soon.*

Exiting the shower, I wrap a towel around myself and find a pair of clothes neatly folded on the sink. I put them on. *A perfect fit.* I admire the black short sleeve shirt and loose pants in the mirror before throwing my hair in a low bun and exiting the bathroom.

The men are sitting on the floor in front of the couch, containers of food laid out in front of them.

"How was your shower, Firefly?" Sorin asks, patting the spot next to him.

"Great." Padding over to them, I take a seat.

"Sylvie packaged these up for us when Sam and I left earlier. It's dinner. We assumed you might not want to go down to the kitchen after everything today."

I shoot him a grateful smile. "Yes, that is correct."

"Good," Sam says handing me a fork. "Let's eat then."

We eat in companionable silence, the food amazing after an exhausting day. As I finish, I lean back and let out a huge yawn. All the men laugh.

"Seems like the little dove is tired. Come. Let's go to bed." The prince stands and holds out a hand to me and I take it.

Sorin and Sam also stand. Sam pulls me into a hug and presses a kiss to the top of my forehead. "I will let you sleep in a little tomorrow, but we must continue your training. You might prove more skillful after a good night's rest so please meet me after breakfast."

Holding back a groan I nod at him, and he chuckles. "Okay. I will see you then."

He releases me. Sorin pulls me into a searing kiss. "Sleep well, Firefly. I will see you at breakfast." I try not to be disappointed that I will be leaving him after all that has happened today. *Does he not want to hold me after... everything?* He sees my insecurity flash across my face and holds my head between his hands. "The prince will look after you tonight. Sam and I have to debrief and if you are in here, I do not think you will be getting much rest." He gives me a mischievous smile. "I cannot wait to hold you in my arms again. Please do not question that." His eyes search mine before he kisses me once again. "Goodnight, Lace."

"Goodnight, Sorin."

CHAPTER FORTY-THREE

Feathers

Alaceandra

We arrive back at our cottage and the prince walks over to the bathroom to get ready for bed. Once he finishes, he switches with me so that I can do the same. Our routine is comforting in the chaos of today but also awkward. We eye each other and stay mostly silent as we put up our clothing and make our way to bed. Now that we have actually acted on the growing tension between us, I get the sense that we both know there is no way of truly going back to the way it was before.

He has been inside me of course there is no going back, I mentally chide myself. *Yes, it was my mouth and not my pussy but still, he took a first from me that I can never have back.* We are now officially *something* by choice rather than obligation and that is going to prove hard to navigate. I hesitate next to the bed. Obviously, most kings have sex with their queens to bear heirs, so I definitely considered the possibility of intimacy with him, but now that there is an agreement surrounding said intimacy with Sorin and Sam involved, I am starting to feel unsure where the lines between obligation and desire stand for him. *Or for myself, really.* Sometimes he treats me as though I am a pawn of his, a piece of property to be manipulated and other times he is spouting his devotion to only me. It seems no matter the circumstances, this man remains a puzzle. I am startled out of my thoughts by his voice only a moment later.

"What is it, Little Dove?" He quirks a brow at me.

I bite my lip. "Everything is just so... different."

"Different, how?" he asks, lifting himself up on one elbow. His intense stare bearing down on me.

Do not shy away, Alaceandra. I mentally scream at myself. "Well, I just gave the first blowjob of my life to you not even an hour ago and then lost my virginity to another man not shortly thereafter. I do not know what games you still have up your sleeve for me and yet it seems like you are impossible to stay away from. On top of all that, I am still in the middle of nowhere with a future completely outside of my hands if we are ever to leave this place," I say in a rush. "Oh, and I can apparently also create fire and spawn demoni. Things are not normal."

"First, I am your betrothed. Our sex life was bound to happen one way or another and I am quite pleased with how it is progressing," he smiles. I roll my eyes, causing him to chuckle. "Second, of course I have more plans for you, my dear little dove, we have truly only just begun our dance, but it is up to you whether that will be something you will fear or not. You have only just found your feathers. You have more control over your future than even I know, do not let your wings be clipped before you can learn to fly."

"And how would I go about flying as you say."

"Train. Get better. Find control. Your ability to do those things will determine just what side of the board you are on. Whether you will be a pawn easily discarded or one that will take down the king and win the game."

"You are being oddly helpful." I cast him a suspicious look.

"Call it a reward for the feathers." He pauses. "And since I seem to be in a particularly good mood, I will even give you a hint when it comes to my name if you ask it of me."

A thread of excitement thrums through me. "Oh, I ask it of you."

"As I thought." He laughs and then is silent for a moment, mulling over what hint he will give me. "Here's your hint: My name lies in the multitude; it begins at the hands of where crop and life ends."

My shoulders slump. "That is not a good hint."

This time his laugh comes from his core. "Agree to disagree then." He pats the bed. "Come to bed. You need to be rested for tomorrow, where I am sure Sam will kick your ass in training. I told you while we are within these walls I will take care of you, and you need rest after your... eventful day."

I huff. "He will not kick my ass; I was able to get a dagger to his throat today!" He snorts and I glare at him. "But, truly, do you not feel different after everything?"

"Different? After seeing and feeling your gorgeous lips around my cock?"

"Yes!" *And now I am flustered.* I pick at the bottom of my nightdress.

He thinks for a moment. "No," he says flatly. "As I told you your first night here, you are mine. I am glad I was the first one to take your mouth, even if I was not the one who took your virginity proper... and I find myself unbothered that Credour... or Sorin is it? Was the one to do it. Somehow there was a rightness in that." He gives me a devious look before lounging back, looking towards the ceiling. "You are quite the little sneak bringing two people into the kingdom under different identities, although I do quite admire that you have your own game you are playing at."

"I-" I try to backtrack. *How would he have... fuck I totally screamed Sorin's name when I came, did I not?* I squeeze my eyes shut.

He chuckles. "Do not worry yourself, I am much too advanced in my own game for you to have kept your little secret for too long. I will soon unravel any others you might hold." He gives me a quick glance and the look on my face must be further confirmation of his suspicions. "What I am concerned about, though, is your marking from that. It was quite obvious that the man is someone who wields vines, which means you have taken on his mark, but not mine. It is curious. Nevertheless, those are thoughts for tomorrow. Please come to bed," I hesitate, "now Alaceandra or you will be exhausted tomorrow." He lifts up the edge of the blanket, inviting me in.

I sigh and crawl in beside him and he holds me close, placing a gentle kiss on the back of my head.

"You were amazing today, little dove, and I am not just talking about the blowjob. The power you wielded..." He hesitates. "If you take your training seriously you may be surprised at just how powerful you can be." He rubs a hand down my side and sighs. "Goodnight." Pulling me tighter he settles in for sleep and for once I am not quite so upset with his riddles. Instead of responding, I snuggle deeper into him before falling asleep.

CHAPTER FORTY-FOUR
Simple Wins

Alaceandra

"Left leg! Arm! Behind you!" Sam drills. He is calling out moves before he makes them. He told me that this will help with the training. The theory was if I have the names of the moves as well as their motions, I can more easily copy them. This would give me a better chance at blocking them before they could land. Although that sounded great in the beginning, it has only proved to slow me down. *His talking is doing more to distract me than to train me.* I think to myself.

"Right Ankle!" he commands, but I am too slow, his wooden dagger striking me on the place he called out.

"Ow!" I hop away from him. I am doing my best to take the prince's advice, but the thought of landing even one shot on Sam today feels impossible.

He pauses. "What is going on with you? You were progressing so well yesterday. This morning it seems like you can barely block a single strike."

His hand grips his dagger tightly and his tone is filled with exasperation. "You need to focus."

I try not to groan, rubbing at my sore ankle. "It is your callouts; I cannot focus when you are yelling them at me."

"When you are on the battlefield there is going to be a lot of noises around you. You cannot rely on your opponent to be silent nor your comrades. If you are working with others you need to be able to hear them calling out to you in case they catch something you miss. If you do not like the noise, you can tune it out. You must learn what works for you on your own."

"Battlefield? Team?"

Sam rolls his eyes. "You know what I mean."

"Okay... well I will do my best."

"Yes, do that." He looks more tired than he normally does during our morning sessions, which is odd because we definitely started later than normal. He walks up to me and places a hand at the center of my chest. "Try to get out of your brain and feel more with your body. What is it telling you to do? You might be surprised at just how much you know." He echoes the prince's earlier sentiment before stepping back and returning to his starting position. Not allowing me to fully process his words, he starts running at me immediately. "Swinging left!" Swinging his body to the left, he plunges his dagger down and I just barely avoid it. "Diving!" He crouches down and swipes at my legs. I jump slightly too late causing me to trip. My ankle sends another jolt of pain through me. I hold back a cringe. "Right arm!" I swing my body left as his blade swipes at my arm.

Focus, Alaceandra. I chant to myself. Listening to my internal voice, I watch how his body moves in space and try to focus less on his words. I dodge a couple more of his swings, but I still end up falling on my ass with Sam's dagger at my throat. After what feels like the millionth time today of being bested by Sam, I see something. There is a pattern to Sam's movements. It seems mister master combat has a tick. He flexes his mouth just a little before he swings. It is not a lot of information, but I hope that it gives me a bit of an edge. Focusing more on his mouth, something that definitely is not a chore on my part, I am able to move a little quicker, dodging and weaving before he can call out. Before long the training becomes more of a dance than a fight. *There! Pivot. Duck. Roll. Swing your leg out. NOW.* I follow my brain's instructions and realize I am actually able to catch him off guard a few times. *When he calls out instruction, he is already preparing for my next movement, causing him to always be one step ahead of me, but when I listen to my own voice...* I strike out, my hip swinging into his, before throwing a leg behind him, tripping him. He hits the ground hard and I take the opportunity to climb on top of him shoving my blade against his throat.

He smiles. "Good job. Now you are paying attention." Pushing my blade from his throat he stands before offering me a hand. We continue like this for a couple more hours and I manage to land Sam on his back two more times before we call it quits.

"You have progressed well today. So much so, we will need to change it up a bit tomorrow. You should be proud. I was waiting to see when you would catch my tell and anticipate rather than react." He is beaming at me.

"Wait that was on purpose." I collapse to the floor and try to catch my breath.

Sam laughs. "Of course, Alaceandra. Every enemy has some sort of indication of a strike before it happens, you just need to find it. Knowledge of a hit may not win you the battle, but it does give you an edge and if you are ever in a place where you need to utilize these skills, an edge is paramount to your survival." His tone turns grave, his brow is creased in worry.

"Hey," I touch his sleeve. "I know the dangers here are present but I have not run into any trouble since meeting back up with Sorin. It is unlikely that I will have to use these skills with you all around." I smile reassuringly.

"Hopefully," he says, but his tone is unconvinced. "If you ever have the option to run in a fight—"

"Take it. Yes, I know, Sorin already gave me the talk."

"It is an important one."

"As I am now aware."

He smirks. "Come on let's get you lunch." He starts to walk back to the cottages.

I sit up. "Wait, Sam."

"Yes?" He turns back.

"Um... can I ask you a question?"

"Always, Parum Bellator." The nickname reminded me I actually had two questions to ask the man, but the second could wait. I needed answers on why Sam stayed on the sidelines yesterday no matter how disappointing the conversation may be. I know he also agreed to this thing with Sorin and the prince, but his actions yesterday did not really give me full confidence in his words. I pick at the grass and Sam gives me a curious look. "What is it?"

I hesitate. "When everything was happening yesterday.... you did not join in. Not that I expected you to or anything, but I was just wondering... with the nickname and everything if—" He takes three long strides and is upon me in a moment, kneeling beside me. Gone is my strict instructor and in his place my gentle protector. I swallow the rest of my words.

"Are you worried about my attraction to you, Parum Bellator?"

"A little."

"Well do not. It took everything within me to not feel every inch of your glorious body last night. The cloaking of the room allowed me to at least communicate with you in some part, but..." He trails off.

"But?" *Cloaking? Is that what the darkness was for?*

He sighs. "But I had to make sure you were safe to experience your desires last night. I would not necessarily say that your powers were contained during that... exchange... and I knew you would hate it if the room was destroyed, so I contained them for you."

"Contained them for.... wait Sorin said I was too drained to use any of my skills."

"That would normally be true seeing how exhausted you were after your training with Baldar, but something about your being with the pest— I mean the prince and Sorin seemed to hypercharge them instead of letting them rest. It did not seem like it caused you any ill effect, fortunately. If you could have seen the way in which your power radiated from you as you came..." His eyes fill with a dark desire. "I was unsure of its capabilities or yours to control it. Instead, I ensured it was not an issue." Ignoring the fact that it seems that Sam has his own nickname for the prince, my brain reels over the fact that I apparently had less control yesterday then I originally thought. Yes, I noticed the sparks coming off my skin, but honestly, I thought that might have been a trick of my lust crazed mind. *I could have destroyed that whole cottage.* The thought sobers me. I chew on my lip.

"Oh."

He smiles. "Fear not, Parum Bellator. The minute you learn to control these powers of yours and are able to defend yourself against danger, I will be unable to hold myself back. Until then." He places a gentle kiss on my forehead. "We should get lunch." He offers me a hand and I take it.

My brain cannot seem to form sentences, so all I do is squeeze his hand. He smiles and returns my squeeze. Together, we make our way back to Sylvie's.

CHAPTER FORTY-FIVE
Bonds and Bonded

Alaceandra

We meet up with Sorin and the prince at lunch and shovel down a sweet doughy concoction and a side of candied meat before I am once again back in the clearing with all the men. Something or rather someone is missing.

"Where is Baldar?" I ask. *If he is not here, how am I supposed to practice?*

The prince pats my shoulder jolting me from my thoughts. I look at him and he points to an x burned into the ground several feet from where we stand. We all walk over to it and as my feet touch the burnt edges a spark shoots through me and into the ground. We all jump back as the forest floor rips itself open to reveal a familiar furry hand followed by a familiar furry body pulling itself from the depths. As quickly as the ground splits open, it stitches itself back up leaving behind only a couple of scorched pieces of grass in its wake.

"Missed me?" Baldar skitters over to me.

"Did you have to make such a grand entrance? Where were you?"

"*Oh you know- places and things. We should really try not to exhaust you so much today; I do NOT want to do that again.*" He is running circles around my feet.

"Do what again?"

He stops running and turns his little head in Sam's direction before turning it back my way. "*No worries.*" He sits. "*We should continue to work on your fire today. Let me know if you start to get tired though!*" He squeaks, then gets up and runs to the middle of the field.

"O-kay." I follow him and so do the other men. Sam and the prince take their positions on either end of the field. This time it only takes me focusing on my flames and a touch from Sorin to ignite the field in soft red firelight. "Holy shit." I say under my breath. We practice making the flames appear and disappear for a while until I am able to do it on my own without having to touch Sorin.

"*Since it looks like you have gotten the hang of that, Sorin please take your place at the south tree.*"

Sorin nods and makes his way over to the tree sitting by the trunk, matching the other two men.

"*Okay Alaceandra now cast your flames.*"

I do and they once again dance around the clearing.

"*How are you feeling? Tired, yet?*"

"No, actually I am feeling pretty good."

Baldar titters. "*Ah, so my suspicions are correct. Seems you two have been busy in my absence.*"

"Busy? What is that supposed to mean?"

"*Well, your powers have progressed swiftly and if that were not enough, I can sense your bond is almost complete... what do you think that means?*"

"My bond is almost... I thought I only marked him, now we have an almost completed bond?" I keep my voice to a hushed whisper.

Baldar sighs. *"Yes, Alaceandra. Notice any new markings lately?"* He sounds annoyed and I widen my eyes in realization. *"There you go, you got it now. No worries though, nothing can be completed until the solstice. The bonding should only enhance your abilities for now."*

My stomach drops and a noise comes from behind me. My flames have grown in size.

"Control Alaceandra!"

I take a deep breath and the flames calm themselves.

"Good. How am I to tell you any information if you are just going to blow up the field? Now try to bring that flame on the right into that one on the left like we were practicing yesterday."

Taking another deep breath, I try to push the conversation from my mind and imagine blowing one flame into the other. They move with a surprising amount of ease, crashing into each other, their colors shifting from red to orange as their heat grows. As I move each one, something else pulls at me. The connection to my flames forms like a physical tether within. A thread that weaves and tangles throughout my body. The more I focus on that connection the easier it gets to pull each one. Baldar has me continue adding flames into the fire until all of my tiny flames have formed one huge violet bonfire, and I giggle, a sense of entanglement filling me as all my threads are crossed and knotted together.

"Great now try to release the flames." I focus on untangling each line and pulling it away from the huge knot. A tingling fills my hands as I do, the extra energy flooding back into my system. The flames disperse but they keep their violet color.

"Release fully, Alaceandra." Once each thread is separated. I cast Baldar a quizzical look.

"You want them to disappear," he says in explanation.

"Oh." I imagine dropping the threads and the little lights extinguish, a rush of power flowing up each line and back into me.

Baldar climbs up my body and I once again cringe at the sharpness of his claws. *"That was really good Alaceandra you barely broke a sweat this time! We will be practicing sending the flames in the air next session and trying to throw them! If we can figure that one out we will try to cast one small flame that you can hold in case you are in an area in need of light."* I smile at the small creature. *"I have a feeling you will pick up on these things quickly too at the pace you are progressing. Once you do, we can move on to your summoning lessons."* He seems more excited than I am. I walk over to the opening of the clearing doing my best to keep Baldar balanced on my shoulder and the men fall into place behind me.

"Great job, Firefly." Sorin's hand warms my lower back as we make our way back towards Sylvie's for dinner.

"It was pretty cool was it not?" I beam.

"It was. You are coming into your skills a lot quicker than even I did. You should be very proud of yourself."

"I am, but..." I look away from him. "I need to talk to you."

"What about?"

Looking around, I notice that Sam and the prince seem absorbed in their thoughts, so I take the leap. "Baldar mentioned something about a bond. In that apparently we are bonded- partially- which is why I have this mark."

"Bonded? Are you sure?"

"Well, no. He only just mentioned it briefly during training, but is this something that has happened before? I have never heard of it."

He nods thoughtfully. "Like I mentioned in the forest it was not un- common for queens to take on multiple partners. Texts had mentioned these pairings as being 'bonded', but I always assumed that was a turn of phrase." He rubs my back thoughtfully. "I will have to look into this further once we have access to a library."

"May I join you once we do? I think it would be good for me to learn more about our history. I tried to do some research back in Helomasi, but I was barely able to find anything." I glance towards Baldar only to realize he is out cold on my shoulder.

He smiles brightly. "Of course, Firefly. Before I forget, I would like to show you a bit about potions seeing as they were key to getting us out of capture the first time." He winks at me. A tingly sensation fills me at the thought of being alone with Sorin once again.

"That would be great."

"Perfect! Let's meet between your lessons tomorrow?"

"That works for me."

"Amazing it's a date then."

"I guess it is."

CHAPTER FORTY-SIX
Brother Death

Sam

*O*ur little sanctuary seems to be getting more visitors. I think to myself grumpily. I grunt as I haul yet another intruder to the cave that I had stowed the first. *Scouts to be exact, seeing as they are woefully unprepared for combat. Any true warrior would be adept at both masking and fighting, but these men rely far too much on their cloaking abilities and a heavy weapon. Once both those tools are taken from them, they are simple to incapacitate.* Making it to the cave, I untie the rope I secured to my waist before this night's watch. Dragging the man inside, I start securing him across from the first asshole. *Which is why I have to start making sure I train Alaceandra on both the use of her dagger and of her body. I would hate to have her be so pitiful once disarmed.*

I hang him by the arms in the cave. *I hope this fucker is alone, but I severely doubt it.* I left the first meathead far too long after he witnessed Alaceandra's abilities. If he sent off a message to whomever sent him, these new scouts mean that she is indeed their person of interest and that does not bode well for the length of our stay here. *I will have to discuss with the group about leaving here soon. Although it would be easier knowing where to go if I could figure out just who sent them.* I turn to my first captive and notice that he is conscious, although he is pretending otherwise. I hold back a laugh and grab one of my daggers. Using it to delicately slice a strip of skin from the man's forearm I watch as he jerks away from me, his charade forgotten.

"Ah looks like you are awake," I say sarcastically, spinning the bloody dagger in my palm.

"What the fuck!" the man yells.

I ignore him and watch as a thin streak of blood travels down his arm. "Want to explain what you are doing here?"

"Who are you?" I nick another cut along his other forearm, and he yelps in pain. "What the fuck, man!" the bonehead screams.

I slice him again. "I can do this all day, you cannot. I would suggest that you start talking." I keep my tone aloof, but the darkness inside of me purrs as the blood pools on the floor. I smile at the awakening of my old friend.

"You think a few cuts are going to get me to talk?" He spits at me. "You will have to do better than that."

I sigh. "If you insist." My eyes darken and a tendril of inky blackness leaves me. I let it wrap around the man. All at once a hundred tiny cuts open up across his form. I watch as his deepest fears become reality behind his closed eyes. His screams echo throughout the cave, shrill and desperate. After a minute I release him. He slumps against his chains. *Guess that was a tad too much then. They do say the minds terrors are a lot more powerful than that of the physical form.* I let out an annoyed noise. *Even still these men are far too weak.*

Deep laughter rattles from the man behind me. "Seems you have matured in power since the last we spoke, Frater Mortis."

I still and allow my darkness to surround me like armor, shrouding my face in shadow. Turning, I face the other captive. My voice is ice. "I see you are still not above inhabiting the bodies of your cannon fodder."

"Old habits." The man speaks, but the way his mouth moves is unnatural. Like noise is being forced from his body rather than it being freely voiced. The man's eyes have gone white, his skin pallid and he twitches with each ragged breath.

"What are you doing sending your men here?"

"You think I do not have curiosities of my own? After you left your kingdom for her-"

"You will not speak of her." Tendrils of darkness swirl around me, poised to strike, but I know I would only be hurting the form he is inhabiting, not the man himself.

More laughter. "Touchy, touchy. It seems your plans of slow pursual have not proved fruitful, Frater. Everyone knows she has come into her powers. It is only a matter of time..."

"You will do nothing," I growl.

"We will see... Until then." The man jerks his head down in a bow. Then he is gone. I check the pulse on the captives only to find none. They are dead. *Fuck.*

CHAPTER FORTY-SEVEN

A Dream Or A Nightmare

Alaceandra

I stand outside in a blue, silken slip dress. My hair cascading in ringlets down my back. The sky is dark and filled with angry storm clouds. The plants around me are blackened and brittle and there is a chill in the air. A castle towers in front of me made of black stone and joined together by a burgundy mortar. I am barefoot and alone. All is quiet and still.

A gust of wind causes the trees to sway and snap, and I jump at the noise. As quickly as the wind rushes through, it is gone rendering my surroundings once again immobile. Only with a key difference. I am no longer alone. Instead, there is a cloying presence at my back. Nausea turns in my gut as my spine straightens. Try as I might to look behind me, I remain in place, my body frozen by some unseen force.

"Ah, there is the princess."

"Who are you?" I try to fight back the terror clawing up my throat.

Haunting laughter fills the air. "You will find out soon enough. You are a hard one to find. Those guards of yours do well at disguising you, although I should not be surprised, they do mask their own identities and motivations well. Even from you."

Mask their identities? *"What do you want?"*

"Only to reveal the truth, little princess. Those who you surround yourself with only want to hide the truth from you. I think it is time that changed."

I struggle against whatever is holding me. "And why should I trust you to tell me the truth? I do not know you nor will you reveal yourself to me."

"I think you will find I am probably the only one you can trust. It is not yet time for me to reveal myself, but that does not make what I say any less true."

I scoff. "I find that hard to believe."

A chuckle tickles the back of my neck. "Oh really? Try asking that Sam of yours what he has been up to over the past couple of days while your prince has been keeping watch of the border. Or better yet ask him what his motivations were for joining the king's guard."

How does this man know about Sam? *"He has told me that before. He wanted to serve his kingdom."*

"He is not even from Tikilium, if he wanted to serve his kingdom he would come back to it."

My brows knit. "You are a liar."

"Am I?" He laughs. "He seemed to appear so suddenly in your life. Have you ever questioned why?" I do not answer, because no I had not, not really. *"As I assumed." His presence leaves my back and I once again try to wiggle free from whatever is holding me still, but I am held firmly in place from the neck down.*

"It seems all the men around you like to keep secrets from you. From that prince of yours to your dearest childhood friend. How sad for you. Don't

you worry, Alaceandra it will not be too much longer. The day of reckoning shall come."

"Why are you telling me this? Why am I here?"

His presence returns to my back, but now it is accompanied by an electric heat. "I will not allow their secrets to continue. Nothing can hide here."

"Where is here?"

A finger traces up my back, causing my skin to breakout in goosebumps. "That's up to you, Alaceandra. Is this a dream, or a nightmare?" A searing pain travels through my spine and into my wrist as a dark portal opens in front of me. "I will see you soon," he whispers before shoving me into the darkness.

Screaming, I bolt up in bed. My hair is matted to my skull. The prince wakes with a start, his eyes wild as he stares at me.

"What is it, Alaceandra?" He jumps from the bed and looks around while I try to ease my pounding heart. After a moment he comes back and kneels at the bedside, grasping my face between his hands. "Alaceandra, please tell me what is going on?" He brushes a finger over my cheek.

"N-nothing. It was just-" *A dream or a nightmare? It definitely felt like a nightmare.* "It was just a bad dream."

"Must have been pretty bad to have you screaming like that. What was the dream?"

I shake my head. *Those who you surround yourself only want to hide the truth from you.* The mystery man's voice rings through my thoughts. "I-I do not know."

He blinks at me, his brows scrunching slightly. "Alaceandra, dreams can be important in more ways than you know. If... if something happened in your dream. If you saw something. If you spoke to someone. It could be important. You need to tell me about it." He continues to rub his thumb over my cheek.

From that prince of yours to even your dearest childhood friend... The mystery man's voice continues to ring through my head. "I might have," I whisper.

"Might have what?" He keeps his tone gentle, something that is very uncharacteristic of the prince. His eyes encourage me to divulge more, his expression encouraging. I give in.

"Spoken to someone," I continue to whisper and pull away from him, hugging my knees to my chest. He sits beside me on the bed, his chest on full display and I try to ignore it. My brain whirls at all the information- *or lies-* I remind myself, that the mystery man told me.

"What did they say?" The prince coaxes me.

"What all do you have planned for me?" I ask the prince looking up at him.

"What?" His face is filled with confusion.

"You mentioned that I was a pawn for you, but what is that game? What are the plans?"

His face shutters. "What does that have to do with your dream?"

He is avoiding the question. "You refuse to tell me? Even after all that happened yesterday?" I try to hold back my emotions but can hear my voice crack.

"It is not a refusal, little dove. I am just concerned about the origin of the question."

"Am I not to be concerned with what our marriage does to suit you? Why you chose to follow us here? Especially now that-" *I have had your cock between my lips.* I cut myself off as tears gather in my eyes. "When we first met in those gardens you were clear about your intentions with me. Your intentions to use me. Regardless of our current state: The sleeping in the same bed, this gentle, protective persona of yours, or your countless declarations since we got here, I cannot help but wonder if this is just the same long game to whatever plot you were hatching. All I am asking for you to do is let me in on whatever plot that is." I look towards him, knowing my gaze is desperate. "I can help better if I know the end goal. I could want to help. I do not have to be an unwilling pawn- we can work together."

He sighs, looking towards the ceiling before his eyes come back to meet mine, his expression a mask. "You should be careful in asking things with answers you are ill-prepared for." I feel as if I have just been stabbed.

"Ill-prepared?" My sadness quickly morphs into anger. "How can I ever be prepared if I do not have answers? I just have puzzle pieces to a future and no way to see how they all fall together. There is no way I can grow stronger when I just keep being fed minimal information-" I clear my throat as the tears come crashing down as my anger grows. "I cannot go along with a plot that I have no knowledge of!"

The prince stares at me, but after a moment answers, his voice a bit hollow. "Revenge, Alaceandra. My father has done nothing but make my life miserable since the moment he took the throne. He has killed countless people, kept me under his thumb, and has destroyed Helomasi from what it once was. I will defeat him and restore it— restore the life around it, but for that I need you. Without you, I cannot come into power."

I deflate. "Come into power? Does Helomasi require their monarch to be wed?" *That would be odd seeing as I have not seen the queen in the entirety of my time there, but maybe there is a reasoning behind that.* "If so, you could have married any girl for that once Sorin, Sam and I disappeared, why follow me?" My voice is filled with skepticism.

"No, I couldn't. He is not just going to give up the throne once I marry, he's..." he breathes. "It's complicated. Who you are plays a big part in everything, it had to be you."

"Who I am?" I give him a bewildered look. "Who am I that it would be important that you marry me? There are other princesses..."

"I cannot tell you who you are, Alaceandra. You need to decide that." He rubs his face. "That is all I can say."

"That is it?"

"Yes."

I think about this. "I do not know if I can live with just that answer forever."

He nods, tiredly. "I will tell you more when I can... if I can," he says almost under his breath.

I nod. "Okay."

He looks at me. "I do not believe this line of questioning has come out of the blue though. If you spoke to someone in your dream it is paramount that we know who it is. It could be nothing, but... there are those who walk through dreams as a means to control others and seeing as this is not your first nightmare, I am nervous of what these dreams could mean. I want to be sure you are not in danger."

"It definitely did not feel natural," I say, picking at my thumb.

The prince places a hand over mine to stop my picking. "That is what I assumed. You can keep your secrets for now, but if it happens again... we will have to inform the others."

A creak sounds at the door causing us both to look over. Baldar slinks inside and crawls onto the bed with us. Laying himself on our conjoined hands he speaks. "*I felt a disturbance. Although I am trying to be considerate of Alaceandra's progress outside of training.*" He gives me a look. *"I think it might be better for her safety if I was able to watch over her tonight."*

The prince jerks his hand from mine and stares at the ferret. "So that is what you sound like." His voice is surprised.

"What kind of disturbance?" I ask Baldar.

"I am unsure of what exactly it is right now, but I will see if anything happens again. Please sleep, Alaceandra. I fear there is a long couple of days ahead of you." He runs over to the bottom of the bed and curls up.

I feel the tendrils of sleep reaching for me once again. "Okay." I curl back up under the covers. The prince follows, getting into bed behind me.

As I start to drift off, he pulls me close and whispers. "My plans will forever change when it comes to you, let's hope we both choose correctly when the time comes."

Before I can question those words, I am asleep.

CHAPTER FORTY-EIGHT
Hand to Heart

Alaceandra

"No daggers today," Sam states as he throws the wooden weapons to the side.

"Why?" I ask, continuing my stretches.

"If something were to happen and you did not have a weapon. I want to make sure you could still get away."

"You talk as if you are preparing for an attack." I laugh, reaching for my toes. Baldar sits high in the tree watching us.

He is quiet for a moment, staring at me. "We have been gone for a long time, Alaceandra. We do not know who could be searching for us at this point. The solstice grows near, and you are out of the hands of Ptheryeth's rulers, they will want to find you."

I think back to my dream the night before. "I would hope if they do, they will treat it more as a rescue than a kidnapping. Although I am not sure what it would be like to find myself back in their hands now that I have learned all this." I motion around me.

"Understandable." I look up to see him smiling at me. "It is important for you to remember that not all who may be looking for you are allies, Parum Bellator. Even those who once were could be feeling more desperate as the solstice closes in. Not to mention those who had captured you when you first arrived might be still on the hunt for you now. We need to be prepared."

I stand. "I hate to think that my marriage would be so important to the rulers of the Ptheryeth."

"It is more than you being wed that they would be concerned with," Sam says more under his breath than to me.

"And why is that?" I squint at him.

He looks away. "We must start training now. Try to stop me." With that he runs at me.

We drill for a couple hours like this. Sam rushing me, while I try to stop his attacks. He provides gentle instruction along the way. Luckily, learning pre-indications of an attack is in fact a transferable skill for both weapon and body work, so I do pretty well at figuring out when he is going to go for me. Unluckily for me, once he has me it is difficult to remove myself from his hold. So, we spend the later half of the morning focusing on different holds and ways to break them.

"Unfortunately, there is no way for me to accurately depict every pattern an opponent might make," Sam says, blotting his brow with his shirt, "but if we continue to practice these moves you will at least have a leg up."

We go through movements and attacks until my stomach makes a loud rumble for food. Sam releases me from his hold and musses the top of my hair. "I think it is time for breakfast," he says with a smile. "Good job today."

I smile at him. "Thanks." He starts to walk towards the cottages, but I stop him. "Can I ask you something?"

Turning back to me, he tilts his head. "What is it?"

He is not even from Tikilium, if he wanted to serve his kingdom he would come back to it. "You are... from Tikilium right?"

"Why do you ask?" His face becomes devoid of expression. *Not a good sign.*

"I mean.... when I asked why you had joined the kings guard in the past you had said it was to serve your kingdom, and I always assumed you meant Tikilium, but... now that I think of it that may have been foolish of me to assume. I think after all our years of friendship and now our... current situation, it might be fruitful of me to ensure I have my facts correct about you and Sorin." *Lest I find something else out from another party.... like I might have already done.*

"You are hiding something from me. That is not the reason you are asking, is it?" His eyes have taken on a darker shade, and he quickly blinks it away when he notices me looking. Walking closer to me he grabs one of my hands. "Tell me, Alaceandra.... why are you filled with doubt?"

I can trust Sam, right? He has protected me for years... but he is avoiding my questions.

"You can tell me, Lace," Sam whispers.

"I had a dream last night," I blurt and Sam's posture goes rigid.

"What about?" He tries to play his tone off as casual, but I notice the edge in his voice.

I continue on anyway, watching Sam's face. "It was odd... a man visited me, but I could not see him because I could not move. He talked to me."

"What did he say?"

"A lot, but mostly he told me to question things." I try to be vague.

"And you decided to trust this man?" His voice and face have again become a blank slate, and I sigh.

"Your avoidance of my questions are not giving me high hopes for his statements being false."

Sam closes his eyes. "I apologize. This is concerning though, there are those who walk through dreams-"

"To control others. Yes, I am aware, the prince mentioned that to me."

"You have spoken with the prince about this?"

"Briefly... I um did not necessarily wake up calmly last night."

Sam's eyes darken once again before returning to their normal hue. "From fear or from pain?"

I scrunch my brows. "Pain, I think, it was brief, but-"

"Fuck." He starts to walk away.

"What, but you did not answer-"

"I cannot force you to trust me, Alaceandra. I also cannot claim whatever the man told you is completely false. I can only hope that you can trust that I have never had any intentions to do anything but keep you safe. Now please go back to the cottages and eat breakfast."

"But where are you going?"

"I need to investigate this."

"Alone?"

"Yes, now please go find Sorin." He turns and swiftly walks into the tree line.

I grit my teeth. "Fine." Turning around I make my way back to Sylvie's cottage.

CHAPTER FORTY-NINE
Sex and Chocolate

Alaceandra

I find Sorin at the table. He has my breakfast set on one side of him and some potion bottles on the other. When I walk in his face lights up, causing me to smile despite my bad mood.

"Hey Firefly. How was today's training session?"

I join him at the table. "Different." I answer honestly. "We worked without the daggers today. I learned how to get out of some holds and defend against oncoming physical attacks."

"That sounds pretty cool!" He smiles at me but noticing my sour mood he pivots the conversation. "Are you ready to dig into potions 101, or would you prefer to eat breakfast first and talk for a bit?"

I grab the breakfast bowl as my stomach growls yet again.

He laughs. "That's what I thought. How are you doing, Firefly?"

I shove a bite of food in my mouth and chew, thinking about my answer. Swallowing, I look back at Sorin. "Not great."

"No? Why is that?" He fiddles with his potion bottles on the table, giving me room to think without the pressure of his eyes on me.

"Fear maybe?" I question myself more than him. "I do not know." I pinch my nose. "Things are just getting more and more confusing as the days pass by."

"In what sense? Are you still okay with everything that happened the other night?"

My mind flashes back to him in between my legs and a blush steals over my face. "Yes."

"Good." His warm hand finds its place on my thigh. "What is going on, Firefly?"

I pause in my eating. "What has been going on since I was shipped off to Helomasi. While I feel like I have gained more control over my physical self, I still feel as though I do not know what is going on around me. All of this feels so... temporary. Like if I breathe the wrong way all the training and playfulness with the three of you will be turned to dust and I will be left to play political games once again. It makes it hard to enjoy anything. On top of that I had a really weird dream-"

"Dream?" Sorin questions.

"Or nightmare? I do not know. It was of a man I did not recognize. He told me not to trust the three of you. And although I want to believe his words are full of shit, the other two have made it really hard for me not to place any weight in what he said."

Sorin's thumb caresses my hand. "I will not tell you that dream walkers have a proclivity for manipulation because I am sure you have heard enough of that already from Sam." I nod jerkily. "What I will say is that Sam and I would never do anything that was meant to endanger you or put you at risk. We care for you deeply, Lace. Us following you was to keep you safe, whether that meant putting aside our feelings for you or not."

"Because I am so valuable to others." I spit out.

Sorin places a gentle hand on my cheek. "Because you are valuable to me. Not because of any powers or prophecy, but because you are you, Lace. If you had no standing at all, no higher calling or crazy powers, I would still want to be with you. Adventuring and growing with you has only made me want to be stronger and better for you. It always has."

"Then why must you keep me so in the dark when it comes to my father's plans and my future?"

Pain etches his features. "I have tried to give you every hint towards those intentions without saying the words, Firefly. Those words would-" He chokes and grabs for a bottle on the table, drinking down the potion quickly. I clutch at his hand my heart racing. After a moment, he continues to speak, and I relax. "All I can say is to remember our capture and the rock. Forces want to ensure your tale goes their way, but let us ensure that your future is your choice."

I nod at him, still concerned about his pale features. Smiling at me once more he leans in and kisses my lips gently. I allow him this kiss and rake my hands through the back of his hair to deepen it. He responds by pulling me into his lap, his lips taking full control over mine. Our hands wander over each other, and I cannot help but moan as he pinches one of my nipples between his fingers. Lifting me up, he ends our kiss and walks over to the ladder leading to his cottage before jumping down the chute.

I laugh. "Where are we going?"

"Where do you think?" He waggles his brows at me causing me to laugh again. "I love your laugh," he says, reverently. I blush and kiss his cheek. He makes quick work of getting to his cottage and climbing the ladder with me still tucked neatly in his arm. I hang on with all my might though, the fear of falling a bit too strong with his show of strength. When he finishes climbing, he sets me down and shuts and locks the little trap door before turning back to me. "Still okay with this?"

I bite my lower lip. "Yes, are you?"

"Ptheryeth, yes." He growls before grabbing my hand and pulling me into the bedroom. Pushing me onto the bed he pulls my shirt over my head before kneeling to slide my leather pants down over my legs, which was not an easy feat. I giggle, trying to kick my way out the tight confines of the leather and he smirks at me. Once my legs are finally free, he starts to go for my underwear, but I stop him.

"Your turn." I am soaked and am craving the feeling of Sorin's tongue on my folds again, but what I am craving even more is to drive him as crazy as he has driven me over the past couple of weeks.

I slide off the bed and start to unclasp his pants before he understands my meaning. "Wait, Firefly. You don't have to-"

"I know I do not have to," I cut Sorin off. "I want to." Pulling his pants down, my eyes widen as his thick long cock springs into view. I use one of my hands to grasp him and slowly stroke root to tip just once. He groans, then shifts our positioning so that he is sitting on the bed. Vines with little purple fruits grow beneath him making a soft pad of leaves. He tosses a pillow on top for good measure.

"I do not want you to hurt yourself."

Giggling again, I crawl on top of the nest of vines and a soft chocolate scent drifts up to me. "What is this?" I ask, pointing to the vine before suctioning my mouth over his cock.

He moans, his eyes flitting back before he uses one hand to softly caress my hair. "Akebia-" His eyes are unfocused as he watches his cock slide in and out of my mouth. "I thought-" another moan as I flick my tongue up the underside of his cock. "I thought it would be the best vine to use."

My mouth comes off of him with a pop. "Smells like chocolate," I say before taking him once again into my mouth.

"Mhmm," he responds distractedly. I laugh again, doing my best not to choke as I continue to suck his length. Although this is only my second time doing this, you would think I had mastered the craft with the sounds Sorin was making. I suck more eagerly, taking him in as far as I can go before slowly pulling back. After a little while his grip on my hair tightens and he gently but firmly pulls me off of him. "If you continue that." He sounds out of breath. "I think we both might be disappointed with the results." He laughs to himself.

"Agree to disagree," I say, stroking him.

He growls. "You are in for it now." Standing, he grabs me from the floor and deposits me onto the bed. I squeak a protest, but he is already pulling down my panties and rubbing my clit with his thumb. My orgasm coils within my belly quickly, my body already pent up with tension and desire. Before I can process the sensation, I am cumming violently, my body shaking as wave after wave of ecstasy crashes through me. Sorin captures my lips and strokes one finger in and out of me testing my wetness. I clench around his finger, my nails digging into his back. "Are you ready for me, Firefly?"

"Yes," I moan. "Now, Sorin," I demand.

He chuckles against my lips. Lifting off of me he grabs another pillow and lifts my hips to place it beneath me. "Tell me if you are too sore and I will stop," he says before slowly pushing himself inside me.

I gasp at the fullness of him. There is a light sting, but nothing terrible and the sensation quickly morphs into pleasure as he lazily rubs circles around my clit. Holding his position for a second, he watches my face before slowly pulling back out. On his third stroke, I moan, my body now filling with heat as pleasure takes over. I feel sparks start to form around the room and do my best to keep them from igniting as my brain starts to fog.

"I will make sure you are safe, Lace, you can let go."

Whimpering, I focus completely on Sorin and do as he says. Clutching the sheets I feel myself skyrocket closer and closer to the edge as his fingers become more insistent on my clit, the sensation mixing deliciously with the pleasure zinging from my core. He starts to pump in and out of me rhythmically, every thrust making me want to moan and pull at the sheets as wave after wave of ecstasy fills me. Pulling one of my legs up, he thrusts himself even deeper inside of me and I cry out at the fullness.

"You feel so fucking good, Lace. I have dreamed of this tight pussy wrapped around my cock, but the feeling of it is better than anything I could have ever dreamed of," he grunts through ragged breaths.

"Please, Sorin." I move my hand so I can dig my fingers into his thigh as he continues to pound into me, his thrusts becoming more and more powerful as he gets closer to the edge himself.

"Fuck," he groans as he pulls me up and spins me around, so I am on all fours. Pulling my hips to him he slams in and out of me and I pant and moan as tiny sparks dance along my skin. Sorin reaches around and uses his other hand to once again rub my clit. I can no longer hold onto any threads of control as I careen over the edge. My arms give out beneath me as wave after wave of my orgasm flows through me. Before I can fall completely on my face, Sorin pulls my back to his front, continuing to fuck me, prolonging my orgasm. After another moment, he finds his own release and we collapse against the bed, Sorin holding me tightly to him.

Once we catch our breaths, Sorin kisses the side of my face.

"That was amazing," I gasp. My brain still dizzy with aftershocks.

"It was." His voice is filled with masculine pride. "Stay here, let me get something to clean you up."

"Okay," I breathe and feel his warmth disappear from my back. A faucet turns on in the bathroom and runs for a little while before shutting off.

"Open your legs," Sorin says when returning to the room. I comply and he places a warm rag between my thighs, causing me to sigh with contentment. He chuckles. "If you like that wait until we get you in a warm shower."

I smile at him, and he mirrors my smile before finishing wiping what he can from between my legs. Taking the rag with him, he walks to the bathroom and turns on the shower. He returns a moment later, scooping me up from the bed, and depositing me in the bathroom. "You should probably pee and then hop in the shower. I will join you shortly."

"This is a little overkill, is it not?" I ask, referring to him carrying me around.

"Not in the slightest." He kisses my forehead. "I will be right back." Then he shuts me in the bathroom. I do, in fact, pee, before hopping in the shower. Relaxing under the warm spray, I marvel over the craziness of the day. *Nightmares, training sessions, confrontations and sex in one day? A morning no less?* I groan at the thought of magick lessons with Baldar later.

The door to the shower opens causing me to jump and Sorin squeezes into the water behind me.

"Hi," I say, feeling oddly shy. Although we had been intimate not long ago, this was the first time we had actually done it between the two of us alone and for some reason that thought was causing tiny elvisera to wreak havoc on my abdomen.

"Hey Firefly." Sorin grabs some shampoo and lathers it in his hands. "Mind if I wash your hair?"

"Sure," I say, unravelling the mass from its tight braid and wetting it beneath the spray, before turning my back to him. His fingers work magic against my scalp until all the stress of the day melts from me.

"That's better," he says softly, rinsing my hair beneath the water once again, before grabbing some conditioner and running it through the bottom of my strands. "What do you say we wash off and then get to that potion lesson. We should have another couple hours before you are set to practice with Baldar." I pout and he taps my nose. "Don't worry, we will just be going over what each potion is and a couple of properties of each. You can sit the whole time."

I sigh. "Deal."

CHAPTER FIFTY
Sunshine and Rain

Alaceandra

The rest of the day goes by without much incident. Sorin gives me another pretty braid before showing me what each of the potions he had set out earlier did and where I could find them. Before I know it, I am back on the field with Baldar as he coaches me through how to make flames grow and extinguish, as well as how to set moving targets on fire. My magick has grown even more than the day before— *big surprise.* I find myself a lot less exhausted than I previously thought I would be by the end of the day. Sam, though, has been absent since this morning. He did not pick up his lunch, nor was he present at dinner. I cannot help but wonder where he is, or how he is investigating what I had told him that morning.

The prince follows me back to our cottage, Baldar positioned on his shoulder.

"I see you two are getting along," I say, climbing up the ladder.

"Seems that way. He grows on you... kind of like a fungus."

I snort.

The prince continues. "Speaking of growing, looks like someone's powers got a boost since their last lesson. What have you been up to today?" He leans against the doorframe one leg propped up for balance.

"He's the fungus," Baldar mumbles, his tiny squeaks barely audible from the prince's shoulder. *"He is right though, you have improved. I was not sure if you would get through one of those lessons let alone all three. You should be proud of yourself."*

"Thanks for the vote of confidence," I say sarcastically. Baldar jumps down from the prince's shoulder and I see the prince wince slightly. "The nails?" I ask.

"Yep," he says, before sitting on the couch. "No, but really. I am curious." He quirks a brow at me.

I roll my eyes. "Your suspicions are probably correct."

"They often are," he drawls. "As I said before, there are always signs. That is the same braid you had when Sam and I found you in the woods, you know?"

I sigh, twirling the braid between my fingers. "You caught me."

He laughs. "Nothing to catch. I hope you had fun. It is interesting to see the correlation between your skills growing and your... interactions with us though."

I roll my eyes. "I am sure it is."

"Someone is in a mood this evening."

I smile. "A good one or a bad one I wonder." I playfully tap my chin.

"Definitely a good one." The prince stands and grabs my hand spinning me.

I laugh. "What was that for?"

"I was just checking out my little dove's wings, they seem to be growing in nicely."

My smile softens. "Thank you."

"I am only pointing out the facts." He kisses my forehead.

"I- I am sorry about last night." The prince stills.

"Why is that?"

"I should not have taken the fear I had about that dream out on you." I look in his eyes, but instead of them softening they harden. He takes a step away from me. "What is wrong?" I reach for him, but he turns away.

"You should not apologize. Your fear is justifiable."

"What do you mean?"

He sighs. "Nothing just—" He rakes a hand through his hair. "It has been a long day. We should go to bed." He walks into the bedroom, leaving me reeling.

"Wonder what crawled up his ass and died," squeaks Baldar, breaking me from my daze.

"So, I was not the only one who thought that was weird."

"Yep, definitely sketchy," Baldar agrees skittering up my body to lay on my shoulder. *"But I did tell you he was a weirdo."*

"Were you not just resting on his shoulder."

"Only because I didn't want to walk. Do you know how hard it is to get up and down those ladders with these legs?"

"Can you not just teleport?"

"That is not the point."

"Sure."

"Sooooo are you going to join mister sunshine in there or are you sleeping at casa Baldar tonight?"

"Casa Baldar?"

"Yeah, the chair."

"Not sure if he will let me sleep on the chair and unlike you, I prefer not to be carried by men who I have confusing feelings for."

"Suit yourself, but if there are any more disturbances, do not come crawling to me."

"Is that not what you are here for, to protect me?"

"Mostly just the teaching bit, but sure. I just don't feel like sleeping with the monster tonight. He snores."

I huff.

"Are you done arguing with the ferret, Alaceandra? You need to rest."

"Are you?" Baldar prods, looking at me with wide eyes.

"I guess so." I remove him from my shoulder and place him on the couch before striding over to the bedroom door that the prince is holding open.

"Your one sided conversations are odd," he says shutting the door behind him.

"Says the man who walked out after informing me that my fear about where his loyalties lie is justifiable."

"I am only speaking the truth Alaceandra. Is that not what you wanted from me?"

"Yes, but-"

"This is what I was saying about you being ill prepared. If you cannot handle me telling you that not trusting me is the smart decision, how will you be able to handle the whole of what we must do- what I must do to get my father off the throne?"

"Can we not have this conversation right now? Frankly your back and forth between kind and caring and utterly infuriating is giving me a migraine." I pinch the bridge of my nose.

The asshole laughs at me. "Fine. Let us go to sleep then." I crawl into bed and he crawls in after me. "Sweet dreams Alaceandra."

"Sweet dreams," I whisper.

CHAPTER FIFTY-ONE
A Warning

Alaceandra

*M*y hair is pulled into an intricate bun. I find myself in a soft yellow dress, with golden swirls. I am in the middle of the field that I train on every day with my men. I am once again barefoot, but I am not alone. The shadow of a man stands in my periphery. I cannot make him out. When I turn in his direction he disappears.

"I see your men have quite the silver tongues." That same voice whispers in my ear, causing shivers to invade my body. "If you will not ask Sam what he is doing, I will show you. Follow me."

My feet compel me to walk through the woods, my body controlled by some foreign entity. We travel a small path covered in rock and trees before coming upon a cave.

"Look in here and you will find the answer."

I near the cave until I am right at its mouth. Inside I see two bodies hanging from rope, lifeless. I gasp and back away.

"There has to be more to this. What are you not showing me?"

"I am showing you the truth. Inside this cave hangs two dead men. See how that one bleeds?" The man in my periphery points to the man on the right. "He was tortured by none other than Sam's hands."

"How do I know what you are showing me is real? This could be just some image you made up to scare me."

"If you do not believe me, investigate yourself. I promise you will find the answers you seek and more." Hands push my back towards the opening of the cave, but instead of the men there is only darkness. I am falling.

I jerk up from my bed once again. *Another nightmare.* I mentally scold myself. Glancing over to the prince I see he is already awake watching me.

"Is everything alright, little dove?"

"Yes, sorry just another bad dream"

"Again?" He sighs. "I never thought I would say this, but where is Baldar? He seemed to keep your nightmares away last night."

"On the couch. He said he did not want to be bothered tonight. Something about your snoring."

"I do not." The prince scrunches his brow. "He would leave you unprotected over a noise complaint?"

I shrug. "I am okay— this dream was shorter and less direct."

"What was it about?"

I hesitate. "He was just showing me around some place. I do not know. It was a lot more surreal than the first. Less words more images."

"Odd. Do you think you will be able to sleep the rest of the night, or would you like to get up now?"

"What time is it?"

"Ptheryeth knows, but I would say you have a couple more hours if you want to try again."

I think about this. "It might be for the best. I can tell it is going to be a long day."

He sighs. "You and me both."

I settle back under the covers and close my eyes. Thankfully, the rest of my night is dreamless.

CHAPTER FIFTY-TWO
Danger Approaches

Sorin

*T*his looks great. The villagers finished putting the last stone into place on the wall surrounding Olvaria last night and I came to check it out this morning. *It seems Sam is also good at construction instruction.* The wall is very well built, but I do have a concern over the shape of it. While it might prove useful for attacks against monsters. It has only one way in and out of it and does not do much as far as protecting against aerial attacks. *We might want to look into finding a way to fix that as well if we are going to be here for much longer.*

I have learned a lot about this village since coming here. They are a very artistic sort. Although they only inhabit the night, they love music and bright colors, which is why they engraved their cottages with beautiful images. They love to use their magick to try to predict what might happen in the future so that they may be prepared. Etching these predictions on their houses ensures that the information can be widely spread among the villagers. At the end of each month, they have council meetings to troubleshoot any problems that might arise from them. *It is quite interesting.* They do not have many soldiers though, so whenever one of their villagers gets into trouble, they are vulnerable to the elements around them. Although this may seem like a disadvantage, apparently the dark lands have deemed these people as quite useful. They have put sanctions on attacking them, which is how they have survived over the years, despite the general dangers that these lands hold. These sanctions do not apply to the wildlife though, hence the need for the wall. *I wonder what all they will decorate this wall with. There is not an inch of this space that is unmarked. I am sure this wall will not stay bare for long.* I smile as I see a ball rolling towards the entrance of the village. Running up, I capture it and place it back on the doorstep of one of the nearby cottages. *I hope Alaceandra is having a nice morning sleeping in.*

Movement makes me glance again towards the entrance of the village. *Odd. That looks like a person.* A shadowy figure quickly darts back into the woods. I make out a boot and a ruby cloak before they vanish. I know Sam had mentioned a couple times that he had spotted scouts on the borders edge. *Maybe this is connected?* I step out of the village ready to capture the intruder, when something shimmers to my left.

Baldar appears at my feet looking frantic.

"Alaceandra is in danger." He runs up to me and yanks at my pant leg.

"What?" *How can I hear him right now?*

"We must leave now before it is too late."

CHAPTER FIFTY-THREE
Ambush

Alaceandra

I wake up the next morning alone. Glancing beside me, I realize the prince has already left, likely after he informed me that Sam came down earlier this morning to cancel lessons. *Glad he has no issues speaking to him.* I think bitterly. I am not sure whether to be relieved or frustrated by this. On one hand that means I get more sleep. On the other, that is less training. As tired as I am, it has been nice getting up to learn something every day and using my body to do it. I stretch. Tamping down my annoyance, I crawl out of bed readying myself for the day. Baldar is still sleeping peacefully on the couch, and I give the little guy a pet before opening up the floor to leave. My stomach growls. *It must be pretty late in the morning. I guess I was really tired— odd dreams will do that to you.*

I let my mind drift over the dream again. I assumed that if Sorin's job with my father involved murder then Sam's had to as well, but what would have Sam having to murder anyone out here? Sylvie has not mentioned to me much more about monsters lurking outside Olvaria's walls. *That does not mean that there is no one around. If the dream has any merit to it, it may be related to those who tried to abduct Lyza. That is the reason the men are patrolling the border, right? To ensure that no more of those monsters can hurt the children of this town? That must be it. But if it is, why would the dream-man show it to me. Why tell me to investigate it? All this is so weird.*

I push my body down the ladder and to Sylvie's cottage, excited about what she has cooked up for this morning. Climbing through the hatch in the floor, I do my best to be as quiet as possible, trying to be mindful of waking Sylvie or her family. After I shut it, I walk on quiet feet to the kitchen. Before I can make it, I pause. Voices are drifting through the hall. Voices that sound a lot like the prince and Sam. I smile, leaning closer to try to listen in. I have always wondered what they discuss, especially after having to spend all that time together. *They act like they cannot stand each other, but surely they have to have gotten somewhat close over those weeks. Maybe I can gain some insight...* I strain my ears and pick up bits of conversation.

"...dream last night."

"...not good... dangerous activity... border..."

Wait, dream? Are they talking about me? I walk closer, keeping close to the walls.

"I had to capture another one, since the last two are dead."

"Fuck," the prince curses. "I have not noticed a ton of activity but that along with the dreams are not a good sign. She has been asking more questions. If they are getting closer to her, who knows how long we have until she figures it out."

"She's been asking me as well. Ptheryeth knows what he's telling her."

"Let's hope not too much."

"If it continues, we will need to get her out of here, the sooner, the better. Please stay on border patrol today I have things I need to take care of."

"Agreed."

I bite my tongue and back up. Moving away from whatever that conversation was. *Dangerous activity at the border? Two are dead? How long they have until I figure it out? Figure what out?* As much as I try to stop myself, the man's voice from last night flits through my brain once again. *...investigate yourself. I promise you will find the answers you seek and more.* I almost growl in annoyance. I should not put any weight on what the man has said. Obviously, he is out to use me for his own means as much as the other men, but... curiosity worms itself into my gut and takes root. *If I can just check out the location in my dream, I can probably figure out just what I am up against here, since it is obvious that my current company wants to keep me in the dark. If there is nothing there then I know whatever the man tells me from this point on is as full of lies as those he claims he is trying to uncover.... if there is something there.... maybe I can finally do some digging of my own.* I look down at the flowy outfit I chose for the day and shake my head. *I cannot investigate in clothes like these I must change.* Keeping an ear to the kitchen, I walk back over to the ladder and carefully climb down.

Making my way back to the cottage the prince and I share, I climb back up and notice that Baldar has now vacated the couch and is nowhere to be found. *It must be nice to be able to transport wherever you want to go without the use of these tunnels.* I make quick work of changing into my fighting leathers once again making the journey back to the main cottage. Peeking my head up, I hear a door close. Quickly, I crouch back down so that only a sliver of my face is visible through the crack in the ladder hatch. I listen for a moment but am met with silence. Slowly I finish opening the door and climb out before shutting it gently. Walking back to the corner where I could hear the men's discussion previously, I listen hard for any more voices, but there are none. Taking a chance, I round the corner, and just like I thought, the room is empty. *Perfect. Step one complete.* Scooping up my breakfast that Sylvie left, I quickly eat some food before storing the rest in the ice chest with our prepared lunches and head outside.

The journey to my training grounds goes by in a blur, my body having committed the route to memory in my short time here. Standing in the clearing, I spin around trying to orient myself correctly to where I was standing in the dream. "This feels correct," I mumble to myself, my eyes snagging on a distinctive tree in the distance. On light feet I enter the tree line, my body pushing me forward. I walk for some time, but right as I feel like I have found the cave, the forest shifts and I am once again lost. I am about to give up when the trees part and I find myself in yet another clearing. A scorch mark stains the center of the space, but it remains otherwise empty. I walk further into the space to investigate the marking on the ground when the sky darkens.

An uneasy feeling grips me, and I turn around to run back to the cottages and realize that I am definitely lost. "Fuck," I whisper. "Why did I not think to mark the path." Wringing my hands together, I take a deep breath trying to calm myself. "The sky is getting darker... it could just be something passing in front of the sun... no need to get yourself worked up." *No, maybe not about the sun, but how are you going to get back to the cottages if you have no idea where you are?* My brain bites back at me. "Unhelpful," I whisper to myself. "I got myself here. I can damn well get myself back."

A cold breeze drifts through the air and the hairs on the back of my neck stand on end. I spin around and *holy shit there are eyes looking out at me from the tree line.* "It's probably just an animal," I mutter. "A really... tall animal."

A man steps into view. *Or not. Remember your training, Alaceandra. For Ptheryeth's sake you can command fire, he is probably just a lost villager.*

"Hello there, little lady," the man says. His voice has a drawl to it and he holds a mace in his hands. *I assume not many villagers would be handling one of those things but who am I to judge.*

I back up. One of my hands going to my hip to grip one of my daggers.

"Ah ah ah, I would not do that." He smiles and his teeth are rotted and decayed. "Would not want to have to hurt you too soon. The king will be so happy with this find." *Okay so probably not a lost villager. Why did I decide to come out here again? A stupid dream?* "Now, darling. Are we going to do this the easy way or the hard way?"

I take another step back, unsheathing my dagger and readying my stance, choosing not to answer the man.

"Tsk, tsk," he whispers. In the next breath, he is rushing me. His mace is held high. He swings it down and I duck out of the way. Popping up, I stab my dagger into his swinging arm. He shouts and pulls away from me and I do my best to hold the dagger as it rips through his arm, backing up swiftly. He laughs. "Someone taught the lady to fight. How sweet." Running towards me again the man tries to take another swing at me, but I once again dodge him, this time rolling to safety, before jumping to my feet.

I look towards the wood line, contemplating my chances of escape, but that is unfortunately the wrong move. A whistling sound has me diving to the left. Glancing to where the noise came from, I see the man's mace is now haphazardly laying on the floor. Before I can process that the brute *fucking threw it at me,* he dives into me causing me to lose grip on my dagger. The wind gets knocked from me as I watch my dagger join the man's mace, just out of my reach. I struggle against the man, kicking, screaming and punching at him. My strength is no match for his and soon he is laying on his back, his legs trapping mine as he chokes me. "Shhh, go to sleep," the man says, his tone far too joyful for the situation we are in.

Think, Alaceandra think. I scream to myself as claw at the man's arm around my throat. I feel the last bits of oxygen in my system start to vanish and my vision goes hazy. *Oxygen?* Something clicks in my brain. *Fire, set him on fire!* Using my last bit of strength, I elbow the man in the face at the same time that I cause the ground beneath us to burst into flame.

"Motherfucker!" The man yells, releasing me. His lip is bleeding profusely, and he clutches at his back, his eyes filled with excitement and rage.

I crawl away from him, coughing, trying to gain as much distance as possible.

"Lace!" I hear frantic shouting in the distance.

"Help!" My voice is raspy as I scream towards the oncoming voice.

The man wipes at his lip. Before glancing towards the tree line. "This isn't over. Oh no, it has only just begun," he says before he stands, grabbing his mace and running away.

CHAPTER FIFTY-FOUR
Keep Watch

Alaceandra

Tears well in my eyes and I do my best to not let them fall.

"Lace!" The voice I now recognize to be Sorin's calls again.

"Over here!" I yell, cringing at the sharp pain in my throat.

He appears behind me with Baldar at his feet. When he gets a good look at the scrapes and bruises covering my body, he collapses to the ground in front of me and tenderly holds my face. "What the fuck happened? Why are you out here by yourself?"

I cough again. "I was ambushed," I say. "I think..." I search my memory for the any information he gave me before he attacked. "I think he wanted to take me to his king. He might have been... connected... to those men that captured us before."

His eyes widen at the sound of my voice.

I brought him to you as soon as I realized you were missing. Baldar says. *I apologize it was not any sooner I was summoned this morning and by the time I got back...* He curls in my lap. *By the time I got back I knew you were in danger, so I grabbed the closest one I could find.*

"Thank you, Baldar," I whisper.

Sorin scoops me up. "You need water, please stop talking until we get you some." He sprints through the forest and back to the cottages. When he opens the door to the kitchens, Sam is sitting at the table looking at something. At our entrance, he shoves whatever it is in his pocket.

"Why are you-" His eyes fall onto my form, and he jumps from his chair. "What the fuck happened? Why are you carrying her?"

"She was attacked," Sorin says pushing things off the table so he can set me down. Once he does, he runs to grab me some water, which I take and drink gratefully.

"How? Was no one watching her?" The room darkens slightly and my heart races.

Sorin pushes at Sam. "Apparently not. Now are you going to help or just yell?" The room brightens again.

"I am okay," I say, my voice already sounding less strained. "Maybe a couple bruises here and there, but I did not get terribly injured." *Maybe if I act like if it is less of a big deal, they will not question why I was out there in the first place.*

"You sound like you were choked," Sam says, his voice filled with barely veiled anger.

"That is because I was," I say, trying to sound cheerful, the tone causes a tickle in my throat, and I cough again.

"So then obviously you are not okay," Sam growls.

"You should see the other guy," I quip. Now that I am away from the whole situation, I cannot help but be proud of how I performed. *Yes, it got a little touch and go at the end there... and really if Sorin was not there I am not sure how much longer I could have held the man off, but I did hold him off.* A couple of weeks ago I would not have been able to, and I cannot help but smile at the accomplishment.

"Oh, I would like to," Sorin and Sam say simultaneously, their bodies full of tension.

"Well, hopefully we will not have to," I say. The adrenaline high is quickly turning into exhaustion. I blink sleepily at the two men, rubbing my eyes.

"Did he get away?" Sam asks, not noticing my shift in mood.

I nod. A couple seconds later, I hear a door slam.

There is a pause, and then I look up to notice that now only Sorin and Baldar remain. I sigh.

"Alaceandra is exhausted," Baldar states. *"I assume she had to use her powers while she was defending herself against the enemy. As your connection is not fully complete this likely has drained her. She will need to rest."*

"It has still not been completed?" Sorin asks, pursing his lips.

"No, it cannot be until the solstice but fear not it is quite strong. A short nap should fix her right up."

"You guys can hear each other?" I ask.

Sorin smiles. "Yes, a relatively new discovery," he supplies. "Come let's get you to bed."

A shiver runs through me. "I do not know if I should." *I definitely do not want to run into whoever is haunting my dreams right now.*

"Do not be afraid, Alaceandra. I will not leave your side. You will rest easy this morning."

"Okay," I say hesitantly. Sorin starts to pick me up, but I stop him. "I will walk."

He puts his hands up. "If you insist. Let's sleep in my quarters. I want to keep watch over you."

I smile at him. "Sounds good."

CHAPTER FIFTY-FIVE
Revelations

Sorin

I almost fucking lost her. Again. I stare down at the beautiful, sleeping woman in my arms. I try to memorize every peaceful curve and dip of her still form. *I am just glad that I was able to get to her in time. Seeing her like that...* I kiss the top of her head. *It was torture. It is torture.* I knew from the moment we laid eyes on that rock with her prophecy etched in it that her fate was sealed, but it had to be done. I know that this will only be the beginning of the trials that her life is going to put her through before she chooses, but I cannot help but wish I could steal her away from it all. That I could hold her here, in my arms, and protect her forever. That I could warn her. *But I can't. I fucking can't.* No matter how many spells I cast. No matter how many potions I concoct, this stupid spell leaves me utterly powerless to do the one thing that I need to do. That I vowed to do, and I need to come to terms with that.

I am in love with this woman. *I am in love with Alaceandra, and I can't fucking protect her.* A tear trails down my cheek, and I let it fall. *I hope one day she can learn to protect herself.*

Alaceandra

After a peaceful nap, Sorin walks me back over to my quarters.

"I think you should take the rest of the day easy. We can continue your lessons tomorrow. I need to go collect some wood for Sylvie for dinner tonight. Please stay in your room."

"I will." I hug Sorin. I am feeling a lot better after my nap. I have not been able to sleep with him since our adventures in the woods together. Although the prince has become quite a nice sleeping partner, I really needed the familiarity of Sorin's arms today.

"Good. If you are feeling up to it, feel free to join me and Sam for dinner. It would be good if we are able to go over all that has happened today."

"I think that would be wise," Baldar adds.

"Okay. I will plan on it. Thank you for caring for me Sorin." I place a gentle kiss on his chest.

"Til my dying breath," he says kissing the top of my head. "Now go before I pull you back into bed with me and this time not for cuddles."

I quirk my brow at him, and he gives me a disapproving look. "Fine, fine," I say and climb up the ladder, "See you soon."

"Looking forward to it," he says before turning to go.

The prince waits for me, his hair is frazzled. He looks a bit worse for the wear.

"Woah. What happened to you?" I stop short just inside the bedroom.

His head jerks up to look at me. "What happened to me? To me, Alaceandra?" He laughs but it is a tinge hysterical. He crosses over to me and crowds me against the wall. "Do you want to explain to me why I came back from the border only to hear that you were attacked, little dove? Not only that, but you were alone when it happened? Why did you not ask one of us to accompany you? And why were you so far out in the woods? Planning another escape attempt?"

"No. I-" My mind flashes back to the conversation I overheard in the kitchen this morning. "I was looking into something." Although internally I may acknowledge that it might have been smarter to leave the whole dream cave alone, the prince's tone has my hackles up, reminding me the whole reason I wanted to investigate in the first place.

He takes in a quick breath, his body a cage around mine. "How many times do I have to tell you, your safety is our priority here. What could you have been possibly trying to 'look into?'"

"Does it even matter? If I would have told any of you about it, you would have surely stopped me."

"The smart move to do, all things considered, don't you think?" His tone is full of condescension.

"No, I do not. Injured or not, I am fine now after only a short nap. There is no need to get all worked up over what happened." I push at his chest. "There is nothing you can do now anyway, except yell at me over it and honestly this whole you must stay locked up in your tower bullshit is not helping your case."

The prince rolls his eyes. "I am not trying to keep you locked up in a tower, and if I were I doubt you would be fighting me as much as you are now."

"What is that supposed to mean."

His arrogant smirk is back, but it quickly sobers. "All I am saying, Alaceandra, is, until we can get everything sorted out to get out of here, please just make sure you have one of us with you. Today could have gone a lot worse."

My shoulders slump, because unfortunately I know all too well that it could have gone a lot differently. Try as I might to do my best to train with Sorin and Baldar, I am likely years behind where I need to be. *I still did kick the guy's ass though.* A little voice in my head says. *You will catch up eventually you just need to give yourself time.* "Fine. I guess that is fair." *For now.*

"Thank you."

We stare at each other, intensely. Our chests are heaving and there is barely any space between us. I can feel the heat of the room increasing and my body awakening at being so close to the prince. I can tell he feels it too because one moment he is staring at me and the next his lips are on mine. His lips move slow, consuming me with controlled precision. I find myself wondering just how much it would take to make him lose that control of his. Soon I am melting in his arms as he pulls me against him. His cock rubs against my suddenly aching center as my nails clutch at his surprisingly soft strands of black hair. My own hair lifts as I feel my power strumming to life beneath my skin. A small moan breaks from my lips when suddenly a sharp sting has me yelling in pain.

I rip away from the prince and look down at my leg to see that Baldar is standing there with a disapproving look. "What was that for?"

"I will not have you summoning anything today, Alaceandra. You will have to save your make out session for another day. Preferably one where I have not already had to save your life?"

"You did not save my life today!" I scold the ferret, and the prince backs away from me watching the exchange.

"Did he bite you?" the prince asks, noticing the tiny spot of blood welling up on my leg.

"Yes!" I answer, indignantly.

"Agree to disagree," Baldar huffs. *"Now go shower, you smell like grass and blood."*

"You do not have to be rude."

"Just being honest," Baldar says nonchalantly, before walking over to the couch and setting in for sleep.

I huff, but march over to the bathroom anyway, leaving the prince standing by the wall, an amused, but confused look on his face.

I stare at the prince as he hangs up our clothing to dry over the shower curtain bar. His back muscles ripple as he arranges each piece. After I showered, he decided he needed one too. I have spent the last ten minutes sitting on the bed absorbing the events of the last few days. It would be amazing if we could continue like this. The training, the comradery, the sex, but if I have learned anything from today, it is that my time with these men is limited. I have already been found in my dreams and now attacked the only time I have found myself alone. How soon until my days of growing my powers and strength are over? How soon until I have to go back to being the meek, controllable princess my father has trained me to be? Until it is all over?

He turns towards me. "I feel your eyes, Little Dove."

I roll my eyes, before dropping them and picking at a hang nail. "How do you suppose this will all end?"

His brows knit. "How will what end?"

"This..." I motion around us. "I mean being here. Obviously, we cannot stay in this dead kingdom forever, especially with the current circumstances. We will need to go back to our royal duties eventually, before someone eventually forces our hand. And then what?"

"Then you will assist me in unseating my father from his throne and—"

I let out a growl of frustration.

The prince gives me a puzzled look. "What?"

"That is all? I get to experience all of this and then I just go back to being a pawn?" Tears prick at my eyes.

"You are destined to play a pawn. Although this respite from doing so actively has been quite entertaining for the both of us, we still have to play out our individual games. That shouldn't bother you. It is not like it is a surprise. I have warned you from the very beginning."

"I do not know. I think it is amazing how much I have been able to learn here. I mean I can command fire and summon creatures!" I let a little flame spark to life in my hand. "I have a rudimentary knowledge of potions, and I can even take down Sam at least once a training session." I let the flame die. "But what is it all for? So that I can be more powerful for those who use me in the future? More powerful for you? Or so that on the off chance I get recaptured those who need me to play in their games have inside protection on their asset?" I choke back a sob. "Being capable and..." I search for the words. "Independently someone, apart from my kingdom, apart from stifling responsibilities, and even apart from Sorin and Sam's constant protection is invigorating. I thought that just going out on a couple of adventures in the woods with those two would be the height of my existence, but this?" I let the flame spark up once again. "This is so much more. Or it can be, if I can let it grow." The flame grows in my palm, before I once again snuff it out. I stare at the empty space. "If after all of this I am forced to go back, forced to continue to play that pawn you are so great at reminding me I am, then I do not know how I will survive it. I do not know if I can survive it and that thought frightens me to my core. Do you not feel the same?" I look at the prince, his still form taking up the frame of the bathroom. "Has this experience shown you nothing? Shown you that we can be so much more than-"

"We cannot." The prince's face goes dark. "We cannot, Alaceandra. If we do not play our parts everyone loses. You will lose. This power that you harbor... If it goes uncontrolled..." He closes his eyes and takes a breath, and I feel like my world is shattering beneath me.

"You are right. Sorry." I wipe my tears. "We should meet back up with Sorin and Sam. It is dinner time." I smile at him weakly.

"Alaceandra-"

"It is fine. They will be missing us soon. We should go."

The prince grunts in frustration. "Fine, but we should take the food to them. We all need to talk."

I nod and head down the ladder, leaving Baldar to nap on the couch.

CHAPTER FIFTY-SIX
Stew

Alaceandra

We enter the kitchen to find Sylvie mixing a stew, three little purple bottles sit next to chopped veggies and meats to her right. When she notices us, she turns.

"Oh! I am almost done! Is it dinner already?" She fidgets with a cloth tucked in her pants.

"Oh no! Sorry I did not realize we were early. We were thinking of maybe taking some food and eating with the others in their cottage. Would that be alright with you?"

"Sure, sweetie." Her smile is twitchy and she is avoiding our eyes. "Just give me a couple more moments to finish up. Feel free to sit at the table."

"Okay..." I hesitate. "Are you doing alright Sylvie?"

"Me?" She busies herself with the food, but her movements are slightly off somehow. More robotic, instead of their usual fluidity. "Um, yes."

She clears her throat. "Well, no I guess not." She turns back towards us. "Hayford and Lyza left last night and have not made it back."

"What?" The prince says. "Sylvie you should have-"

"No, no. I did not want to worry you all with it. You seem really busy, and she is with her father, I just—" she sighs. "I think I know where they are now."

"Where are they?" The prince demands.

Sylvie smiles, but it is one filled with grief and turns jerkily back to the food. "It matters not. I know how to get them back I just—" She sighs.

"Sylvie?" The prince questions. She stays quiet for a moment and continues stirring the pot of food. "Please tell us Sylvie we want to help."

"Let's not discuss this tonight," she says, her voice hollow. "I do not want to burden you all with my bad mood. " She grabs some bowls and places them on a small tray before scooping soup into each one. She hands it to the prince. He stares at her and her shoulders drop. "I promise I will tell you tomorrow... I just need time. Please?"

He nods. "Tomorrow."

She nods and turns back to the soup.

We leave her and go down the hatch to the other cottage.

CHAPTER FIFTY-SEVEN
An Arm... Cool

Alaceandra

"We come bearing food." I try to don a good mood when we arrive to Sorin and Sam's cottage, but I find that their moods seem to be no better than ours.

Tension crackles through the space and standing at the center of it is an angry Sam.

Sorin's eyes widen when we come in and he quickly stands in front of the table. "Hi, Firefly." He walks up to me quickly. "Let's put that over he-" A flash of red catches my attention causing me to almost drop the food.

"What is that?"

Sitting on the small table is an arm. *A detached arm for that matter.* The blood from where it is severed is pooling on the table and from the look of it, it does not seem like it was detached too long ago. My stomach turns slightly.

"I found the man who attacked you," Sam says, his voice icy. Sorin cringes.

"Did you?" I say, my mouth feeling a bit dry. "Does that... um... belong to him?" My gentle protector is looking anything but. Blood coats his shirt and his fists are clenched as he stares daggers at the arm on the table. For some reason a thrill surges through me at the sight instead of the fear I was expecting.

"It is his arm, yes," he answers simply, his tone still strangely detached.

"And how did it get there?" the prince asks.

"I relieved him of its weight and put it there."

"Ah," the prince says, taking the food from my hands. "Where is the rest of him?" He does not seem as surprised by the dismembered body part as I am. As confusing as that is, I cannot force that fact to worry me. Instead, the whole situation feels surreal— something within me is almost excited by all the violence the day has brought.

"I do not know." Sam's voice has deepened dramatically, his rage coating every syllable. "He got away." He punches the table. "Again."

"So, you decided to bring the bloodied part to your cottage? To do what? Examine it?" the prince questions, dryly.

"What else was I supposed to do," he roars. "If I do not find him, Alaceandra-" His gaze finally leaves the arm on the table and clashes with mine. The blood drains from his face. "Alaceandra... fuck." His eyes flick back down to the arm. "What are you doing here?" His voice has returned to his normal cadence, along with an edge of alarm.

I swallow. "Ummm... dinner?" My eyes flick to the arm again. "Not the arm though... stew. From Sylvie." I point to the little containers.

"Oh," he replies lamely. "I uh, I will clean this up." Gathering the table as a whole he walks past me and opens the hatch in the floor before tossing the whole thing down and shutting the door once again.

Glancing down at himself, it is as if he notices the blood for the first time. "I need to shower," he says before running to the bathroom.

I stare after him. "Am I dreaming right now?" I ask the room.

"Hmm..." The prince pinches me and I swat at his hand. "No. Dear old Sam just went a little overboard there." He stares at my face. "I take it you have not seen that side of him before."

"No, she hasn't," Sorin answers for me. He grabs one of my hands. "Sorry you had to see that. Are you okay?"

I let out a sharp breath. "Yeah," gently pulling my hand away from him, I walk over to the couch, checking the area for any bloody residue, seeing none I plop down. "It has just been a long day."

"I am surprised you are not running away screaming," the prince says, smirking.

So am I, but if that arm is really from my attacker, I cannot be upset with Sam for removing it. I reply mentally. "Par for the day, I guess," I say instead.

Sorin kneels beside me. "Look, Lace, you just caught him at a bad time, we did not realize you were on your way up. He-"

"It is fine. It is not the first severed limb I have seen, just the first at his hands. I can deal with it. I think we have more important matters to discuss. Like the owner of that arm and what they were doing in the woods in the first place."

"Ah ah ah, like you are going to get off so easily. Mind telling us why you were in the woods yourself?"

So much for hoping being cheerful would make them forget about the whole thing. I bite my bottom lip. "Can we wait til Sam gets back? I would rather explain everything with him here. Less repeating myself."

They both nod. After a few more minutes, Sam makes his way back into the sitting room, but try as I might to catch his eyes, he refuses to look at me.

"Now tell us," the prince demands.

"I had another dream last night," I say and the men lean in to listen.

"The same man from before?" the prince asks.

"Yes, but I still could not get a good look at him. This time though instead of just speaking to me he showed me things."

Sam perks up at this. "Showed you things?"

I nod. "A cave. With two dead men hanging by the arms in it. He told me..." I pause, licking my lips. "He said Sam killed them." My eyes drift to the hatch that is currently hiding the severed arm right now and Sam groans.

"What?" Sorin asks Sam.

"I did not kill those men," Sam grumbles.

"I did not say that-"

"I know you did not say it, but I saw your eyes, Parum Bellator. You are currently thinking that it could be possible that that is true and while I will not say that I have not killed, because I think we both know that is untrue, those men did not die by my hands. Neither has any scout that has come upon these lands." His own eyes flick to the hatch. "Yet," he growls.

"Wait," The prince interrupts. "How does that have anything to do with why you were out in the woods?" He asks.

"Yeah, about that..."

"Firefly..." Sorin warns.

"So.... this morning, I overheard Sam and the prince talking about dangers on the borders and how I am asking too many questions and I thought if I could just look into this cave then maybe I could do a little digging myself because try as I might to pry information from you three, you refuse to tell me anything of value," I spit out in a burst.

"And you thought the best way to do that," Sam says through gritted teeth, "was to try to find the cave with the potentially dangerous criminals...on your own."

"Yes." I nod. Sorin sighs. "In my defense you and the prince were acting really suspicious. I thought if I did not find anything out there then that would be proof enough that the dream man was spouting lies and if I did...."

"Then you were going to believe what the idiot was saying?" Sam rubs at his face.

"Well, no... I would just probably have continued doing my own investigations."

"But instead, you walked into a trap," Sorin says.

"It seems that way." I throw my hands up in exasperation.

Another sigh. "We are only keeping things from you to keep everyone safe." Sam is now raking his hands through his hair. "There have been... threats, but until now, not anything to be overly concerned about. Informing you of every little detail surrounding these things would only lead you to be in even more dangerous situations. We wanted to make sure that you completed as much training as possible before you are exposed to everything. It seems though the time for that is quickly drawing to a close."

"Why is it coming to a close?"

"Because the solstice is still three months away, but it looks like people are making their move now. Unfortunately, that means that we need to start taking action along with them. We can try to travel further into the dark lands to get them off our tail, but who is to say how long that will last."

"Off our tail? Is this because we left before my marriage to the prince? Who is after us?"

"Everyone is after you, Parum Bellator, and your betrothal to the pest is not the only reason why.... Do you remember the big rock that had that prophecy on it? The one you saw when you and Sorin were escaping?"

"Yes...."

"Well, that was about you. Once the solstice is upon us you will be able to be matched with someone. That pairing will give them all the power they need to either take over Ptheryeth or end it."

"What? You are telling me this now?"

"I need to, because that man you are seeing in your dreams is doing whatever he can to get you away from us, Alaceandra and I need you to know the reason why. It is not out of some fucked up kindness or good natured drive for the truth. It is so he can use you, likely to bring the end of the world as we know it. If you choose to go with him-" He bites his tongue. "We cannot choose your path for you, but you should know what you are deciding for or against."

A thought niggles at me and I cannot help but voice it, "Is that why you are all here too?" I look at the floor. "I mean I know that the prince has some grand revenge plot that he wants me to be a part of but what about you, Sorin? Sam?"

Sorin touches my chin bringing his gaze to mine. "As I have told you before, I will tell you again. Whether you had all the power in the world, or none at all, I will stand by your side. Whatever you choose, Lace, I will be with you no matter what." I smile at him softly and he kisses my forehead.

Releasing me, my eyes turn to Sam's stormy ones. "I will not lie to you and tell you that there are not ways I wish things to go," he says, "but I have committed myself to you, Parum Bellator. I will not go against any wishes of yours if I can help it."

I feel lightheaded, overwhelmed by all the new information and I lean back on the couch to take it all in. Another moment passes and the prince's voice rings through the room. "As lovely as all this is, Alaceandra has barely eaten all day. We should all eat."

"Agreed," rumbles Sam.

Sorin grabs the containers of food the prince set down earlier and hands them out. The prince digs in and I cannot help but smile at his vigor. "Hungry much?" I ask, opening my own container.

He rolls his eyes.

Taking a bite of my food, I groan a little. It tastes amazing. It is hearty and a little nutty with vegetables and meats that meld together to form a flavor I have not once encountered before, but am sure to remember.

"Guess it is good." Sam chuckles, opening his own container, before handing the last one off to Sam. Despite the tension, we eat in companionable silence.

"Tomorrow, if you are in agreeance, I think we should leave. I am sure there are more villages that we can find and we will have a far better chance of making it through here on our terms if we are all together," Sorin says, setting aside his container.

"How many have found us?" I ask, stabbing at a piece of meat, before I too set the rest of my food aside. *Back to business already then.* I stare longingly at the stew still left in my little bowl.

"Three it looks like, but that is already too many. Whoever is sending them definitely knows our location by now," Sam answers, collecting both the prince's and Sorin's bowls and setting them in the bathroom before returning to sit with us.

The prince quirks a brow at me, looking at my bowl. I just shrug. *Nothing kills one's appetite more than the discussion of people trying to kidnap them.* "Do you think they all work with the same person?"

"It is likely. Their weapons have all been similar thus far. Heavy, bludgeoning things. What was your attacker carrying?"

"A mace, so yes, it would seem that would track with your description." I think for a moment. "What king do you think they are serving? The men who captured me and Sorin also mentioned a king, but I would assume that it would not be King Demetrius nor Nikoli, especially considering that they seemed to have no knowledge of my name on both accounts."

The men exchange a look. "It is hard to say," Sam says carefully. "There are many rulers in Ptheryeth, we cannot be sure if this king of theirs is one of actual nobility or has deigned himself as such through amassing power."

"To be honest, I do not want to find out," Sorin mutters. "The sooner we can get away from this king the better. He does not seem very friendly."

An image of Sylvie's grief-ridden face fills my vision and guilt eats at me. "We cannot." Sorin looks at me, confused.

"Sylvie told Alaceandra and I on the way in that her husband and daughter were abducted yesterday," the prince chimes in.

"What?" Sam stands up.

I nod. "She would not give us any details, but she told us that she may have found a way to get them. She said she would explain more tomorrow. We cannot just leave her to deal with that, if this has to do with me, she has no idea what she has brought to her doorstep by allowing us to stay here. We have to make sure that her family is not punished for her kindness."

"Fucking great." Sam starts to pace. "Why did she not inform us of this yesterday? No wonder that man was lurking around. He probably was staking out the area after their abduction."

"You would have to ask her. She refused to speak with us about it, but I am hoping she will be more forthright in the morning," the prince says, letting himself sink against the base of the couch.

"This is all the more reason to get you out of here," Sorin says raking his hands through his hair

I frown. "I am not leaving her here to deal with my mess alone. We will speak to Sylvie tomorrow. If she has already found a way to recover them it is a moot point anyway, if she has not... well then, we will help her. We can leave when it is resolved." A yawn overtakes me and I feel my vision blur slightly. *I must be more tired then I thought.* I melt against the cushions.

The prince yawns and rubs his eyes. "Sounds like a plan," he mutters.

Sorin gives me a curious look and then glances towards the prince. "We have all had a long day." I watch as his eyes start to gloss over, his own tiredness catching up to him. "I would feel more comfortable if we were all together tonight. That way one of us can stay up to keep an eye on things. In all honesty, the way things are progressing is cause for unease. If Lace has another encounter tonight, I think one of us should be around to wake her up."

"Are you insinuating that I am unable to do so on my own?" the prince challenges, but his speech is slightly slurred and his form sways slightly like he is one second away from passing out on the floor.

"From the way you are looking? Yes," Sam answers. "Come. We should lay down."

Sorin scoops me from the sofa and I nuzzle into his warmth, a couple moments later I feel myself deposited next to an already sleeping prince, his snores drifting through the room. Sorin tucks me under the blankets and places a gentle kiss on my forehead, then freezes. His face filled with shock. The lights flicker and my stomach flips.

"Sorin?" My gaze drifts over to Sam who I realize was already on the other side of the bed. A look of panic crosses his features before anger takes hold. His body twitches slightly like he is trying to move, but he does not.

Guys? I try to call out to the two of them, but no sound escapes. My eyes widen as I try to move my fingers and toes but realize I cannot. My eyes dart to Sorin and Sam. One of their hands grip the bed as they stare at each other, but it seems we are all somehow stuck. *What is going on?* I try to say but once again my mouth refuses to cooperate. I watch as their bodies finally give in to some unknown force and collapse onto the mattress. Sorin's weight surprises me and I try to scream but realize that, that too, is an impossibility. A numb, tingling sensation claws up my throat and then everything goes black.

CHAPTER FIFTY-EIGHT

He's Here

Alaceandra

Opening my eyes, I find myself back in front of a castle in the dark lands. My hair is tied up into a knot on my head and I am wearing a ruby dress that falls from my form in waves. I spin around to find that I am alone, the grass tickling my bare feet. Taking a tentative step forward, a loud caw sounds right above my head. I look up to find a creature that looks eerily similar to my elvisera flying through the sky and deeper into the woods. The creature is injured, scarlet droplets cascading down from her wings as she soars. My stomach sinks to my toes as a sense of foreboding grips me. I hear myself whisper "Addie" before I am sprinting after her.

I throw myself through an allée that branches off to my right and try to catch up to her. I gasp as my dress catches on stray branches that reach for me along the path, allowing the dead wooden talons of the forest to penetrate my skin. Why must I always wear such a long dress?! I curse the garment and force myself to continue to place one foot in front of the other, that *eerie feeling growing ever stronger within me. Rivulets of my own blood fall to the ground matching the trail Addie has left as wound after wound open up along my legs. With another loud caw, her wings stutter before she is plummeting to the forest floor. I scream as I watch her fall, my pace quickening. I grit my teeth when I finally make it to the place I thought she landed. The area looks as if a meteor has crashed into it, trees are ripped from their trunks and the smell of smoke is heavy in the air. As I survey the area there is no sight of Addie, instead at the center of the wreckage there is a note, tied in silky ruby ribbon.*

I climb over the trees, mentally thanking Sam for all the extra upper body strength he has instilled in me over the past month and walk hesitantly over to the little bundle. I look around once more, but there is no one. Bending down, I pick up the note, untying the ribbon and letting it go. Taking a moment to watch as it snakes its way through the breeze, I take a deep breath and unravel the parchment.

I blink a couple times before the words come into focus.

Your time for running has ran out. Prepare yourself for He has arrived.

CHAPTER FIFTY-NINE
Betrayal In Strange Places

Alaceandra

I wake up, my body drenched in a cold sweat. *That one felt so real. Could it have only been a dream?* Blinking my eyes open, I realize that Sorin, Sam, and the prince are laying across the bed. *What happened last night?* I push at Sorin to try and get his weight off of me a bit, but he only moves slightly. I lift the blankets to look at my legs. They are unmarred. No cuts, no dirt, nothing. *And it looks like I am fully clothed....* I look around. *And so are they? So why-* One of the iron pieces on the walls comes crashing to the floor and I realize what woke me. The room is shaking. Suddenly last night's events come back to me in a rush. *We talked, ate, and then.... and then everyone collapsed.* Panicking I push at the prince, Sorin, and Sam, but they are out cold. The room shakes again. I untangle myself from the bed and drag myself across the room on weak legs, looking for something that can help me wake them. Spotting Sorin's bag, I rifle through the myriad of potion bottles he has stowed within.

"Come on, come on, come on," I mutter sniffing each potion bottle before finding one that is particularly potent. Gagging, I cap the bottle, and squat as a particularly vicious tremor runs through the room. Once the room stills, I practically crawl over to the men and frantically waft the potion bottle's aroma under Sorin's nose. He awakes with a jolt.

"Wha-at the fuck," he groans, rolling over to his side.

"Get up!"

"L-lace?"

"Yes. Get up! The room is shaking."

He holds his head, wincing. "My head hurts."

"No one will wake up." My voice is borderline hysterical, the room shakes violently again.

Sorin bolts upright. "Can I see that?" He points at the bottle. I give it to him, and he looks at it shaking his head before pulling himself from the bed and dragging his body over to his bag. Searching through it, he takes out two other bottles. Drinking part of one, he walks back over to the bed and pours the rest of it out in the other two men's mouths before uncorking the next. He gulps down part of whatever is in the second bottle as well before offering me some. I drink a little and he takes it from me before pouring that too into the sleeping men's mouths.

"This one should help keep us stable through the quakes," he explains before tossing both the bottles away from him.

After a moment, both men wake and jump from the bed.

"What is going on?" Sam demands.

"We were drugged," Sorin deadpans. The room shakes yet again.

"Why is the room shaking?" The prince asks, rubbing a hand over his face.

"We are under attack," Sam states. He starts pulling on his leathers hastily. Sorin follows.

The prince stares. "How do you know that? I thought we were still safe from the threa-"

"Obviously we are not. You both keep Alaceandra safe. You know what to do." Sam darts out of the room.

"Wait where are you-" the hatch shuts with a bang.

"We need to find a place to hide." Sorin is all business, yanking me towards the bathroom. "We should be relatively safe in this cottage for now if they think you are in the other one with the prince, but we will need to find another place soon. We do not want to be sitting ducks."

"I want to help," I say pulling away from Sorin.

"You will be helping by keeping yourself safe, we already discussed that you are what they are after,"

"That is bullshit. Sam is out there on his own, we need to help him."

He glares at me. "You are not advanced enough in your training to take on a real threat, Firefly. Not that I would send you out any-"

"I am helping," I demand. "You all were training me for a reason. I have a good control over my fire and dagger, and I was able to hold off the other attacker well enough on my own. I am not going to have Sam go out on a suicide mission without the two of you. If you are worried about my training, I promise, I will stay back as much as possible, but if I can help at all, I am going." Sorin stares me down.

"The whole point of us being with you is to keep you safe, Firefly. If we let you go out into the danger we might as well be handing you off to the enemy."

"That thing, whatever it is, sounds big and who knows what destruction it has already caused. Either you take me with you and I stay out of the way, or I will find some way to sneak out of here and join the fight without any of your protection. Do not test me. I will not have Sam out there on his own."

"He can handle himself. He does not need us out-"

"What if all this shaking makes the tunnels collapse? I would be in as much danger of starvation and death being trapped down here as I would be up there."

Surprisingly, it is the prince that breaks. "We need to take her," he says to Sorin, before looking back to me. "But stay out of the way and near the cottages. If something happens to you... well let's just hope nothing does."

"But-" Sorin starts to interject.

"Lace isn't kidding," the prince mumbles. "She will find a way to get away, how do you think she got involved in the fight last time?" He gives me a reproachful look and I cast my eyes down. Not because I am ashamed but because he is right. I am fully prepared to find the next exit out of here to help Sam if needed. I just feel bad about worrying them. "And we do not know how sturdy these tunnel systems are. It is very possible we might get stuck down here if we wait."

Sorin sighs. "Okay, then. Let's go."

We make our way through the tunnels. Dirt rains from the ceiling. We have to pick our way through carefully as to not be hit by any rocks. When we reach the ladder to Sylvie's cottage the prince climbs up, but just as I am about to follow him Sorin stops me.

"Remember Lace, if things get dicey out there do not try to be a hero. Just-"

"Run. Yes. I know." I hold back an eyeroll.

He looks at me steadily. "Will you?"

I look away. "Yes."

He sighs and releases me. "I don't believe you."

I turn away from him and climb up the ladder, because he is right not to. If push comes to shove and I can be of help to any of them out there, I am not sure if I can run away, even if that ended in my detriment.

326

CHAPTER SIXTY
Siege

Alaceandra

Emerging from the tunnels, I look to see where the prince is but instead freeze. Rubble and ash surround me instead of the hallway I was expecting to see. I look to my left and notice the prince standing there, a grim look on his face.

"Why did you stop?" Sorin yells from below me.

"It is... gone." The beautiful cottage that once stood here is now piled around me. Little bits of linens and cookware are strewn about. The village that once towered around us is also a charred husk of its former self. The belongings of the villagers lay in the streets, abandoned. Sculpted walls are now piles of rock littered as far as the eye can see. Above us, elvisera soar through the skies, their riders barely perceptible in the distance. I blink rapidly, my brain not able to grasp what I am seeing. *And the noise.* Clattering metal and blood curdling screams echo through the village in a low terrible roar.

"What is gone?"

"Come here, Alaceandra. Let him through."

I slowly finish making my way out of the hatch. Sorin makes quick work of climbing up the ladder. We all stand in what was once Sylvie's cottage.

"This is really bad," Sorin says.

"You don't say," the prince replies sarcastically, kicking a pipe. A loud clang echoes through the space. Someone sprints towards us in the distance.

"We should find cover. It is not safe out here." Sorin grabs my arm and we run towards the trees. Crouching, we watch as the man runs closer to where the cottage once stood. With a scream, he trips and falls over an abandoned doll. A soldier in burgundy and black armor follows close behind wielding some kind of pointed bat. Catching up to the man, he swings the huge weapon. With a sickening thwap, the man collapses. Blood sprays, painting the soldier's face and the surrounding area the same burgundy color as the attacker's armor. He laughs before sauntering back towards the village.

A loud roar makes us all jump. We glance up to see one of the elvisera diving down and spraying more fire over the already burned remains of buildings.

"We need to get out of here," Sorin whispers.

"But what about Sam? He ran out ahead of us."

"Maybe we will find him on the way out. We cannot wait around for him."

"But the village is enclosed, the only way out of here is to go through...that." I motion towards the wreckage.

"I know, we will have to tread carefully, but the more we stand in one place the higher our chances of being seen. Let's go," Sorin says.

"Sorin is correct, I am sure that Sam will be able to handle himself in the meantime but it is much too dangerous for us to be hanging about."

Using what is left of the forest as coverage we slowly make our way deeper into the village. The villagers are fighting the men with burgundy and black armor in the streets with everything they have. Swords clang against axes and hammers. Arrows fly through the air and seemingly strike at random. Dead villagers are thrown to the side once defeated, the armored men's laughter echoes through the air as they take life after life. The stench of death and blood are heavy in the air.

A child's cry has my gaze swinging to the nearest building. A soldier has a man hanging over a table, his arms pinned behind him while another stands crouched in front of his face speaking to him.

"Where is she?" the armored man yells.

"Who? I do not know who you are-" The armored man stands and swings his axe. The villager's head falls to the ground.

"Daddy!" the child cries.

My eyes widen as the men advance on the child and, before I know it, my legs are moving. My body is propelled by instinct rather than thought as fire surges from my palm and into the nearest soldier. My bracelet glows as I make contact with the man's armor and a moment later the burgundy and black suit cracks allowing my fire to penetrate to his skin. He screams and tries to bat at the flames. My heartbeat is thumping through my ears as I take in what I have just done.

"Lace!" I hear Sorin's shout in the distance and I snap out from my daze. Turning, I approach the next armored man.

Using his panic to my advantage, I slice my dagger across the man's throat. He looks at me and his eyes bulge before his body falls to the ground. My body hums as my fire engulfs the man. Suddenly I am yanked back, my arms pulled firmly behind my back.

"There you are." Another soldier breathes into my ear.

I kick back and stomp on the man's foot. His grip on my arms tightens painfully and I struggle against his hold. "Stop moving, brat. I-" His grip loosens and I swing around to blast him with fire but see a bloody vine ripping itself through the man's chest. *Sorin.*

I turn to face the child but see that the prince is already crouching next to him, wiping at his tears. The child nods at whatever the prince said, holding an object close to his chest, then runs towards the wood line. The prince watches the little boy run until he has disappeared, obscured by the trees, and starts to walk over to me.

Something touches my shoulder and I swing around again, ready to face my next attacker, but it is only Sorin. "We need to keep moving." He says. I nod.

We also start to move back towards the trees but another shout catches our attention. "She's over there!" A woman screams.

The prince pushes me back. "Run!" He yells as several men in armor turn in our direction.

"What are you going to-" The air stirs and something glows in the prince's hands and along his back.

"Is that a bow? I did not know you could do that." I marvel at the prince's newly formed weapon.

"There are a lot of things you don't know and a lot of things you never will if you do not get moving right now." He fires off a shot and a man falls in the distance. The prince's eyes have turned a brilliant lavender.

"But—" my hand is yanked by Sorin pulling me away. Something whizzes by my head.

"You can't kill her asshole; he would kill us all."

A man grunts. I turn my head in the direction the object flew and see a small hammer lying on the ground. *Did he throw that?*

"You have to keep moving," Sorin says.

I return my focus to what is ahead and run. The prince stays at our back, letting loose several arrows to keep the soldiers away. We weave through the village, trying to make it to the entrance. Sorin's vine whips out in front of us taking down any men in our way. More fighting breaks out, staining the dirt crimson. We navigate through a maze of fallen bodies of villagers and soldiers alike. I try to bite back the overwhelming guilt that fills me when I look into their blank stares. We lose the soldiers by ducking into one of the buildings that despite all odds is still intact. Crouching in its entrance, we watch as the men run by.

"Where did she go?!" We hear one shout.

"Why are they killing so many people?" I whisper to Sorin and the prince.

"I don't know," Sorin whispers back, grabbing my hand and squeezing. Sorin's eyes are now a deep gold.

"They are looking for me."

"They will not get you," the prince says, his voice a low rumble.

I nod, but squeeze Sorin's hand a little tighter.

A shout echoes in the distance and we peek out of the building to see Sam fighting off some men by the village entrance. His eyes are black and shadows surround him, cloaking his body. Little black daggers explode from his form and embed themselves into the armor of the men surrounding him. One by one they crumble.

On the other side of him a tiny creature runs over soldiers' feet, causing white bursts of light to shoot from the soil. The armored men turn to ash before reforming into pale, unnatural versions of themselves. With jerky movements they turn their weapons on each other, bludgeoning their fellow soldiers as if they were enemies, until they too are unrecognizable.

"Sam? Baldar?" I whisper. Another roar sounds above us and the room we are in heats up dramatically as fire starts to lick at the building's walls.

"We need to go!" Sorin screams.

We throw ourselves back out onto the streets, but there are soldiers everywhere we turn. We skate along the sides of abandoned food carts and burned buildings, but we are spotted almost instantly.

"The princess!" Someone wails and some of the soldiers turn towards us, surrounding us.

"Shit." Sorin wraps one of his vines around a man and throws him away from us. Rotating, he uses another vine as leverage to kick a different soldier in the chest. The man hits the ground hard. Snatching a thorn from his vine Sorin uses it as a makeshift dagger and slits the man's throat. On the other side of me, the prince transforms his bow into a broadsword. With deft precision, he slices off his opponents' arms before stabbing them in the stomach.

Something smacks against my arm and I grunt as pain fills me. Turning, I find another man wielding a bat-like object. He lifts his arms to swing at me again and I stab him with my dagger before setting him on fire, the humming within me growing stronger. Another man tries to make a grab for me, his forearm surrounding my throat. I slice his arm and kick him in the knee, making him buckle. Turning, I stab my dagger into his eye and push him to the ground. My arm dangles uselessly at my side and I try to ignore the pain.

Another bright light shines and I squint through it before noticing that we have made our way closer to Sam and Baldar. The light around us brightens and darkens dramatically. I cannot help but feel disoriented as the men around me appear and disappear in the changing light.

Another piercing noise sweeps through the air and the prince collapses to my left.

"No!" I scream reaching for him, but another man swings a hammer towards my head, and I duck and roll out of the way to avoid the swing. I reorient myself, and glance over to see the prince back on his feet, but he is now much further away. The battle is raging around him making it impossible for him to get closer to us. Sorin is now the only one standing at my side. I catch the prince's eyes and he yells over to Sorin. "Get her out of here!"

I glance towards Baldar and Sam and see that they are still entrenched in battle, hundreds of soldiers surrounding them. Through the fray, Baldar and I make eye contact.

"No, Alaceandra!" Baldar screams in my head. *"You should not be out here. They are too close."*

"Who?" I internally scream back at him; I duck again as the man wielding the hammer takes another swing at me. I throw flames in his direction and he deftly avoids them before taking yet another swing. I watch as one of the soldiers makes a grab for Baldar and successfully captures him.

A squeak trills sharply through my head. *"Keep fighting you cannot be taken."* Baldar's voice is weak and strained. *"I cannot hold this form much longer. Survive, Alaceandra. I will see you soon."* A couple of seconds later, a sense of emptiness fills me.

What? No! Where did he go?

That humming sensation within me grows even stronger as I throw fireball after fireball at the men surrounding me and Sorin. Light no longer overtakes the sky, instead it is consumed by darkness, the burgundy of the soldiers' armor seeming to glow in the low light. I stab at any man who gets close enough and duck and weave as weapons swing in front of my face. My energy starts to wane in spite of the humming reaching a fevered pitch. I stumble slightly, tripping over a shoe left in the street when an axe gets dangerously close to slicing me. Seconds later Sorin appears behind the man's back and slits his throat.

My eyes snag on a man sneaking up on Sam from behind. A stick held firmly in his grip.

"Sam!" I scream.

Sam's pitch-black eyes swing to mine at the same time the man swings the stick. It does not make contact. Right before the swing connects, a void of darkness expands from Sam's form. Bodies drop as the inky blackness takes a hold of them. "Run!" Sam yells, his voice distorted.

"Come on!" Sorin yells and grabs me. We run past Sam and make it out of the village and into the woods surrounding what was once our refuge.

Crouching between the trees, I become overwhelmed with emotion and tears start to stream from my eyes as the pain in my arm and all that I have witnessed catches up to me. I take a heaving breath. "Sam and the prince... They are still back there." Tears continue to streak down my face as I gasp for air. The humming fills my ears and it feels like every nerve ending is on fire.

"They will be okay; we do not know that they are not. We just need to get out of here for now. We will catch up to them later."

"The soldiers are here for me. This is all my fault. All my-"

"Shh we cannot worry about that now. We need to run hard and fast; we cannot stop for a long time. Do you understand?" A roaring sounds above us as more elvisera soar towards the village entrance.

"What about-"

"We cannot worry about them."

I sniff, wiping my tears from my eyes with my working arm. "Okay. Okay. We can go. I am sorry." I start to run deeper into the woods, but Sorin stops me.

He hesitates. "Whatever happens..." Sorin grasps my face in his hands and kisses me deeply. I hold onto him tightly like he is my only lifeline, *because he is.* "I love you, Alaceandra. You will get through this."

Me? My eyes search his. "We will get through this," I say, another tear leaking onto my cheek. "Sorin, I love-" He places a finger over my lips, halting my words.

His face lights up with a cheeky smile. Despite all the death and destruction. All the unknowns, my Sorin, my rock, still has it in him to smile. The humming dies down slightly, his presence calming whatever chaotic energy was growing within me. "We need to move. You can tell me la-" His beautiful smile drops, and he looks down.

"Sorin?" I say, reaching towards him. Red seeps from his stomach and slowly starts to coat the front of his shirt. *Blood.* My heartbeat sounds in my ears as the world starts to move in slow motion.

Sorin grabs at the front of his shirt and his eyes meet mine, full of tears. "I love you," Sorin whispers. I watch as his eyes roll back, and my vision starts to turn hazy. *No. No, this is not happening.* His grip on me loosens and his arms fall to his sides. "Run." His voice is strangled as he falls to his knees and then crashes to the ground.

"No!" I shout and fall down with him, placing my hand over the wound. "Stay with me, Sorin. Please! Please! You promised!" Tears stream down my face as blood starts to soak my hands, my clothing, my body as I do everything I can to stop the blood. *Sorin's blood.*

"I am so sorry." I hear a voice whisper. Whipping my head up, I see a crying Sylvie holding a bloodied knife. Her eyes are a milky white and her face is unnaturally pale. She takes a step back. As our eyes connect, her knife falls to the forest floor. "She's here!" she screams, her voice unnatural and choppy.

"Sylvie what are you-" My voice is shaking. *Blood so much blood. Everywhere.* The humming within my head comes back full force as magick flares to life under my skin. The mark on my thigh starting to burn painfully.

"He is dead! It is done! She is over here!" Sylvie screams again. Soldiers appear from the trees, surrounding us. Sylvie backs away from us, then turns and stumbles into the woods as the men close in.

Dead? No, he... he cannot be dead. He is right here. He just said— A prickling heat stabs my skin as a foreign force invades every crevice of my mind. A woman's ghastly scream echoes through the space— *my scream—* as I try to force Sorin to wake up. Hands grab at me, pulling me away from him, and I fight them with all of my might, shooting streams of fire at anyone who tries to get near until I am overwhelmed.

As the men finally start pulling me away from Sorin— *my Sorin—* a sickly-sweet voice whispers in my ear. I echo its message as if in a trance. *"Ashes to ashes, dust to dust. If those I love shall die, you too must."* An explosion of fire bursts from my body, and I watch robotically as the soldiers surrounding me succumb to the flames. Their forms turn to dust before me. Once all who surround me are ash, piercing silence rings through the forest. I crawl back over to Sorin and collapse on top of him and then darkness.

Epilogue: Carriages and Corruption

Alaceandra

A jolt forces me awake. I tug at my arms, but realize I am tied up. *Not this again.* Taking stock of my surroundings, I keep my eyes closed. *Am I moving?* I feel hazy as I realize that I am not alone. *Dreaming?* I squint my eyes open and see my father and King Demetrius sitting across from me in what looks to be a carriage of some sort. Another man sits beside me, but I cannot seem to recognize him. *This does not feel like a dream.*

"We have captured her, now what?" my father says grumpily.

"Well, it is simple really," the unknown man says. "She must marry a prince, not run off with one. If your prince is unable to do his duty, I will." *His voice is eerily familiar.* I shiver.

The man's palm touches my thigh, right over Sorin's bond mark. My thigh starts to burn, and agony fills my whole body. Then, I once again lose consciousness.

About the author

Rauri Rose

Rauri Rose loves all things romance. She has been writing ever since she was a teen and has always found beauty in the way throwing one-self into a book allows them to experience the world around them and worlds unknown in the safety of their reading nook. At home she spends her time writing and keeping up with her fiancé and four cats Atticus, Shadow, Midnight and Belle. She has a ton of ideas to share and hopes that you enjoyed the book!